ADVENT

of a

MYSTERY

ADVENT
of a
MYSTERY

Marilyn Leach

BARBOUR
PUBLISHING

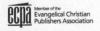

PROLOGUE

September

In the grand hall, the front door opened and the September rain raged upon the white marble floor. The North Sea squall had finally hit inland. The man stepped inside, pushed the formidable door shut, then slipped out of his soaked overcoat. Though middle-aged, the fellow's etched face wore the inscription of one much older. He shook the dead leaves that had littered the front steps from the soles of his shoes. Dampness of the English autumn permeated every corner of the hall that bore old World War II relics on its austere white walls.

At the far end of the cavernous space, a stately valet descended the polished staircase so rapidly he nearly lost his footing. "Sir, come quickly, your father's asking for you."

Immediately upon entering the bedroom where his father lay, the man was aware of a sense of panic in the elder's face. "Father?"

Sickly, yellowed, and drawn, his father motioned the valet to his side. "Up," he growled.

"No Klaus, I can do it." The son pushed past the servant and maneuvered his father into a sitting position.

With the flick of his forefinger the master dismissed the valet from the darkened room. Faltering, he grasped at a wadded piece of newspaper from the night table at the bedside. The sweep of his arm toppled multiple medicine bottles, most crashing to the floor. His son sat on the edge of the bed, close to the beleaguered body of the man who was once robust and determined, the leader of armies of men. The old soldier pushed the paper into his son's hand then grabbed the back of his firstborn's neck, pulling him to his face. The beads of perspiration about the ill man's forehead smelled of death.

"There's one left," he rattled. "One left."

His son's face blazed. "I thought—"

"My death's cheating them, but you and your sons are next." He gasped for air. "Get them before they get you." The old man's grip tightened, making his son wince. "Promise me."

"As sure as I live, father, it is done."

The near corpse slumped upon the pillow. The gripping hand loosened then fell limp to the bed. He writhed as if a giant hand were pressing his chest. A faint breath escaped between his sallow lips. It was his last breath this side of forever.

CHAPTER ONE

Berdie smiled. *What an odd lot*, she mused.

"God rest ye merry, gentlemen, let nothing you dismay. . ."

The song filled the frosty night air as several carolers stood in the front garden of Twenty-nine Westwood Road.

The village solicitor, Preston Graystone, stood shoulder to shoulder with the long-standing town electrician, Edsel Butz. A fine young university student, Mathew, and his childhood sweetheart, Cara Graystone, shared a caroling book with the electrician's stout wife, Ivy. Mr. Raheem, the start-up greengrocer sang tenor notes with Mr. Webb, the recently elected council member. And there was the aged spinster, leaning on her cane, melodious and determined even in her old age, Miss Livingston. With her stood her constant companion, a dear but forgetful neighbor, Natty. The choirmaster, Lillie Foxworth, a bright, cheerful woman, conducted the carolers with great exuberance. All walks of life joined together, celebrating in festive song.

Berdie snuggled closer to her husband, Hugh, and tucked her hair into her stylish, yet warmly practical, holiday hat. She felt the nip of the December night air on her nose and was sure it must be glowing holiday red. Her husband had often told her that her brown eyes held the warmth of a hearth fire. At this moment, she wished they literally could start a fire, because her large tortoiseshell glasses felt as chilly as fairy frost. Berdie's wool blazer was doing a fine job of keeping that part of her body quite warm, but it fit a bit snug this evening. Though she was involved in both energetic community service and active investigative journalism most of her life, having two now-grown children had taken its toll. It all came with becoming "mature," she decided. But then there was also the Devonshire cream she loved to lavish on her afternoon scones. *It's the holidays, after all*, she thought. Neither bone-chilling weather nor the complexities of aging could lessen her joy in being here with this mix of people and lifting her heart in song with them. They were, in a sense and at this moment, family. For her husband standing next to her, Hugh, they were part of his flock.

Hubert Elliot carried his tall muscular frame with military bearing as befit a man with an honored past in Her Majesty's Royal Navy. He had tried putting things right using armed force, and discovered, in the end, that putting things right was more a spiritual matter. The very day of his retirement from service, he registered for seminary. Now here he stood, with his congregation. Beneath his dark winter coat lived the keen ability to put people at their ease. The silver hair, which some said gave him the air of a film star, was just barely visible beneath his homburg and drew even more attention to those ardent blue eyes.

"Remember Christ our Savior was born on Christmas Day. . ."

Hubert's voice became invigorated. Berdie shot a quick glance to the man with whom she had shared her heart and life for twenty-six years. He couldn't deliver a tune in a wheelbarrow, but apart from that small detail, she knew he was the best-suited person in all of Great Britain to be the vicar of Saint Aidan of the Wood Parish Church. And, although she and Hugh had been serving the parish for only three months, the majority of members were warming toward their new vicar.

All continued as with one voice. "To save us all from Satan's power when we were gone astray, O tidings of comfort and joy, comfort and joy; o tidings of comfort and joy."

Berdie moved on with the jolly troop. The carolers followed ancient cobbled streets to warm homes and cottages as was the tradition in Aidan Kirkwood on the first Sunday of Advent. Some dwellings boasted large back gardens. The tiny stone row houses were dressed for the English winter, and a battery of newly built dwellings were awash with fresh paint. When the troubadours moved across the High Street, the usually vibrant shops were abed for the night.

In no time at all they approached Oak Leaf Cottage, the vicarage that was just a stone's throw from the ancient church. Everyone was in anticipation of the Advent party this evening, complete with the lighting of the ring.

Upon arrival, three people were waiting at the decorated door of the vicarage.

Standing eye to eye, Hugh shook hands with the fellow who was also a man of the cloth—Gerald Lewis. He was currently visiting Aidan Kirkwood on ecclesiastical matters. "So glad you could join us this evening, Reverend Lewis."

"Thank you for the generous invitation—I'm delighted," the colleague replied.

Hugh turned. "Mr. and Mrs. Reese, glad you're here, please come in."

"We can't," Mr. Reese rushed. "We just need a word with Mathew."

Mathew Reese, home from university for the weekend, handed his caroling book to his fiancée. The tall, blond young man put Berdie in mind of her Hugh when he was university age: smartly dressed, trim, handsome.

"Mum, Dad, are you here for the party?" Mathew queried.

"No Mat, we are not." Mrs. Reese was untouched by the prevailing holiday spirit.

"Why don't you step into the library? Get out of this frightful chill," Hugh offered.

"We'll stay right here, thank you." Mr. Reese had fire in his voice.

"Well, let's the rest of us move in," Berdie suggested.

As soon as the manse door was flung open and the troupe entered, the smell of fresh pine mingled with the scent of cinnamon and oranges. It tickled the merrymakers' noses like a Christmas partridge feather. The comfortable stone manse had been holiday dressed by Hugh and Berdie that very afternoon with help from their close friend, Lillie Foxworth. Polished woodwork showed off the fresh garlands draped around doorways, mirrors, and mantelpieces. They also wound their way along the central oak staircase that stretched up to the next floor. The evergreens were punctuated with deep burgundy bows and sprinkled with little gold stars that caught the light and seemed to beg a Christmas wish.

The entry hall was alive with guests. Mr. Graystone removed his overcoat and hung it on a hook of the ample pub mirror. Berdie thought he rather looked like his name—gray stone. He was tall and angular, sharp-featured, with prematurely gray hair.

Always dutiful, he helped old spinster Livingston with her long lavender coat, the poor woman getting her cane all twisted up in the works. By the end of the kind gesture, it became a tussle.

"Silly man," was all the silver-haired eighty-four-year-old offered Mr. Graystone as she scraped her cane across his newly polished shoes. The scars that littered her left cheek went crimson as she moved on to the sitting room.

"Now Miriam, you need to thank the gentleman," Natalie Bell offered. The village called her Batty Natty as she had so few lucid moments. Natty was a neighbor to Miss Livingston, more like her shadow half the time. Natty reached in her pocket and pulled out a one-pound coin. "Thank you, sir, for your services," she said to Mr. Graystone.

"Oh Natty, put that away." It was Cara Graystone, undeniably the prettiest young woman in the village. "You're in the manse, Natty, for a party. My father helped Miss Livingston with her coat as a matter of courtesy. He's not a doorman."

The old dear seemed a bit embarrassed when she came clear and returned the money to her pocket. "Of course," is all she said.

Cara took the oldster's coat and hung it on an empty hook. "I'm going in the sitting room, Natty. Come along," Cara offered. She apparently decided against waiting for her fiancé, who was still talking with his parents outside.

Ivy and Edsel Butz both looked at the decorations with delight.

They were the only married couple in attendance besides Hugh and Berdie. Well, Mr. Raheem was married, but his wife was not a singer and so he was unaccompanied this evening.

"Beautiful!" Ivy Butz exclaimed, hands spread wide. Edsel nodded his large head in agreement.

"Indeed," said Mr. Raheem with a slight Punjabi accent. "My compliments to the hostess."

Berdie delighted in their appreciation. "Thank you."

These guests moved on to observe stands of airy orange pomanders throughout, holiday bowls of spiced nuts at every turn, and of course, the much-loved Nativity set which had belonged to Berdie's mother. It sat in pride of place on the sitting room mantel. The Christ child was conspicuously missing from the crib, and the three wise men were at the far end of the mantelpiece. On Christmas Eve, the holy babe would be placed in the waiting manger, and on Twelfth Night, the three wise men would add their presence to the stable scene. Ah yes! This was the Elliotts' living holiday greeting card, wishing joy, peace, and beauty to all who entered.

The merrymakers drifted into the ample sitting room. While Hugh lit holiday candles, Berdie flew into the kitchen with Lillie Foxworth, her best friend and comrade, on her heels. Hot spiced cider and tea simmered on the stove.

"I don't think we'll be playing the Albert Hall soon," Lillie the musical director extraordinaire piped, "but we are having a jolly good time!" Her dark hair formed ringlets of natural curl around her thin tawny face. She and Berdie had been dear friends since university. "So, what's your take on the temperature of the gathered crowd?" Lillie's bright hazel green eyes couldn't hide the intrigue she found in Berdie's gift of smelling out trouble. "Who seems a bit shifty, who's hiding something, who's smoldering beneath their calm exterior?"

As rectory hostess, Berdie began placing holiday mugs on a gracious wooden tray. "I'm a vicar's wife now, Lillie. My forays into newsworthy investigations have given way to dalliances with altar flowers and women's guilds."

"You don't fool me, Berdie. Vicar's wife or not, I can see that twinkle in your eye when you're on to something." Lillie took the ladle from the hot spiced cider and poured the simmering liquid into the awaiting cups. "Come on," Lillie quipped, "just a general temperature of our assembled saints."

Berdie turned on her heel. "The general temperature, Lillie, is somewhere between roasting chestnuts and the winter hoar frost." She grabbed an oven mitt decorated with snowmen. "You know I've given my word to Hugh that I'd keep this perky little nose clean and out of the fray."

Just then, Ivy Butz waddled into the kitchen with her usual jovial spirit, and Berdie was glad the electrician's wife had interrupted the conversation.

"And are you snuggin' the holiday cheer?" Ivy laughed. Just the sound of Ivy's voice brought a certain amount of glee into a room.

"You found us out, Mrs. Butz," Berdie piped. This was one of the few times Berdie had seen the stout woman without one of her children clinging to her skirt hem.

"Can I pitch in as well?"

Before Berdie could answer, Mrs. Butz picked up the freshly

brewed pot of tea perched on the edge of the stove. "Such a lovely holiday teapot. I love the little birds, Christmas robins by my sight. Shall I pour?"

Berdie had barely parted her lips to say, "Please do," when the willing helper was out the kitchen door, teapot in hand.

"No grass grows under her feet," Lillie offered. "Five children and a husband who can hardly keep up with the demands of his job, still, it amazes me how she seems to keep so jolly."

Berdie put a stack of burgundy napkins with gold trim on the drink tray. "Mr. Butz isn't home much."

Lillie brightened. "Why? Something's going on there, isn't it? I knew it!"

"Lillie! They are simply a part of our parish, and I'm stating a simple fact."

"Edsel's father passed on just two years ago, leaving the family electrical business to him, and Edsel was the sole heir. With our recent building boom, he's been busier than a goat in the garden, new houses springing up like April dafs. He had to hire a new man—well, an apprentice really." Lillie picked up the fully laden tray.

"Oh yes, Edsel hired Jamie Donovan." Berdie opened the kitchen door. "He was in church this morning. I invited him to the party."

Lillie started, nearly dropping the tray, "Oh no, you didn't!"

At that moment, the front door chime rang. "Go on through, Lillie. That could be Jamie."

Berdie entered the hallway. Mathew Reese burst into the hall from the front door, the lighted wall sconce casting a shimmer upon his fair hair. "I'm my own person now," he raged and slammed the door behind him.

"Are you all right?" Berdie's voice caught the young man up short. He stiffened.

"It's not really your business, is it, Mrs. Elliott?"

Suddenly Mathew didn't seem like a young Hugh at all, in looks perhaps, but certainly not in manner. The door chime rang out impatiently, once, twice, and a third time in rapid succession. Both hostess and guest stared at the door.

"If it's my parents, don't let them in," Mathew said tightly.

Without comment, Berdie went to the door and graciously opened it only to find Jamie Donovan listing off the front step along with Lucy Butz—Edsel and Ivy's teenage daughter. But Jamie, one step ahead of danger, was agile enough to regain his balance and hold Lucy with him.

"Ya' beasts knocked her round," Jamie bellowed after Mathew's disappearing parents. The Irishman had a few more choice words for the Reeses but realized Berdie now stood in the doorway. He took Lucy's arm. "Okay Luce?"

Poor Lucy seemed momentarily bedazzled. In the ado, her long auburn braid had wrapped around and given her a whack on her frosted cheek.

"Jamie, Lucy, please come in," Berdie blurted.

Jamie put his arm around Lucy's shoulders and helped her inside. Berdie closed the door behind them, delighted that she didn't have to deal with Mathew's parents at this present moment. She could resume being a hostess for her guests.

"The rest of the people here aren't nearly as inane as those two," Mathew churned.

"Jamie, this is Mathew Reese," Berdie introduced.

Jamie removed his knit cap, revealing coal black hair, his heritage from a mother long absent from the twenty-three-year-old's life. His rough hands pushed the cap into a pocket of his woolen overshirt, and he tipped his head toward the golden boy.

"Lucy, a rather mature crowd for you, don't you think?" Mathew asked.

"I'm sixteen in May," she stated with the lift of her chin. Her heavily mascaraed eyelashes coupled with her high-glossed lips that slightly missed the target betrayed her first attempts in makeup.

The sitting room door opened, and Cara Graystone joined the foursome in the entry. Her fitted ivory cashmere sweater reflected both her father's rank as village solicitor and her position as his only child. An emerald solitaire ring, almost the size of Berdie's Christmas platter, dwarfed her slim finger. Mathew placed his hand on the small of his fiancée's slender back.

"Darling, this is Jamie. Jamie, this is my fiancée, Cara."

Berdie sensed Jamie stretching up to make sure every inch of his five-foot-seven-inch frame was fully flexed. The young men reminded her of the picadors she saw at the bullfights in Spain, displaying their prowess to dazzle the crowd.

"We've met," Jamie declared.

Cara Graystone smiled as she gave her long, honey hair a flip over her shoulder. It was an unconscious gesture she made when tense, and it didn't pass Berdie's awareness. The young woman took a deep breath. "Let's join the others. Reverend Elliott is about to light the Advent wreath."

"Did you know, Jamie, that in Latin *advent* means 'to come'? It signals an awaiting." Mathew was telling more than asking.

Lucy Butz shifted her feet.

"Of course," Cara interjected, "everyone knows that. We're all waiting, waiting for Christmas to come."

"Are we, now?" Jamie dug his hand farther into his pocket.

There was something in Jamie's voice that made Berdie's nose twitch.

Berdie and her visitors entered the warm sitting room that hummed with conversation. Upon sight of them, the aged body of Miss Livingston rose up on the strength of her cane. When fully erect, she thrust the stick toward Jamie. "Who invited you?" Her once melodious voice now screeched. "And what are you doing with *her*?"

The room hushed except for the sound of the teapot Mrs. Butz slammed down on the side table, sloshing brown liquid all over a bowl of spiced nuts.

"Lucy!" With the combustion of an Atlas missile, the girl's mother was across the room, grabbing her daughter by the arm.

"Ivy, leave the child alone," Edsel Butz commanded.

"This is all your fault!" his wife hissed.

The stunned Lucy tried to pull her arm out of her mother's grip. "You're hurting me," she squealed.

"My dear lady, please sit down," Hugh offered the elderly spinster.

"And you!" Miss Livingston ignored the vicar. She shook her cane toward Edsel, making the pink scars on her left cheek go twice crimson. "Your father would shudder to see the loss of integrity, the shoddy craftsmanship, and disgrace you've brought to his business."

"You stupid cow!" It was Jamie who railed at the elderly woman.

"Steady on," Hugh cautioned the young man.

"You'll get yours, ya' witch. You just watch and see if ya' don't!" Jamie pulled his cap from his pocket and tugged it on his head. He lunged for the door, bumping Cara's shoulder as he went. The Irishman turned toward Berdie. He barely spoke, "You invited me to this?" The fire in his eyes burned into the very heart of Berdie.

Lucy yanked herself away from her mother. The teenager's gaze ran across the room of astonished faces. "He's really quite wonderful," she apologized, then burst into tears.

Edsel Butz scooped his daughter into his arms. With the nod of his head, he beckoned his wife to the door. Without a word, the Butz family left with what little dignity they could muster.

"If you please, Miss Livingston," Mr. Raheem, the new-in-town greengrocer spoke up. "Sit down and take a bit of tea."

Miriam Livingston struck her cane on the hardwood floor with such force Berdie was sure it would crack open a Christmas walnut. "I'll not have some foreigner telling me what to do. Now where's my coat?"

"I say. . ." It was Reverend Lewis speaking now. "Where's your Christian charity, madam? It's Christmastide, the season of peace and goodwill." He spoke directly to Miss Livingston.

"Goodwill?" the old woman nearly screamed as she scanned the onlookers. "Lies! Deceit! These are afoot in our village." Her fuming eyes returned to the clergyman. "Peace? There is no peace for the wicked." The spinster straightened herself and hobbled to the door. "Come along, Natty," she called. And with that the two women left the room.

"I will see them home." Mr. Raheem gave his holiday cup to Lillie.

"Thank you, Mr. Raheem." Hugh looked relieved. "You are indeed a gentleman." Hugh walked the kind man into the hallway.

"Can I refresh anyone's drink?" Lillie asked.

No one responded.

Reverend Gerald Lewis set his cup on the end table near him and stood. "I believe I've overstepped my boundary here this evening. I will apologize to Reverend Elliott. My apologies to you, Mrs. Elliott." He tipped his head toward Berdie. "To all of you. I'll see myself out."

Lillie slid up next to Berdie. "What's the temperature of our assembled saints now?" she whispered.

When, at the end of the evening, the last guest stepped out into the crisp English night, Berdie and Lillie set to the cleanup. Hugh excused himself and walked the hundred meters to the church.

"He once told me he does his best thinking at the kneeling rail," Berdie told Lillie while loading the old dishwasher in the kitchen.

"If that's the case, don't expect him home soon." Lillie put the last cup in the appliance.

"We can make a divine request as well, my dear friend." Berdie pushed the START button on the machine. "Pray this old thing performs well."

Without a slip, the device began its work.

"Yes!" Lillie celebrated.

Berdie shook her head. "This whole affair this evening, I know there's an elephant in the middle of the room," she mused. "I just can't put my finger on exactly what it is."

"You know what the problem is with your elephants, Bernadine Elliott?" Lillie asked.

"I'm sure you're going to tell me," Berdie answered.

"Every time you go elephant hunting, someone ends up missing or dead."

CHAPTER TWO

With Lillie sent on her way and Hugh still at the church, Berdie ascended the stairway to the upper story. Instantly it felt like endless miles of ornamented wood. It was then that Berdie realized how tired she was. She entered the spacious master bedroom and prayed blessings for Nick and Clare, her two grown children. Their pictures sat on the night table, offering gentle comfort to a mother whose offspring were in distant lands. She promised herself that within ten minutes' time she would be washed, creamed, in her night slip, and head to pillow. It took only nine minutes.

"What, what?" Berdie was roused by a familiar tone, but in her state of coming to, she couldn't make it out.

"Vicarage," the graveled voice of her just-awakened husband spoke into the receiver of the bedside telephone. "Yes. What? Yes, of course. Right away."

Berdie heard the *click* of the receiver as it fell into its cradle. A long sigh escaped the lips of her loved one. He pulled back the covers and arose. She could hear him wrestling with his clothing.

"Hugh, what time is it?" she asked.

"Don't worry, love. Go back to sleep."

"Who called?"

"It's Dudley Horn from the Upland Arms Pub. Apparently there are a couple of our flock that need assistance getting home."

"Is that really your job?" Berdie whined.

"Love, I'm the parish priest in a small village. Everything's my job."

She felt Hugh's gentle kiss on her cheek. The sound of his footsteps down the carpeted stairs and the slam of the door made her suddenly aware that he was gone. She placed her hand upon the warmth of where his body lay only moments before and fell back to sleep.

This time she awoke to a sound that she recognized right off. It was the shower in the en suite bathroom, the water forcefully hitting the floor of the old claw-foot tub. A small lamp on the dressing table was lit. It was the only light visible so far on this bleak December morn. Berdie put on her glasses and gazed upon the bedside clock. "Half six?" she almost yelled.

The sound of splashing water stopped and her towel-wrapped husband emerged from the bathroom with little clouds of steam. Though rejuvenated, he looked fatigued.

"You look like Zeus arriving from the heavens," Berdie teased.

"Ah, I have the strength of ten." Hugh stretched and yawned.

"Right." Berdie loved her husband's optimism. "It's half six, Hugh. A bit early after a tiresome night."

"Not when you have an appointment at the church in fifteen minutes." Hugh began blow-drying his hair. He turned and looked into the tall dressing table mirror.

"An appointment?" Berdie yelled. "Who has an appointment at six forty-five in the morning at a church?"

"And today's the interfaith jumble sale in Timsley," Hugh hollered out, still styling.

"Honestly," Berdie said to herself. She put on her housecoat and added a spritz of lavender botanical splash. With that, she headed to the kitchen.

She sat at the petite kitchen table with a generous mug of freshly brewed tea. It was revitalizing her senses when Hugh popped in. Berdie poured another generous mug of tea, added a slip of cream, and handed it to her husband.

"I've been thinking," Berdie said.

"I really need to get going," Hugh cautioned.

"I know, love. I've decided I'll handle the jumbo sale in Timsley today. Lillie can help me, then you'll have your morning."

Hugh took a quick sip of tea. "I haven't time to discuss this."

"So it's settled then." Berdie beamed. "Go on, get to your appointment."

Hugh smiled. "Actually, it would help me out buckets."

Berdie planted a morning kiss on her grateful husband.

"The boot's loaded." Hugh was cheerful. "Both Miriam Livingston and Ivy Butz are expecting a ride." And with that, the vicar sprang for the door.

⟵

It took Berdie a bit to remove the frost from the windscreen of the Citron. Though the car was older, it was faithful. And Berdie adored the lavender tone of it. Hugh called it a light gray, but then a former military officer would. The quick sprint to Lillie's house, just two roads over, was enough time to get the heat going inside the car.

Berdie still marveled at the divine Kismet that brought her and Hugh to the very village where her cherished friend lived. The former vicar of Saint Aidan of the Wood Parish Church left for a foreign field just as Hugh was ready for assignment. It all came together like pieces of a puzzle and was reason for awe and celebration every time it came to mind.

When Berdie pulled up to the splendid three-story home that held Lillie's flat, two quick beeps were enough to bring her friend bounding to the car.

"I must say. . ." Lillie smiled as she got in. "After last night's discourse, this could be quite interesting. Miss Livingston and Ivy Butz as fellow passengers all the way to Timsley!" Lillie's green eyes positively glowed.

Berdie pulled the car away from the curb and started down the narrow road. "You must behave yourself," she asserted.

"That's easy enough," Lillie assured, "but will our two passengers behave?" Lillie rubbed her Christmas mittens together with vigor.

Out of nowhere, a figure dashed in front of the car. "Eek!" Lillie screeched. Berdie slammed on the breaks, but the female jogger kept on going without even acknowledging the close call. She ran straight into the woods.

Berdie was sharp. "A mobile in one hand and a dog lead in the other. They'll meet with mischief someday!"

"It's Cara Graystone." Lillie sounded surprised. "That's not like her. She's usually very attentive."

Berdie looked after the figure. Indeed, it was Cara and her Highland terrier, Snowdrop. "If she hopes to continue her exercise program, she had better keep her mind on what she's doing."

When Berdie moved on again, the sun had started its celestial climb, but gray clouds shrouded its full glory.

"What lovely little patches of fairy frost all across the gardens and rooftops," Lillie observed.

When they came to a stop at Lavender Cottage, Miss Livingston's home, the glint of a morning ray hit upon the roof of the back potting shed then quickly disappeared. Berdie observed that the high fence around the front garden surely needed some repair and a good coat of paint. *A great spring project for our church youth,* she thought.

Both women exited the car. "Here goes," Lillie chirped. A few steps and they were at the front gate.

"I must say I love Miss Livingston's front garden," Lillie commented. "It always smells of English lavender—the entire lot is planted in it you know."

"Well of course," Berdie answered, "after all, it is her bread and butter."

But when Berdie swung the painted iron gate open, it was clear the lavender was in its dormant winter sleep.

"Look!" Lillie stopped short. "Isn't that Batty Natty sitting on the front step? Is she coming, too?"

Berdie espied the old dear. She was in a woolen jumper, but

she had no coat or jacket, no gloves, no hat.

"She must be freezing," Lillie observed.

Walking up the path to the doorway, it was clear that Natty was in disorder.

"Natty, love, are you okay?" Berdie asked. Something was very much out of sorts. Berdie bent down to take the woman's icy hand. The old soul's eyes were flared with fright, her hair was disheveled, her body shivered uncontrollably.

"How long have you been sitting here?" Lillie questioned. She removed her Christmas mittens and put them straightway on the frigid hands of poor Batty Natty.

Berdie raised her voice, "Natty, are you okay?"

A glimmer shot through the glazed eyes. She looked into the face of her rescuer and tried to speak, but her teeth were chattering so that the sounds were inaudible. She grabbed Berdie's arm as if clinging to a breath of life, teetered forward, and tried again to speak. "M–M–i. . ."

"Let's get her inside to the warm," Berdie ordered Lillie. Both women squatted down to lift the old lady.

"N–n–o–o," the old voice croaked. With one irrepressible move, she fell in a heap against Berdie's body, nearly knocking her over. "Mi–Mi–Miriam."

Berdie recovered her balance, and it was then that she noticed in the dark door well that the front door to Miss Livingston's cottage was ajar.

"Lillie, if I help you get Natty up, do you think you can get her next door to her cottage?"

"I can try."

"Natty," Berdie said with voice elevated, "Lillie is going to take you home. I'm going to look in on Miriam. Okay? Do you think you can walk?"

The dazed woman shook her head affirmatively. A look of relief shot through the elderly woman's face. With all the strength she could find, and with the help of her friends, Natty stood up. Lillie placed the woman's thin arm around her shoulder and wrapped her own arm around the cold woolen jumper.

"Here we go, dear, one step at a time," Lillie encouraged.

Berdie took a deep breath and stepped inside the door well. There was a second door ahead, and it, too, was open. She had witnessed this scenario before—open doors in dicey weather, no apparent occupant at hand. It almost always announced foul play and never lent itself to any good. With her gloved hand, she pushed the second door wide.

The small entry hallway was dark. Berdie cautiously put one foot inside. She paused. "Miss Livingston?" Her voice was strong.

She had observed from outside, the many times she had passed it, that this cottage was apparently laid out somewhat like a row house. There would be the entry, the hall, and rooms just off that central hallway identified by entry doors, perhaps glass, perhaps wood.

"Hello, Miss Livingston," she called out again. There was no response, just a steady *tick, tick, tick,* of what Berdie guessed was a grandfather clock. She crossed the threshold, now fully into the hall. "It's Mrs. Elliott." *Tick, tick, tick.*

"Where's the light?" She felt along the wall and found a switch.

She pressed it. Nothing happened. She pressed again, and again. A shiver ran across her neck. She wished Lillie were with her.

"Steel yourself, old girl."

She felt her way two steps down the left side of the hall and found another door ajar. She pushed it open. The *tick* of the clock was keenly louder. *This must be the sitting room*, she thought. There was a small crack of light where a drawn drape across a window hadn't closed properly.

" 'The Lord is my shepherd. . . .' " Berdie felt her shoulders tighten. She stepped lightly around the back of an object. The toe of her shoe caught on something and she stumbled. She righted herself quickly.

" 'Yea, though I walk through the valley of the shadow of death. . .' "

A startling *bong* split through the darkness. Berdie jumped, putting her hand to her racing heart.

"Wretched clock!" She took a large swallow of air, slowly releasing it to bring herself back to center. In four more steps she was at the window. With one magnanimous swoop, Berdie flung the long drape open.

" 'I will fear no evil.' " She spun round. The gray light of a winter morning revealed a hailstorm of devastation. Books from shelves littered the floor, overstuffed furniture, and pillows. Quilts were gashed open, spewing the filling all across the room. Paintings were slashed, wall decor torn from their mountings. Even dead cinders from the fireplace were strewn across the hearth rug. Nothing was upright or in its appropriate place, except one thing. There on the mantel of the fireplace the Advent wreath stood upright. Though missing one of the four singular candles, the large central Christ candle and three smaller ones stood in their proper place, valiantly, amid the rubble.

Berdie's investigative reporting skills and training came to her as automatically as snow in winter. But what would Hugh say?

"No," she heard herself say. "I need to call emergency services, let them take care of all this."

Berdie was out of the cottage and halfway down the garden walk when Lillie met her. "Berdie?"

"My mobile phone's in the car, Lillie." Berdie was terse. "Do you have yours with you?"

Lillie pulled the mobile from her overcoat pocket, and Berdie grabbed it and dialed rapidly.

"Is Natty set right?" Berdie asked.

"I started a hot bath for her and microwaved a cup of steaming tea," Lillie responded.

"Yes," Berdie spoke into the phone. "Emergency services?" She paused. "Mrs. Goodnight?"

"Yes, you need my husband then?" Mrs. Goodnight asked.

"I need him urgently," Berdie nearly shouted.

"Oh no." Lillie tensed.

"I'm at Lavender Cottage." Berdie breathed deeply to try to calm herself.

"He's on a call at Carlisle Cathcart's farm. I'll ring his mobile."

"I should hope so," Berdie clipped then handed the phone back to Lillie. "I mean, really." Berdie was absolutely livid. "I can't believe emergency services rang Constable Goodnight's home!"

"It's a small village." Lillie rubbed her bare hands together. "Is Miriam all right?"

"No. . .I don't know."

"What do you mean you don't know?"

"How far away is the Cathcart farm?" Berdie was anxious.

"Probably fifteen minutes full on. Is that where Goodnight is?"

Berdie grimaced and stood silent.

Lillie pushed past her, making a beeline for the front door of the cottage, but Berdie caught her by her coat sleeve.

"Don't go in," Berdie warned.

"Bernadine Elliott! Miriam could be lying in there hurt, and if something is badly wrong, Guard Albert Goodnight could literally be a life's breath too late. Besides, he's hardly worth tuppance when he does show up."

"Right!" In less time than it takes to cut a Christmas cookie, the women threw the front doors open wide, planted garden rocks as doorstops, and found their way to the stairwell.

"Have you been in here before, Lillie?"

"A couple times," she responded.

"Her bedroom?"

"Top left, I believe. Why are we going to the bedroom?" Lillie asked as they quickly negotiated the stairway.

"If what I think happened, happened. . ."

"What do you think happened?" Lillie asked just as they stepped onto the landing.

"Where are your mittens, Lillie?"

"I left them at Nat's."

Berdie pulled off one of her gloves. "I know it will feel awkward, but put this on backward on your right hand. If you touch anything, use that hand."

Lillie took the glove and struggled to get it on.

The small porthole window on the back wall offered enough light to carefully navigate the landing. The bedroom door was wide open.

"Lillie, is this the loo?" Berdie pointed to the room on the right side of the landing. She continued, "Try to find the light switch and ascertain if it is in the ON position or the OFF position. Don't touch it. And be careful, the floor may be littered."

Lillie prudently proceeded.

"Miss Livingston," Berdie called out, then eased herself into the bedroom. A dirty garret window wearing small voile curtains supplied just a shaving of light. An odd odor played with Berdie's nose. She sniffed. Her nose contorted. It was the overpowering smell of sweet dried lavender mixed with the dark scent of cessation of life. Barely visible, on the floor very near her feet, Berdie observed the outline of a body etched in the bleak winter light. Miriam Livingston lay in bloodstained nightclothes. Berdie bent low, close to the body. With her ungloved hand, she felt for a pulse, knowing at first touch it was a futile gesture. The blood looked like it had come from the upper abdomen.

"The poor old soul." Berdie felt pity and anger churn in her stomach. She glanced around the dim room. The area was strewn with bits of stems and blooms. The bed mattress was up on end at the foot of the box spring. The room was ransacked. Again, nothing appeared to be in its proper place. Drawers were open, many lay upside down on the floor with contents dumped. The wardrobe was gutted. "What's that?" Berdie noticed small pieces of paper lying in clumps across a long rug running the edge of the bed. She looked closer. "Hundred-pound notes!"

"Berdie?" Lillie's voice was tentative. She stood in the doorway of the bedroom. "The bathroom is a disaster area."

Berdie arose, and Lillie's gaze landed on the corpse. "Oh my." Lillie put her gloved hand to her mouth. The pungent odor must have assaulted her nose, for she swayed.

Berdie reached her in time to grab her elbow and guide her to the stairwell. "Let's sit down." Both women sat very near each other on the top stair.

"Is it natural causes?" Lillie seemed hopeful.

"No," was all Berdie said.

Lillie's eyes moistened. "Even as a little girl I loved her front garden. . .and her lovely singing voice. Crotchety old thing."

"I know, love." Berdie kindly took her friend's hand. The two women sat in silence.

Four minutes is but a flash, but for a quiet mourner and a consoling friend sitting together in a dark place with a body in the next room, it's a moment frozen in time.

"They're not going to get away with this, whoever did it!" The hard edge of Lillie's voice sliced through the silence.

"Let justice roll down like the mighty waters," Berdie agreed quietly.

"What's the first step of an investigation?" Lillie stood resolutely. "Checking for witnesses," she answered herself. "Let's get to it then."

"Look Lillie, we found Miriam. There's nothing we can do for her now." Berdie was blunt. "And no, you check the actual crime scene, that's the first step."

"Finding who did this, isn't that doing something for Miriam?"

"If Hugh thought I was getting involved—"

"You are involved! Do you see Hugh here? Is it a mistake that, as it worked out, *you're* the one who set out for the jumble sale? At least do a look-see. It's your gift, Berdie, and more than that, it's your moral duty." Lillie was almost shouting.

Berdie stood. "I suppose. . . The light's poor but it couldn't hurt."

The two women, back in the bedroom, stepped carefully across the fray and opened the curtains.

"Don't move anything," Berdie instructed. "Was the loo light turned off?"

"Yes." Lillie was close to Berdie.

"I was afraid of that," Berdie said half under her breath.

"Do you think the person who did this needed to relieve himself?"

"Or herself. Of course not, but I do think the perpetrator may have already known the lights weren't working."

"How?" Lillie plied.

"You enter a room where there is no light, you're trying to find something hidden, obviously, and you turn on the light."

"But they didn't try because they knew it wasn't working."

"It's a possibility." Berdie bent toward the floor. "Look, there's melted candle wax here." She moved on. "Here and here, as well."

"How did you notice that?" Lillie wrinkled her brow.

Carefully, Berdie picked up a half-burned candle with her gloved hand and inspected it. "This is the Advent candle from downstairs." She placed it gently back down in the very spot she found it. "It's often the smallest thing that holds the most truth," she continued. "Lillie, take a whiff of the underside of the mattress."

The obedient helper moved to the upturned mattress and took a tiny sniff. She drew her head back. "Overpowering smell of lavender."

Berdie arose and brought one of the hundred-pound notes with her. She sniffed the money. "Just as I expected. . .lavender." She handed the money to Lillie, who put it to her nose, too. "I would say our dear Miss Livingston had a very large account at the Bank of the Box Spring." Berdie pointed to the bed. "She wrapped the money in dried lavender and made her deposits."

"Then it's true." Lillie looked at the scattered notes and sprigs of the purple blooms. "It was rumored in the village that she kept money in the house."

"My guess is Miss Livingston knew the killer."

"What?" Lillie's eyes grew round.

"There's no forced entry at the door, at least not in front."

"Are you saying someone from the village. . ." Lillie stopped short.

Berdie edged closer to the body. Something caught her eye. Gingerly she lifted the hem of the dead woman's nightgown. What she saw lying there sent a shudder through her body.

"I can't breathe." Lillie started to sway again.

Berdie bounced up and steadied her friend. "Let's go down-stairs to the back door."

The door that faced the back garden and the potting shed was standing fully open when they got there. Lillie inhaled the cool air while Berdie inspected the door and locks. "Unmolested. Do you know if Miriam kept a key under a pot, something like that?"

"I can't imagine she would; she wasn't terribly trusting," Lillie admitted. She drew another long, deep breath.

"Yes, well. . ." Berdie turned to her friend. "Are you up to continuing this look-see?"

"Absolutely," Lillie exhaled.

"That's my girl." Lillie was a trooper.

"You check the sitting room windows to see if they have been messed about, and I'm going to look more closely at the Advent wreath."

Both women were about their tasks in the sitting room.

"Why the Advent wreath?" Lillie asked while inspecting a window.

"I can't help but think the candle upstairs and the undisturbed wreath down here have something to tell us."

Just then Berdie heard a shuffle at the front door. She froze. "Shh."

A huge dark figure stood in the arch of the sitting room door. Berdie grabbed the fireplace poker. "And what are you two up to?" Constable Albert Goodnight boomed.

Lillie leaped as if shot through by an electric bolt, and Berdie dropped the poker with a loud *clang*.

"The murdered body of Miriam Livingston is in the upstairs bedroom," Lillie blurted.

"Body?" The guard pulled the nightstick from its place on his rotund waist. "You two, outside," he bellowed, "and don't move from the front garden."

After a few moments, Constable Goodnight emerged from the house. "Dead indeed," he said baldly.

The policeman's jacket fit so tightly around his ample body, the gaps between the buttons revealed his shirt beneath. Observing the hairy growth beneath his nose, Berdie was sure he had never met a pair of mustache scissors.

"Mind you," he piped, "it was a tragedy in the waiting."

"How so?" Berdie asked.

"Everyone in Aidan Kirkwood knows Miriam Livingston doesn't believe in banks. Or I should say *didn't* believe in banks. Old fool kept her life savings in cash, right here. Some dogs have more sense than that one."

"Really!" Lillie was clearly offended.

Berdie wondered how many murder investigations Goodnight had attended to, if any.

The guard glanced at the two women's hands, observing that they each had only one glove on, and one of those was on backward. "You didn't touch anything in there, did ya'?" he bawled.

"We are aware of how to treat a crime scene," Berdie assured him.

Goodnight's eyes narrowed. "Are ya' now?" He touched the police insignia badge with his forefinger. "This is now a secured crime scene and this is my patch, so why don't you two toddle on home and have some tea?"

"But we found the body," Lillie spurted.

"I know where ya' live. I'll come round when I need you," he boomed. "Now go home."

Berdie spun on her heel, and Lillie followed her down the path to the gate.

"And didn't I tell you about Goodnight, Berdie?" Lillie spit it out.

Both women articulated at the same moment, "Not worth tuppance."

CHAPTER THREE

Once outside the gate of Lavender Cottage, the two women immediately dismissed Goodnight's command to go home and went next door to check on Natty. When they knocked, she came to her front window and espied them before opening her door.

"Quite lucid." Berdie was pleased.

"Quite, considering her ordeal," Lillie agreed.

After the pensioner opened the door and let them in, she stuck her head out and looked about before closing and locking the door securely. Still in her dressing robe from the bath, her neck was wrapped with a woolen scarf that had white snowflakes decorating the edges. She had also donned the holiday mittens Lillie lent to her earlier. Natty's white tresses dripped water, making little spots all across her robe and scarf.

"Do sit," shc offered cheerily. "There's a full pot of fresh tea in the kitchen, I believe."

"I'll get it for us, Natty." Berdie went to the kitchen while the two women sat comfortably in the sitting room.

True to course, Berdie found the hot teapot on the kitchen counter. It would seem Natty was better able to process her thinking when she was in the shelter of her own home. Berdie looked around for some cups and spotted a used one on the kitchen table. Sitting near it was a small television and a fully laden cup tree. The old oaken table was covered with a toile de Jouy–patterned tablecloth. Set on a cream-colored background, little sheep grazed across the table in quiet meadows with small water pools and ancient trees, all in a sun-faded shade of blue.

"How marvelously French," Berdie said. Then she spotted the curtains at the gracious kitchen window. They, too, were made of the same fabric. She stopped. "I wonder."

The window looked directly into Miriam Livingston's back garden—or rather directly onto the dilapidated fence that surrounded the garden. A large section of the fence was missing. Berdie sat in the table chair that faced the window. The empty cup was at her hand, and the television beyond it on the table edge closest to the window. She looked out upon the winter morning and the large gaping hole in the fence. "Straight on," she said.

Berdie opened wide the kitchen door into the sitting room. "Ladies, what say we have tea in the kitchen?"

"Right." Lillie was up, but Natty sat as if glued on the love seat. She gripped the arm of the rose-patterned sofa, making her knuckles turn a frightening white. She looked at Berdie pleadingly.

"I shan't go in there, I shan't. I shan't go in that room."

Lillie glanced at Berdie, who immediately consoled the unwilling woman. "It's all right, Natty. We'll take tea in the sitting room."

Lillie reassuringly patted Natty's shoulder.

In moments, Berdie emerged from the kitchen holding a tray laden with teapot, cups, spoons, sugar, honey, and cream. When she set the tray down on the central coffee table, it was apparent Lillie was strained.

"Natty wants to know where Miriam is," Lillie said.

Natty jumped up and filled everyone's cups with the soothing liquid. "You take two sugars, don't you, dear?" Natty asked Lillie.

"Yes, I do." Lillie tilted her head. "But how did you—"

"I poured tea for you at the church brunch on Saint Aidan's Day. You take two sugars." Natty smiled.

Berdie and Lillie exchanged a surprised glance.

Lillie leaned toward Berdie and spoke quietly, "She can't remember where she is half the time, but she can remember how many sugars I take from a tea that happened in August."

After the hostess was seated, Berdie spoke gently. "Natty, we need to talk about what happened this morning."

The elder's eyes flared, and she ran her mittened hands across the neck scarf. The serenity of forgotten events was being threatened.

"You needn't be frightened, dear. You're safe as houses. Lillie and I are here with you." Berdie lifted her teacup and took a sip. "Now, did you start out your morning with a cup of tea?"

"Oh, tea," she said. Batty Natty brought the teacup to her lips, which was quite a feat with the mittens. She smiled. "Isn't it nice to have tea with friends?"

"But you took your breakfast tea alone early this morning," Berdie coaxed.

Natty blew on the brown fluid in her cup.

Berdie continued, "Did you take your morning tea at the kitchen table? With that large window, it must be lovely to watch telly and gaze at the neighbor's back garden."

"Oh yes." The hostess grinned. "The sprightly Christmas robins on the fence." Without warning, the smile faded. Natty's mittened hand began to tremble so that tea was spilling all over the saucer, all over the mitten.

"Natty?" Berdie watched the ugly hand of fear take hold of this dear soul.

The woman sprang to her feet, splashing the tea all down her robe. The teacup tumbled. It hit the floor and shattered, sending a shower of broken pottery across the rug. "There's someone in the garden, menacing, menacing." She put her hands to her cheeks and started for the door.

The flurry of fright seemed to catch Lillie off guard. Her face paled, just as Berdie apprehended Natty and put a reassuring arm around her shoulders.

"Where's Miriam?" The dazed woman's voice was anxious.

Berdie eased the aging body into the love seat and sat next to her, then put her hand on the frail arm of Natalie Bell.

"Miriam has gone away," she said tenderly.

Though calmer, the oldster lifted her eyebrows. The silver spectacles couldn't cover the questioning look deep in her eyes as a droplet of water from her wet hair dripped down her nose.

"She would have loved to say good-bye, but she didn't have the opportunity."

Lillie began gathering the pieces of the broken teacup.

"Where did she go?" Natty asked.

"She has gone to a lovely place," Berdie reassured her. "It's very peaceful there and serene, a place where she will find great comfort."

Batty Natty nodded her head in understanding of what Berdie was saying. "The farm in Northumberland then!" She beamed.

Just as calm and relative sanity had been brought back into its proper place, there was a frantic knock at the door.

"Window!" Natty shouted.

While Berdie kept Natty still, Lillie peeked out the window.

"It's Cara Graystone. She's secured Snowdrop at the gate. The poor little white creature looks in need of water," Lillie announced.

"Dear little Snowdrop." Natty smiled. "Please see to Cara while I fetch Snowdrop some water."

The elderly hostess toddled off, and Lillie opened the front door.

Cara was flushed. Her beautiful gray eyes held a sense of panic. "What is going on?" She was trying to catch her breath. Though the air was cold, the collar of her sweat suit was moist with perspiration. "Why is Goodnight at Miss Livingston's?" she asked, knowing it couldn't be good news. "He has put up yellow tape and won't let me in the garden."

"You were jogging this morning," Berdie stated rather curtly.

Cara entered the sitting room and shook her honey ponytail. "I turned the far corner and saw the guard's car. Then I saw Albert at Lavender Cottage. Please, do you know what's going on?"

Lillie silently took a chair, and Berdie drew a deep breath.

"There's no easy way to say this. . . ." She paused. "Miriam Livingston is dead."

"Dead?" Cara eased herself into a nearby chair.

"Lillie and I came to pick her up for the interfaith jumble sale this morning and we found her body. I'm sorry to tell you there was foul play."

Cara shook her head. "No, no, no." She buried her beautiful face in her hands. Inside those soft gray eyes a dam burst. Tears fell between her fingers and splashed on the floor. She raised her head and looked at Berdie. "Has the world gone mad?" The loveliest girl in the village, her face skewed in pain, had rivulets running down her face, wetness gathering at her nose. Berdie grabbed a paper napkin from the tea tray and handed it to Cara.

"She was like a mother to me." The young woman wiped her nose and eyes, both red with grief.

"I know this is so very difficult for you, Cara. It's difficult for all of us." Berdie placed her hand on the girl's shoulder. "You see, we believe Natty may have seen something—the body, the perpetrator, we're not sure, but she's very fragile right now. We need to put on a good face for the old girl. Do you understand what I'm saying?" Berdie tried to be kind and strong at the same time.

"A good face. Really?" Cara stared hard at Berdie and pushed away the caring hand on her shoulder. Her tears blurred to anger. "What about me? What about the state I'm in?" she railed. "The fool that lives here is daft, she has no real sense of what's going on. It's a grace for her." Cara's tears spilled out. "How—how can I possibly cope?"

In a whirl, Cara lunged her way to the front door. She opened it and turned toward Berdie. "Encourage and comfort, isn't that what a vicar's wife does?" Despair sat squarely on the young woman's shoulders. "Well done, Mrs. Elliott." A loud slam of the door was the departing gesture given to two stunned women.

After making sure Natty was in a fair state of mind, Berdie rang up an altar guild member who was available to stay with the oldster the rest of the day.

Berdie and Lillie left Natty's dwelling and walked toward the Citron that was still parked near Lavender Cottage. The cottage gate, as well as the door, was crisscrossed with yellow police tape. Goodnight's car was still in place.

"I know Cara and Miss Livingston worked together, but really, don't you think Cara's reaction was a bit dramatic?" Berdie asked her companion.

"Oh they're far more than business partners," Lillie informed.

"How so?"

"The Graystones lived in London when Mrs. Graystone died. Cara was a child. Neither she nor her father adjusted very well to the loss." The women paused beside the car. "So Preston— Mr. Graystone—moved here hoping village life would be a more suitable environment in which to raise his daughter. . .start anew and all. Miss Livingston was Cara's nanny for only a short while. Preston and Miriam fell out over differences in child care or some such thing."

Berdie intuitively continued the story. "Graystone, over-whelmed with the start-up of his solicitor's practice here, worked all hours. Despite Miriam getting the sack, the females' relationship continued on a less formal level. The grandmamma figure became a kind of surrogate mother for the lonely child."

"More or less," Lillie confirmed.

"So, for all intents and purposes, Miss Livingston's death is a déjà vu of Cara losing her own mother." Berdie pursed her lips. She looked at her shoes. "I didn't know."

"Yes." Lillie paused and nodded. "Although recently it seemed they had grown a bit more distant. They had some kind of a rift."

The late morning sun was struggling to give snippets of light in between the gray clouds. The friends leaned their backs against the little car and stared at Lavender Cottage.

"Brilliant," Berdie spoke into the coolness. "I started out for a jumble sale and ended up with a dead congregant, accompanied by a half-baked investigation that will probably be a sore point for my beloved husband." Berdie took her car keys from her pocket. "Then, I managed to completely disparage another congregant's suffering, and last but not least, I've left another one believing her dead friend is on a farm up north."

"Having a little moan, are we?" Abruptly, Elgar's "Nimrod" played forth from Lillie's coat pocket, the mobile rudely interrupting her.

"Hello," she greeted into the phone. Her eyes widened. "Oh, hello Ivy." Lillie shot a glance at Berdie who cringed with forgetfulness. "May you speak to Mrs. Elliott?"

Berdie stepped away, shook her hands, and mouthed the words, *Not now.*

At that moment, a white van pulled up next to the women.

"Is this Lavender Cottage?" a man called out from the half-open window. Coroner was written across the side of the vehicle.

"Indeed," Berdie called back. *It's a divine opportunity*, she thought. "Can I assist you?"

"I'm afraid she's involved with another concern right now, Ivy." Lillie's voice was quite loud. She shook a fist toward Berdie. "No, we didn't forget you."

The van parked. Two people emerged, dressed for the occasion in their work smocks. The distinguished man, though smartly dressed, was relaxed and wore the stature of one who has done this business many times before. The younger woman with him, a crime scene investigator, appeared bent on getting to business and moving on.

Berdie met the two on the grass verge.

"Hello," she introduced herself, "I'm Bernadine Elliott." She extended her hand.

"I'm Dr. Meredith." He took Berdie's hand and shook it firmly. "This is Miss Andras." He gestured toward the woman who gave a terse smile.

"Excuse me, but did you say your name was Bernadine Elliott?" he asked.

"Yes." Berdie smiled.

Goodnight's booming voice trumpeted from the gate where he stood, "So you found the place."

Berdie was amazed that such a large man was so apt at startling people with his presence.

"You made good time from Timsley," Goodnight noted.

"Albert," the doctor acknowledged Goodnight then turned his

attention back to Berdie. "You're *the* Bernadine Elliott, the one who ran the exposé on MergingTec's fraudulent scheme several months back?"

"Yes I am." Berdie wasn't sure if the doctor wanted to punch her or hale her.

"I want to thank you." Dr. Meredith's brown eyes were keen.

Berdie breathed easier, but Goodnight leaned forward with a scowl and tapped his fingers on the gate.

"My brother's life was devastated by MergingTec. They bled him dry. Lost everything. Those thieves strutted about with their yachts and dinner parties. But now, thanks to you, those devils are getting theirs. Ill-gotten gain loses its glamour from the inside of a jail cell."

"Quite so," Berdie agreed.

"Justice is being served. They'll be banged up for life. Well done."

It was as if a bright holiday gift had just arrived on Berdie's doorstep. "Thank you, Dr. Meredith." She beamed with the delight that her success was acknowledged.

"Are you investigating this case?" the man asked.

"No, she's not," the guard interrupted. He knit his bushy brows. "Not an appropriate duty for a vicar's wife."

The doctor stared at Goodnight. "That's talent gone wanting." Dr. Loren Meredith wasn't the least bit intimidated by the large Albert Goodnight.

It was then that Berdie noticed that the coroner's shining brown hair had a slight frosting of gray at the temples and was pulled back at the nape of his neck into a handsome ponytail.

Dr. Meredith spoke to the large man, "Scotland Yard put their hand to the MergingTec case and all but botched it. It took Mrs. Elliott's prowess to get it right." He turned back to his heroine.

"Please." Berdie was blushing. "Call me Berdie."

Miss Andras glanced at her watch.

"One thing," Berdie added, "I was the one who found the body. May I take the liberty to suggest you may want to take note of Miss Livingston's back. I think it could be significant."

Guard Goodnight lifted the yellow police tape. "Gordon B! The Christmas goose will be on the table by the time you two shut your gobs!"

Miss Andras blithely slipped under the tape and made for the door.

"Go on, Albert. I'll be there momentarily," the coroner commanded.

Berdie could just make out the blue language of Goodnight's mumbles as he walked to the door.

Dr. Meredith pulled out a business card and gave it to Berdie. "I am in your debt. If ever there's anything I can do for you. . ."

Berdie knew from the strength of his voice that the gentleman was sincere.

"Thank you." She hesitated then went on. "And about the victim's back, Dr. Meredith. Check to see if there are red spots that align with the wax drippings I believe you'll find under the body."

The doctor nodded and pulled an unwrapped surgical plastic cap from his pocket. As he did, he espied the lovely Lillie who caught his gaze. With a quick tip of his head, he acknowledged her and she smiled back.

"Oh this is my friend, Miss Lillie Foxworth," Berdie quipped, "a bit indisposed at the moment I'm afraid."

"Yes, well, off to work then." He took in a last look at the mobile phone–toting Lillie and turned to Berdie. "And I'll follow through on your suggestion."

She watched the gentleman make his way inside the cottage. Berdie was certain he would be rigorous in his job.

"Yes, I'm sure she'll ring you." Lillie looked at Berdie. "At her earliest opportunity." She switched the mobile off and put it in her pocket. "Did she ever put a flea in my ear." Lillie looked tired.

"I owe you," Berdie admitted.

"Hugh's on his way in the church's people mover to get Ivy and take her to the sale. He's tried to reach you on your mobile."

"I shouldn't doubt it."

"We're done with our little moan then?" Lillie smiled.

"It was just a hiccup." Berdie's cheer returned. "I must admit, that gracious man with his appreciation couldn't have come at a better time."

"And handsome, too." Lillie smiled.

Berdie lifted her brows and grinned. "Interested, are you? He seems to be."

"Just saying he's handsome." Lillie's smile blossomed into a grin.

The women were seated in the car when a shout sounded from the cottage door. It was Goodnight.

"Oh that man!" Lillie gulped. Berdie opened the car window.

"You two, in my office, seven this evening, and don't even

think about being late."

"Where's your office, the Upland Arms car park?" Berdie chided.

The guard turned, and Berdie closed the window.

"Belayed by his charm," Lillie said. Both women let go a quick laugh then a sigh as they pulled away from the cottage.

Lillie said she had three scheduled voice lessons to give in the afternoon, so Berdie dropped her friend back at the flat. Berdie wasn't keen on going back to the vicarage where she was sure the phone would be ringing incessantly. So she did several errands, including going to Sainsburys for some food goods and dropping the donated parish bits and bobs in her car boot at the sale, although she didn't stay.

When she got home and finished putting the market goods away, it was only minutes until her husband arrived.

He looked rushed when he came in the kitchen. He was returning his mobile in his pocket. "Goodnight just called; he wants you and Lillie at his office in five minutes."

"And how's your day as well?" Berdie responded.

"Sorry, love." The peck he gave her on the cheek was less than passionate. "I'm driving you both over." Hugh took a breath. "I know this must be hard on you, Berdie, but just let the officials do their job." He put his hands on her shoulders, and his blue eyes were steady. "Stay clear."

Berdie blinked.

Hugh straightened his collar. "Right then, ready to go?"

The constable's "office" was a former front bedroom in the family's row home at the east end of the High Street. The sitting room was a temporary waiting room this evening. Several people who were considered witnesses hung about, while Jonathon Goodnight, the eldest child in the Goodnight family, tried to keep the smaller children in hand. Hugh stepped on a toy truck, and Lillie's coat was soiled when Daisy, the Goodnight's spaniel, jumped paws first to greet her.

Mrs. Goodnight, car keys in hand, came through the front door bringing several more people with her. "Like gatherin' up sheep, this," she greeted whoever would listen.

Among those whom Harriet Goodnight brought as possible witnesses was a very confused and frail Batty Natty Bell. However, the old woman's demeanor perked up the moment she saw Lillie and Berdie.

Mrs. Goodnight rapped on the "office" door and hollered, "Vicar's here! And that lot what I rounded up."

A muffled voice from the other side of the door hollered in return, "Send the vicar in and send some drink in with him."

"None of the drink while you're on duty, Albert Goodnight!" The constable's wife yelled then waved Hugh to the room.

It wasn't but a moment when Hugh reentered the waiting room. "He wants you two as well," he said to Berdie and Lillie.

"We're going in that room, Natty." Berdie pointed to the door. "And we'll be back out soon."

Natty didn't appear to be very happy about the arrangement.

Hugh stood, and the women sat in chairs that Berdie would have bet a ten-pound note came from the jumble sale. Goodnight appeared stuffed in his seat at a littered desk that was inadequate to accommodate a man of his size. A plate was parked on the corner of the desk, holding a meat pie and the remains of green pea mash.

The guard narrowed his eyes and looked squarely at Berdie. "Remember I'm the one asking the questions here." The constable stuck a fork into the meat pie and shoved a large piece in his mouth. "Miriam Livingston was dead when you found the body?"

Berdie tried to be tactful and responsive despite being appalled. "Perhaps we should go and return when you've finished your meal."

Goodnight chewed. "Answer the question, please."

"I checked for a pulse, there was none." She paused. "By the state of the victim, I would say—"

"I have the coroner's report, Mrs. Elliott." A piece of piecrust was caught on Goodnight's mustache.

"As the party who found the body I have an interest in seeing that report," Berdie spoke carefully.

"And do you?" The piece of crust bounced with each word. "Is that so you and your busybody friend here can have a good chin wag?"

"Mr. Goodnight, my wife and Miss Foxworth are not given to idle gossip." Hugh's voice was crisp. "Mrs. Elliott has the best of intents."

The policeman shoved another forkful of food in his mouth. "Did you see any money?"

"Yes, hundred-pound notes in the bedroom."

"See a murder weapon?"

Berdie tilted her chin. "I saw something that could have possibly been the murder weapon beneath the hem of the deceased's gown."

"A screwdriver?" Goodnight barked.

"Yes."

"Gotcha." Goodnight smiled. "You were snoopin', weren't ya'?" He scribbled something on a paper.

Hugh cleared his throat.

Harriet Goodnight popped into the room holding Miss Bell by the elbow. "The batty one wants to come in to be with Mrs. Elliott. She's givin' us the fits out here." She deposited Natty in the room and left with a loud slam of the door before her husband could object.

"Who's in the garden?" Natty squeaked when she saw the constable. "Someone's in the garden."

"Constable Goodnight..." Berdie couldn't help herself. "I think Natty may have valuable information to the investigation."

Albert pointed his fork at Natty. "What, this one?" He then scooped up some pea mash from the plate. "She's daft as Balaam's donkey."

There was a knock at the door and Mrs. Goodnight plummeted through again. "Cara Graystone says she needs to see you."

"Harriet," the policeman bawled, "I've told you at least ten times, don't interrupt when I have people in the room."

Cara squeezed past the guard's wife and stood her ground directly in front of the desk. "I have something that's relevant to Miss Livingston's murder."

Goodnight frowned, but Cara rattled on and Mrs. Goodnight banged the door closed.

"This morning I saw a man in the woods when I was out

jogging. I didn't think anything of it at the time, but he looked, um, furtive. He was coming from the direction of Lavender Cottage."

"Description?" Goodnight stuck the last bit of pea mash in his mouth.

Cara pushed her long hair back with a flip. "He was tall, very tall, light hair, a white blond color. It wasn't anyone from the village. I hadn't ever seen him before. Dressed in black."

Natty started. "Yes." She began to tremble. "I saw him, too."

Cara gasped. She turned to the old woman. "You saw him, too?"

"Right." Goodnight put the fork down. "Ladies, was the man running?"

At the exact same moment Cara said, "Yes," Natty said, "No."

"Blinkers!" Batty Natty shouted, just like a child who speaks at the same time as another child. "Blinkers on you, Cara." She grinned; the trembling ceased.

Goodnight rolled his eyes. "Saints preserve us. Was the man carrying any bags or wearing a large overcoat?"

Berdie's ears perked up.

Again, at the same moment, Cara said, "No," Natty said, "Yes."

"Blinkers again." Natty was downright cheerful. "I got blinkers on Cara twice."

Cara leaned close to the constable. "With all due respect, does she have to be in the room?"

Goodnight ran his tongue across his top teeth, sweeping little green bits away. "Listen, Cara, what you saw was someone, probably one of our holiday blow-ins, who had a row with his wife, or was suffering a bout of indigestion from eating breakfast at the Upland Arms. Now go on home and try to have a good night's rest."

Cara blazed and folded her arms across her dark leather jacket. "Fine, I'm going to give this information to my father. As the village solicitor he'll do something about it."

"Tell him anything you want, love, this one's already on the hook."

Berdie tried to be polite. "Excuse me, Constable Goodnight, did you say this one's on the hook? Already?"

"Well done, Albert." Hugh wasn't helping at all.

With defiant gray eyes, Cara steamed out of the room.

"Don't you want to ask me something?" Lillie chimed in.

"No." The policeman leaned back and folded his hands over his large stomach. "And as for your person with information that is invaluable to the case, Mrs. Elliott, observe." He turned his smug face to Batty Natty.

"Miss Bell, did you see, at Lavender Cottage this morning, a *short* man with *dark* hair wearing a *plaid* shirt?"

Her eyes grew large. "Yes, I did," she said with a nod of the head.

Goodnight leaned forward across the desk. "And did you not also see the little green men with orange hair, dressed in nappies?"

Natty's chin quivered. "They were there, too?"

"All right, Constable, you've made your point." Hugh was sharp.

"I rest my case." Goodnight grinned like the Cheshire cat. "You can all go home now."

Back out in the sitting room, Hugh walked to the front door, followed by Berdie and Lillie. "I'll get the car, you wait here," Hugh said and left.

Lillie came close to Berdie. She was almost breathless. "Who do you think the suspect is?"

"I don't know," Berdie admitted. "But as sure as Christmas holly pricks the thumb, I'm going to find out. We'll see if this case is already on the hook."

CHAPTER FOUR

After leaving the Goodnight residence, it took only five minutes to deposit Lillie and Natty in their homes. Since the Elliotts passed the Upland Arms on the way home, they decided to stop for some takeaway.

"I'll go in and get it. What do you want?" Hugh asked.

"Anything but meat pie," Berdie declared.

She could hear her stomach growl while she sat in the quiet people carrier. It was cold but clear, the moon was waxing—or was it waning? She wasn't really sure. Smoke rose from the stone chimney of the Upland Arms. It curled into the dark sky and disappeared among the stars.

This pub, established in 1680, was the true local of Aidan Kirkwood. The lively public house not only served up the standard drink and pub grub, but rounds of conversation and scuttlebutt. It often had the latest news before the *Kirkwood Times*, the weekly homegrown newspaper, even knew anything occurred. And just this past Sunday night, the Upland Arms sponsored a darts tournament in which several teams from nearby village pubs participated. That made Berdie wonder just who it was that Hugh had to help home in the middle of the night.

The arched wooden door of the establishment opened, and light spilled across the car park accompanied by the usual pub banter and jolly music. It broke Berdie's moment of reverie. Edsel Butz stepped out, bags of carryout dinners in his arms. For a man who was often jovial, who cherished both family and the dinner hour, he looked quite low. Berdie wasn't sure what to expect if she conversed with Edsel. After all, when he left the party last night he was angry and humiliated. Then today she had left his wife, Ivy, literally out in the cold. She opened the van window with a wing and a prayer.

"Hello, Edsel."

He set his eyes upon her but it was as if he didn't really see her. His large frame sagged, work coveralls sticking out from under his plaid woolen overshirt. Berdie imagined he had worn his straight dark hair parted on the side like that, with a close cut around his ears, since school days.

He finally acknowledged her. "Mrs. Elliott."

"Edsel, I'm very sorry about—" Berdie started.

The man shook his head. "You haven't done anything to me you need to apologize for."

"Yes, well, there's Ivy."

"She's barely speaking to me at the moment. You can take that up with Ivy. I've got other things on my mind right now."

Berdie tried to console him. "The whole village is trying to deal with Miss Livingston's death."

Edsel moved closer to the open window. "You invited Jamie Donovan, my apprentice, to your party, didn't you? You must think he's a good chap."

Berdie smelled the oily aroma of chips and cheese toasties. "I have no reason to think otherwise."

"You know, those things he said to Miss Livingston at the party, calling her a stupid cow and all, it was just a snap reaction to her rude behavior."

"Yes, I think we all know he didn't mean anything by it." Berdie wondered why they were talking about Jamie.

"You pound a ground stake into that belief, Mrs. Elliott." The man looked down then straightened. "Jamie's going to need it."

The pub door opened wide again and Hugh approached with two brown paper bags. "Evening, Edsel."

"Vicar."

Hugh handed the bags to Berdie through the window then turned back to Mr. Butz.

"Sorry about all this mess." Hugh sounded concerned.

"Not your fault, Vicar." Edsel tried to sound chipper.

"I just heard some of the scuttlebutt inside. If there's anything I can do, please, don't hesitate to call."

"Thank you. I'll keep that in mind." Edsel tipped his head to Hugh and Berdie then trudged to his work lorry laden with ladders and electrical gear. He started the engine.

"He was going on about Jamie," Berdie informed when Hugh got in the people carrier.

He inserted and turned the key. He sat back and paused. "The suspect in the Livingston murder case has done a runner. There's a manhunt being conducted. Apparently, Jamie Donovan killed Miriam Livingston."

⎯

The large kitchen in the vicarage was quite cozy for its size. The table for two by the back garden window was just big enough for Berdie and Hugh to sit comfortably. Two baskets of hot fish and chips were ready to be devoured. Berdie doused her food liberally with the malt vinegar that always accompanies a fish dinner.

"I just can't believe it's Jamie." Berdie started to put a chip in her mouth.

Hugh took her empty hand.

"Oh yes." Berdie bowed her head.

"Thank You, Father, for the bounty of this, Your earth; bless it to our bodies. Amen." Hugh blew on a hot chip. "This whole thing with Jamie has you in a real stew."

"Well why wouldn't it? Why Jamie? I know he's new to the village, and he made some inappropriate comments to Miriam Livingston, but he's not a murderer."

"Or doesn't appear to be," Hugh countered.

Berdie took a bite of fish and chewed for a moment, almost ignoring what her husband had just said. She swallowed. "What ties him to the murder? Electricity off and he's a repairman, a tool, a witness, what?"

Hugh put his fork down. Berdie saw him raise his left eyebrow, a sure sign that she probably would not be pleased with whatever came from his mouth next.

"Berdie, leave this investigation alone." Hugh was in his military mode.

"But, Hugh, Albert Goodnight is less than brilliant at investigating something like this. He's doing a terrible job," Berdie pleaded.

"Bernadine, that's the point. It's *his* job. I admit, as a former military officer for British intelligence, I'm less than impressed with his work as well. But we have our own work to do."

Berdie popped a chip in her mouth and chomped as if it were shoe leather.

"Love, we are caretakers of this parish." Hugh enumerated, "First, we have a funeral to arrange. Next we have the Butz family, Mr. Raheem, even Reverend Lewis who suffered from the biting tongue of Miss Livingston. Now there's no possible reconciliation. How are they coping? Cara Graystone has suffered great personal loss. And what of Jamie Donovan? We have a community in mourning and they're looking to me"—he stopped and wagged his head—"they're looking to *both of us* for pastoral care at a critical moment in time."

Berdie was now paying attention to what Hugh said, and of course, as was almost always the case when her husband was making a point, it made good sense.

Hugh bit a chip in half. "Here it is Christmas, the season of goodwill, and someone's been murdered. Many in our congregation are wondering if this is a lost holiday."

Berdie looked her husband keenly in the eye. "And it is not."

"Indeed!" The conviction of the reverend's sure and true beliefs stood at attention. "And as the protector and defender of the faith, it is fitting to care for the welfare of the flock. It's crucial that we allow people to grieve and at the same time restore a sense of normalcy. All this is my job and it's a fair expectation. But I can't do it without your help." Hugh gulped down the other half of the chip.

Now it was Berdie's turn to put down her fork. "Cooking

church casserole dishes when Lavender Cottage needs a good scour for evidence?"

"No time for chasing the bad guys, love. And you do far more than supply feedings."

Hugh was such a wonderful husband and an outstanding pastor, but how could he observe Goodnight's lack of ability and be satisfied with it? On the other hand, she knew every word he spoke was true. She had responsibilities that required her full attention here in the church ministry, and, as he said, they weren't just cooking casseroles. She reached across the table and took Hugh's hand. "By the grace of God I'll do my best, Hugh. I can't promise more than that."

Hugh smiled. "I can't ask more than that."

By the time they finished their meal and tended to the tidying up around the vicarage, it was bedtime. After saying their nightly Compline prayer together, Hugh was out with the light. But Berdie was restless. She kept thinking about Jamie Donovan.

The next morning, Berdie set about weaving her regular routine into the demands of the current calamity.

Her first errand this morning was to walk to the *Kirkwood Times* located on the High Street. It was a tradition, since 1869, for the vicar's wife to submit a weekly recipe to be printed in the column, "Recipe Corner." In general, as a former investigative reporter, Berdie found submitting recipes to the weekly rag a bit of a cheek. After all, she had worked on tough cases with some powerful newspapers. However, for the sake of tradition and good standing in the community, she continued the practice.

Her submission today was Bread Sauce, a flavorsome favorite for the holiday table.

This morning, the walk was a delight to the senses: The air was brisk, whiffs of smoke alerted the nose to hearth fires, doors wore lively Christmas wreaths, and boisterous woodland birds called to one another. It took only a slip of time to reach the newspaper office.

When she got there, the small storefront office was stuffed firmer than a Christmas goose. Visiting newspaper personnel, two desks and multiple filing cabinets, plus a counter, shared a space that was large enough to hold only one desk comfortably.

"Mrs. Elliott," David Exton greeted. The lean young man, whose black-frame glasses gave his baby face a note of authority, was the son of the former, now retired, editor. His journalism degree just finished, he was hungry to make his mark in the world of news.

Berdie squeezed through the crowd to enter the swing gate of the counter behind which David stood.

With rapid fire, the digital recorder crowd was launching a gaggle of questions toward the editor concerning the recent murder. He was doing his best to accommodate.

Berdie deposited her recipe at the appropriate in-box and moved back toward the counter swing door. Just the odor of the place pulled at her newspaper roots.

A reporter loudly inquired of David, "Did you know the victim?"

"Not well," he responded, "but I can tell you she reacted churlishly toward my photographer. When he snapped her picture after winning Aidan Kirkwood's August flower show, Miss Livingston tried to break his camera. Sold that picture to a London paper, by the way."

"What can you tell us about the perp, Jamie Donovan?"

Berdie couldn't help herself. She stopped by the swing gate to listen.

"All we can give you at the moment is"—David Exton read scribbles from an Upland Arms paper serviette—"according to our local police, the murder weapon was a workman's screwdriver, found at the crime scene that inextricably ties Jamie Donovan, age twenty-three, to the crime."

Berdie blinked. How does a screwdriver do that?

The editor continued, "Witnesses say they heard him arrive on the scene near the time the crime was committed."

Berdie knit her brow. Heard?

"His work lorry was found at his employer's home, where he apparently bunked for parts unknown."

"He's from Ireland?" another newspaperman questioned.

"Originally. He lived in Aidan Kirkwood for the past three months."

"A manhunt is being conducted?"

"All rail stations, airports, and water passage ports have been alerted. Several calls have come into the Aidan Kirkwood police station."

Berdie smirked. Police station? The cramped bedroom with Goodnight chomping meat pie flashed across her mind.

"None of the calls have been conclusive." David Exton drew a breath.

"And the motive?" the same voice asked.

"Money was stolen, the amount unknown, but enough to fit under a mattress."

"Under a mattress?" A chuckling voice spoke the general sentiments. "Hardly worth killing for."

Indeed, Berdie thought, *hardly worth killing for.* This lot could teach Albert Goodnight a thing or two.

Berdie heard herself speak, "Jamie's a good lad."

Every eye fell to her.

"Hey," a senior woman among the horde barked, "aren't you Bernadine Elliott? You broke the MergingTec scandal. "

Berdie flushed. She thought of her promise to Hugh. "Must go."

"You know the murderer?" another asked.

Berdie pushed through.

"Uncovered something?" someone shouted.

Young David Exton interrupted, "She's the village vicar's wife."

Berdie maneuvered her way through and flew out the door.

The pull of that newspaper office was like a small child spying a jar of Christmas sweeties!

"My next stop is the greengrocer. Preparing a church dish for the funeral meal, at this moment that's my responsibility, yes." Berdie looked down the High Street to where the Raheems' store was nestled. "I can't possibly run into trouble at the greengrocer."

When Berdie entered the store, the jolly bells on the door clanged loudly. The produce bins were filled with fresh goods, but it seemed business at the store was less than robust. The Raheem family had arrived in town near the same time as the

Elliotts. Clergy had a fairly secure built-in acceptance factor. But any small village can be a fishbowl that doesn't easily welcome new swimmers, and in Aidan Kirkwood, the Raheems were dog-paddling.

Mrs. Raheem came out from the back room. "Good morning," she greeted cheerlessly. She held a pair of kitchen shears in one hand and a bundle of parsley in the other. Her market pinny covered most of her lively colored sari that floated around her ankles. She was a lovely woman with dark dramatic features— exotic. But today she was anxious and looked as if she hadn't slept.

"Good morning." Berdie smiled in return. She had seen Sharday Raheem at church, but she had never before seen her working in the store.

"Can I help you find something?" Mrs. Raheem asked quickly.

"I see just what I want. Those kiwis are lovely. Also, I need fifteen pounds of potatoes."

Mrs. Raheem put both the shears and parsley in the ample pinny pocket. With great zeal, she flipped open a brown bag and attacked the potatoes, rapidly stuffing them in the sack.

"So you're minding the store today?" Berdie asked.

"My husband had to go to London this morning and left me here alone to do all the work." She shoved three more potatoes in the bag. "He couldn't wait until my sister arrived to help me, no, he had to go today."

"It must have been something important," Berdie tried to encourage.

"Business, always business, and soon we won't have one!" She picked up a potato white with mildew. "You see, no buyers, the food rots."

Sharday appeared so taken in her displeasure, Berdie was hoping that particular potato would not absently make it into the brown bag. But it did.

"And now the bank calls for us to come. Ten thousand pounds we have to give them or we have no shop. Do they think the money grows on bushes?"

The bells on the door rang out again and Lillie swept into the store.

"Good morning one and all," Lillie practically sang, causing Mrs. Raheem to put even more punch in her potato gathering.

"Lillie, you're cheerful," Berdie observed.

"I just got three new clients for voice instructions. Relatives are giving singing lessons as Christmas gifts. That seals my winter holiday in Portugal." Lillie twirled and snapped her fingers.

The storekeeper took the bag prepared for Berdie to the checkout counter. "What does madam want?" she asked Lillie acidly.

"Four onions."

Berdie chimed in, "That's four *pounds*. She means four *pounds* of onions."

Lillie's stunned eyes fell upon her friend who held an index finger to her lips. Lillie whispered, "What will I do with four pounds of onions?"

Mrs. Raheem set about gathering the vegetables.

"Later," Berdie whispered back.

"Where's Mr. Raheem?" Lillie asked Berdie quietly. "At least *he's* pleasant."

The onions were gathered, weighed, and at the counter in less than a minute.

Both women moved to check out. Lillie's purchase rang up fine, but Mrs. Raheem had to check the price of kiwis to complete Berdie's order. The cash drawer was open and the woman lifted the coin tray to check a price list. Oddly, there was a sudden scent of lavender. Both friends looked at each other. Then they saw it—a one-hundred-pound note clearly lay on the floor of the cash drawer.

"A special," Sharday Raheem announced, "two kiwis for a pound." She returned the coin tray to its place.

"My." Berdie could feel herself moving beyond her official church duties. "I couldn't help but notice. It's not often a retail business will accept such a large note." She was being careful.

"My husband put it there." Mrs. Raheem stopped. "Are you spying my money drawer?" The woman was clearly offended.

"No, no. It's just that I only have a twenty-pound note."

Lillie's eyes were still secured on the cash drawer, mouth agog.

When the transaction was complete, Berdie had to grab her friend's coat sleeve to move her toward the door. "Thank you, Mrs. Raheem."

Once outside, both women bustled away from the shop door then halted.

"That was Miriam's money." Lillie looked dazed.

"It's a sales cash drawer," Berdie pointed out.

"Yes, but she said her husband put it there."

"True. Let's not jump to conclusions. It could have been given to him." Berdie glanced across the road and caught sight of The Copper Kettle Tea Shop. She started across the narrow street. "Come on, Lillie."

"Where are we going?"

"Fresh tea and scones always makes things easier to sort."

The women trundled across the road with their multiple pounds of veggies. Once inside the shop, the two friends settled on polished wooden chairs at a table just big enough for two. Tea canisters lined the walls, and pretty little painted cupboards held teapots and stacks of cups, plates, and other various tea paraphernalia. It was just recently that The Copper Kettle added four tables with chairs to the shop. Originally, Villette Horn, the owner, only sold tea. Now she sold it, brewed it, and served it accompanied by fresh baked goods and simple fare.

By virtue of its cramped space, The Copper Kettle could be a hotbed of gossip. But at this moment, Berdie and Lillie were the only customers present.

"Tell me, Lillie," Berdie said, "did Miriam often disperse one-hundred-pound notes around the village?"

"Never," Lillie retorted. "And how often do you pay for a purchase at the greengrocer with hundred-pound notes?"

"What's your pleasure?" Villette Horn grinned and pointed to the slate board on the wall where the offerings for the day were chalked in. Short-clipped, caramel-colored hair contrasted with her long jaw. "I say, the cranberry scones are going well."

"Oh yes, two of those." Berdie looked to Lillie who agreed.

"And we'll split a pot of Yorkshire Gold," Lillie added.

Villette set to caring for her guests.

"The conversation at the party. . ." Berdie was searching her memory. "Miriam scorned Mr. Raheem when he suggested she calm down."

"Yes, I remember," Lillie said.

"Hardly a cause to murder someone."

"After she was so rude to him, he offered to take her home. Doesn't that strike you as odd?" Lillie scrunched her nose.

Berdie gave a slight nod. "But there's something else. We watched him leave with Miriam and Natty. That means he was likely the last person to see Miriam alive."

Villette was at the table and laid it with the ordered goods. The two scones smelled of sweet oranges and pungent cranberry, but something was amiss, another odor. The attendant wiggled her nose and did a double sniff. "Onions!" she exclaimed.

"We've been to the greengrocer," was all Berdie said.

"Well, I hope no one else comes in. It's an unseemly odor for my tearoom," Villette spouted and returned to her work.

Lillie gave Berdie's foot a nudge. "What am I going to do with all those onions?"

Berdie slathered her warm scone in fresh butter. "Mrs. Raheem was telling me about their money woes before you entered the store. The large onion purchase was an act of mercy."

"Merciful with *my* money." Lillie swirled the cream in her tea. "And what money woes for the Raheems would that be then?" She took a bite of scone.

Berdie whispered, "The bank requires ten thousand pounds or

the Raheems are in danger of losing the store. Mrs. Raheem was quite concerned about it."

Lillie swallowed the scone in one gulp. With a quick gesture, she brought the teacup to her lips and washed the bread down her throat. She took a breath. "Would Raheem murder for money?" she squeaked.

"Quietly dear." Berdie's caution was barely audible and Lillie leaned forward. "Money, or the need for it, has been known to turn man into beast."

Lillie abruptly sat up. Mrs. Horn was again at the table.

"Everything canna, quite all right and more?" she asked.

"Quite delicious." Berdie suspected the woman had other motives for being at the table.

"Horrible stuff this, with Miss Livingston and all."

Berdie's suspicions proved true.

"Natty Bell's son came for her. She'll live with him through to spring. Poor Natty. And to think the murderer lived right under our nose." She lifted the lid of the teapot and glanced in. "True, Jamie Donovan hasn't been among us long." She returned the lid to the pot. "But, oh my, and a customer pointed this out when she was here this morning. How can Ivy Butz live with the fact that her husband took in a killer?"

"Mrs. Horn, if you don't mind." Berdie set her teacup down firmly. "It sounds like Jamie Donovan has been tried and convicted in the court of The Copper Kettle."

Villette's tight lips revealed she was not pleased with Berdie's stark evaluation. "I say!"

"Really," Berdie kindly reasoned, "wouldn't you agree all this is a bit premature?"

The hostess arched over the teapot. "You go see that poor, sleepless Ivy Butz with the tear-stained face, and you ask our Ivy if it's premature." The woman left the table.

When two customers arrived, Berdie and Lillie finished their teatime quickly, especially when Mrs. Horn obtusely sniffed.

Berdie walked home, bags of produce in her arms.

Upon opening the back kitchen door, Berdie ran headlong into Hugh, who was leaving. Both yelped as potatoes spewed everywhere. Their surprise turned into easy laughter as they gathered the errant veggies.

"I'm sorry, love," Hugh offered.

"So when and where does your flight depart?" Berdie teased.

Hugh put the produce on the kitchen counter. "I'm glad you're home, Berdie. Edsel just called. His family is in a state. Will you come with me to tend them?"

"You needn't ask twice," she said, and both of them were out the door.

CHAPTER FIVE

Getting to the Butz household was a quick jaunt. Hugh informed Berdie on the way over that Edsel was in distress concerning both his wife and daughter, Lucy, who were not coping well with the death of Miss Livingston or the accusation of Jamie Donovan as a murderer. And apparently there were preexisting problems as well.

It was obvious when arriving at the Butz's home that though the central portion of the house was built over sixty years ago, rooms and sections had been added on since then. Edsel, in his work overalls, was waiting for Berdie and Hugh. He opened the front door before the vicar could even lift the knocker.

"Thank you for coming so quickly," Edsel greeted. He ushered them into the hall that clamored with the sound of distant voices of children. When he pointed the way to the drawing room, one couldn't help but notice the two suitcases, full to the bulging, that austerely sat near the door. Berdie wearily gave a sideward glance to her husband, who acknowledged her with an arched eyebrow.

At the bottom of a small staircase, Edsel belted out like a trumpet, "Ivy, the vicar's here."

Berdie and Hugh followed Edsel into the newly added drawing

room where there were two chairs, taken by Hugh and Berdie, and a sofa where Edsel planted himself. The only other object in the room was a small commode table where a rather stark Christmas cactus was desperately trying to bloom. There was nothing about this drawing room with its freshly painted bare walls that really drew one in. It rather shouted, *Go away!*

Edsel's forehead wrinkled. "She had to have a drawing room, you know. Well, here 'tis," he said awkwardly. "Now she wants a wine cellar. And here's me that only drinks the fizzy pops with the young 'uns."

Ivy bustled into the drawing room with their youngest child, two-year-old pajama-clad Duncan, in one hand and a very large handkerchief in the other. Ivy's face was swollen with crying, her mousy brown hair pulled back and tied.

"Edsel seems to think you can help us," were Ivy's first words spoken, and that to the floor. When she finally brought herself to look at Berdie, her eyes welled up with moisture. Edsel stood up and helped his wife settle into the sofa.

"Martha, come get your brother." Ivy's roar made Edsel's trumpeting sound timid. "I hate fussing in front of the children," she offered demurely and sat on the sofa with Hugh.

Edsel returned to his seat.

Eight-year-old Martha entered the room. Her twin brother, Milton, was close behind.

"Say hello to the Elliotts," Edsel instructed.

"Hello," squeaked Martha and wrestled Duncan from her mother's ample arms.

"Are you going to get Lucy to come out of her room?" Milton asked Berdie.

"Don't give Duncan any of your peanut butter," Ivy cautioned. "You know how it bloats him."

"It gives him stink bombs," Milton announced to Hugh.

With the baby between them, the twins waddled Duncan off on his pudgy little toddler legs.

"There's a problem with Lucy?" Hugh questioned.

Ivy burst into tears. "There's problems from London to Lincolnshire." She wiped her eyes and nose with the large handkerchief. "Which one you want first?"

Edsel scowled. "Lucy locked herself in her room last evening, and she refuses to come out. We've tried to reason with her. Lila, our second, who hibernates with her planetary charts—she fancies herself an astronomer, you know—even she gave it a go, but our Lucy's a stubborn one. And Lucy's not eaten."

"It's all because of that Jamie Donovan." Ivy's cheeks turned an angry shade of red. "If he hadn't gone after her—"

"He didn't go after her, Ivy Butz." Edsel looked at Hugh. "Jamie cared for my girl, but not in that way."

Ivy's nose glowed like a holly berry. "Then why's she mad for him?"

"Why is any fifteen-year-old girl gone mad over a handsome young man?"

Berdie could see this going in circles for hours. Then she thought of how tenderly Hugh had gotten their daughter, Clare, through some rough spots when she was a teen. "Let Hugh take a go at getting Lucy to see sense," Berdie offered. "He was adept with our daughter, Clare."

Edsel was on his feet. "I'll take you to her," he offered Hugh.

"Mind you, I was Clare's father, but I'll see what I can do to help."

Edsel already had a look of relief about him, and with that, both men ventured forward.

"I wish that troublesome Jamie Donovan had never stepped foot in this house, this village for that matter." Ivy welled up. "I've had to keep my little hinnies home from school, all the talk that Jamie's a"—she paused and dabbed at her eyes—"a killer." The distraught woman buried her face in the handkerchief.

Berdie moved to the sofa and put her arm around Ivy's shoulders. "We don't know that Jamie perpetrated the crime." Berdie was trying to bring comfort.

Ivy lifted her head abruptly. "Don't we?" She was sharp. "Goodnight had Edsel identify the murder weapon." Her jaw tightened. "And wasn't it the very screwdriver Edsel had given Jamie as an early Christmas gift. 'Well done, Jamie'—can you imagine—is carved into the black onyx handle with Jamie's hire date inscribed on the shaft. One of a kind, it is."

Berdie thought back to when she saw the tool beside Miriam Livingston's body. She had noted the unique black onyx but hadn't noticed inscriptions. "Jamie's tool may have been used, but unless something puts him at the crime scene—" Berdie stated, when Ivy interrupted.

"Oh he was there." Ivy was resolute. "The Turners, Mr. Clark, Widow Sheridan, all that lot who live on Westwood Drive. . . Ask them. They all heard the awful grinding screech from that old work lorry Jamie drives. When it comes to a stop those blasted brakes raise the dead." Ivy took a breath. "Mr. Clark says he saw a short man with dark hair."

"It was Jamie?" Berdie asked.

"Well of course it was him." Ivy was irritated. "He's done a runner, hasn't he? Sure sign of guilt. And you heard what he said to Miriam at the party. 'You'll get yours,' he said."

Berdie placed her hand on Ivy's arm. "Those were youthful words from a slighted twenty-three-year-old."

"You're not on Edsel's track are you?" Ivy stiffened.

Berdie was perplexed. "Edsel's track?"

"My husband's dafter than a topside-down Christmas pudding!" The large woman scrunched her red face. "He swears by all that's holy that Jamie didn't do it." Ivy Butz tilted from anger into painful distress at the chasm that separated herself from her cherished Edsel. "He defends the boy, still."

"Guilt or innocence is decided in the courts, Ivy. We must leave it in divine hands." The truth was that something inside her indeed was "on Edsel's track." Circumstances that screamed solidly that Jamie was the murderer gave way to loosely substantiated possibilities. Odd. Something was odd. But Berdie turned to the matter at hand.

"I think our first concern is Lucy. Right now she's the issue. Do you agree?"

"Of course." Mrs. Butz blew her nose. "She's on Edsel's track, you know." She sniffed. "And she's angry at me because I'm not. Edsel's going to stay at the flat above the shop to give me some space says he. Our Lucy wants to go with him. What a holiday this looks to be."

The sound of a phone ringing somewhere in another room

interrupted the conversation. It rang only twice and was followed by a small murmuring voice, then a shout.

"Da', it's for you." Milton's childish utterance became as large as his father's. "Police."

Berdie heard rapid footsteps and the distant sound of Edsel's voice. "Butz here."

A perturbed Martha, tugging a delighted Duncan, entered the drawing room. "Milty gave him peanut butter." Martha scrunched her nose. Little Duncan smiled brightly, peanut butter smudged on his upper lip.

"Saints preserve us," Ivy bawled. She swept the baby up and let out a long "Whew!" With a quick trot to the door, Ivy called to Berdie, "Mind you, that husband of mine is keeping something from me, I swear he is, and it'll be something to do with that Donovan boy."

Berdie sat a few moments in the room and offered a prayer for both the Butzes and her husband's success with dislodging the love-struck teenager from her domain. Then Berdie heard Hugh's voice and went into the hallway, where he stood next to Edsel, who had his arm around Lucy's shoulder. She certainly wasn't cheerful, but her tear-stained face was calm. In her hand was a small pink suitcase, bits and bobs of rapidly packed clothing peeking out the sides.

"Daddy and I are moving out," Lucy stated in a matter-of-fact manner.

"Now, love, we're just staying in the flat above the shop till things are right way round." The lines in Edsel's face deepened. "Go on to the car, Lucy. Give me a moment with the vicar."

The young lady granted Hugh a tiny smile. "Thank you, Reverend Elliott," she said and made her way out the door.

Edsel lowered his voice, "The police arrested Jamie, and the old Bill have him in Timsley."

"How did they find him?" Hugh asked.

Edsel laid his finger aside his nose and tapped. "Goodnight told me Raheem phoned him from the train station in Timsley this morning. He spotted Jamie getting on a train bound for Holyhead."

"Mr. Raheem," Berdie spoke her thought.

"The police picked the lad up in Timsley then?" Hugh questioned.

"No, Holyhead. They brought him back to Timsley and discovered he had a ferry ticket on him."

"Headed back home to Dublin." Berdie verbalized what everyone was thinking.

Edsel shook his head. "I've got to get to Timsley. I don't mean to be rude, but I really must go."

"Of course." Hugh took Berdie's arm.

"Thanks again, for Lucy and all." Edsel opened the door.

The couple walked out into the winter afternoon.

"Who commits a murder and goes to his family home?" Hugh scratched his head.

"I'll tell you who does if you tell me how you dislodged Lucy dear from her hunger strike." Curiosity was not a hidden quality with Berdie.

Hugh smiled. "I just pointed out that if we, in the collective sense, felt Jamie was innocent, her good person being locked away from the world wouldn't help his cause. 'Faith without works is dead.' " Hugh's smile grew wide. "Now answer my question. Who murders then goes to his family home?"

"Simply put, not a murderer. Someone frightened or confused goes home."

Hugh agreed. "I mean, if they caught him at Heathrow with a ticket for Brazil, well."

"Well indeed." Berdie adjusted her tortoiseshell glasses and nodded.

"Ah, now, Mrs. Elliott, we have a funeral to plan and execute in the next forty-eight hours," is all Hugh responded.

―

"Another stock of lavender and I believe we've got it," Berdie asserted. Her voice carried across to the other end of the ample stone chapel, where Hugh stood looking out a graceful arched window. "Cara has been a brilliant help the past two days, despite her deep grief, with all the wreath crafting." Berdie chose a large-bloomed stock. "I believe it is a lovely tribute to Miss Livingston, the lavender maven. It's a pity she has no relatives remaining to see all this." Berdie gazed about at the beautiful holiday wreaths of lavender that adorned the altar and decorated the ancient walls of Saint Aidan of the Wood Parish Church. She nestled the final stock into the huge aromatic spray of regal purple. "You know, her front garden is all English lavender, but I noticed her back garden is all French lavender. Cara said it was the French lavender that won the prize at last year's Flower Festival." Berdie became quiet.

"What's that, love?" Hugh piped.

Berdie recognized a hint of concern in her husband's voice. "The funeral flowers are all ready."

Hugh strode the length of the chapel, his heels sounding like a military regiment on the worn stone floor. In a moment he was next to her.

"Brilliant!" he offered with just a note of distraction.

"Have you finished your sermon?" Berdie asked.

Hugh looked upon the flowers and felt a bloom with his fingertips. "My first funeral service, Berdie, and I'm eulogizing a murder victim. How do I explain the problem of an eighty-year-old woman being struck down by the hand of evil?"

"I know you'll do well, love. It will be a relief when we get all this settled, but you are so adept at staying the course and keeping your troops resolute in rough waters," she breathed.

"I just row, but it's the Lord who keeps the troops resolute." Her husband popped a kiss on her cheek. "I'll be finishing up in the sacristy." A few steps and Hugh was upon the sacristy door. He opened it and solidly stepped inside.

It's been awhile since I fixed border cake for afternoon tea. I must do that sometime soon for Hugh, thought Berdie.

As she placed the spray near the front kneeling rail, she heard the chapel door slowly creak open, and hesitant steps sounded across the floor. "The funeral's not for another four hours," Berdie called out, not bothering to look.

"I'm not here for ze funeral," came an odd voice with a foreign accent.

Berdie turned to see a small man dressed in a light-colored blouson shirt with an open leather waistcoat that matched his weathered boots. His black brimmed hat shadowed his eyes but not his dark shoulder-length hair. He fumbled with a long iron box in his hand. "I'm here to see ze priest."

A handful of people huddled at the church door adorned in long coats, and some wee children poked their heads out from their mother's wraps. When Berdie caught sight of them, they quietly closed the door.

"I'm afraid Reverend Elliot is occupied at the moment," Berdie asserted.

"I'm here to see ze priest." The man's diminutive voice intensified. "I will see him now!"

"But—" Berdie interjected.

"I will see him *now!*" he shouted. The peculiar character had become a raging giant.

Berdie, quite taken aback, found her voice much louder than she intended. "Reverend Elliot is preparing for a funeral."

The door to the sacristy flew open, and Hugh stepped out. "Berdie?" Hugh's mellow tone rained calm upon the interaction. "May I be of assistance, sir?"

The figure pushed past Berdie and sped straight to the sacristy, giving Hugh a quick nod. "We need ze privacy," he quipped as he swept into the small room.

Hugh gave Berdie a questioning glance then a reassuring nod and closed the door.

Berdie was not about to leave the chapel even though she'd finished the floral duties. *Who is that man and what on earth could be so urgent?* tumbled through her mind. She sat down in a pew and opened the prayer book, a special edition prepared by the

Northumbrian Community. Even though it was midmorning, she would do her noon prayers now, if she could concentrate well enough, that is.

Not more than fifteen minutes later, the two men emerged from the cloistered meeting. Hugh and the stranger shook hands. Berdie closed the book and stood up as the man whisked past her. She tried to read her husband's face. It was the look he wore when contemplating his next tricky cribbage play. The chapel door closed hard.

"Hugh? What—"

"The funeral's off," Hugh blurted.

Berdie reared in disbelief. "Off?"

"A family development of sorts."

"But Miriam has no family. Hugh?"

Berdie had seldom seen her husband at sixes and sevens but it appeared he was at a loss now. "We need to get the word out quickly."

"I don't understand—" Berdie's words tumbled upon one another.

Hugh interrupted. "We've much to do in a short amount of time. We need to call the villagers, those living most distant first, notify the altar guild to cancel the food donations, alert those providing transport for the elderly, oh, and tell Peter George to stop digging. Explanations can wait, love."

"You're not putting me off forever, Hugh Elliott," Berdie assured her husband and sought out the congregational Rolodex. "As soon as things are well in hand, we're having a word."

Three hours and forty-five minutes later, Lillie and Berdie

sat in a back pew, ready to intercept any who may have slipped through the net, to advise them of the cancellation.

Hugh opened the sacristy door. "Anyone show?"

Just as Lillie shook her head no, the church door opened. Reverend Gerald Lewis held the door open and gaped across the empty church. "I guess the old thing wasn't too well liked then," he said to the two women in the pew.

"Ah, Reverend Lewis," Berdie greeted. It had never occurred to her to notify him.

"Gerald, please come in," Hugh invited. "Actually, the funeral has been canceled."

The reverend squeezed his narrow eyes and tipped his head. "Canceled?" His white collar contrasted with the look of consternation on his face. He entered and closed the door behind him. "Why, how does that happen?"

Hugh clipped across the stone floor. "Just one of those odd things. As you know, Gerald, a man of the cloth cannot break confidences even in the most distressing situations." Hugh tried to be casual. "Taking tea is far more palatable than sorting out canceled funerals, wouldn't you agree? Care to join us?"

Before Reverend Lewis could respond, Dr. Meredith opened the church door, finely dressed in a respectful black suit. His smoky eyes perused the empty church then fell upon Lillie who quietly took Berdie's hand and caught her breath.

"Dr. Meredith!" Surprise rang in Berdie's greeting.

"Mrs. Elliott," the pathologist acknowledged and entered the quiet sanctuary.

"Hugh, this is Dr. Loren Meredith. Dr. Meredith, this is

my husband, Hugh Elliott."

Hugh stepped forward and shook the doctor's hand. "Dr. Meredith."

"And this is Reverend Lewis," Berdie directed.

"How do you do?" Dr. Meredith shook the clergyman's hand.

Berdie looked toward Lillie. "And of course you know—"

"No, actually we didn't really meet." Dr. Meredith tipped his well-groomed head toward Lillie.

"Oh right, this is Miss Lillie Foxworth."

The doctor and musician gazed at each other. All but a barn pot could sense there was enough electricity between them to light up London for a week.

Finally the doctor spoke, still caught in the glow of Lillie's blush and dazzled hazel eyes. "Delighted to finally meet you, Miss Foxworth."

"As am I you, Dr. Meredith." Lillie's demeanor crackled with static energy.

"Are you here for the funeral?" Hugh inquired then went on, "Because if so, I'm sorry it's been canceled."

"Really?" the physician said plainly.

"Reverend Elliott has just made it clear he's not at liberty to address the issue, but we're setting to on a holiday tea." Lillie was intent. "I'm sure we'd all enjoy your company," she said, trying to sound relaxed.

"Please do stay," Berdie added with a glimpse toward her best friend.

Dr. Meredith smiled. "Well, in that case, how can I not?"

In a matter of moments, the quintet made their way to the vicarage, with Berdie and Dr. Meredith lagging behind.

"Mrs. Elliott," Dr. Meredith spoke quietly.

"Berdie, please."

"Berdie, about the spots you asked me to check on the victim's back."

"Yes." Berdie was so caught up with the day's events she almost forgot that this man held valuable information.

"There were pressure marks indicating the candle wax in the bedroom was hardened when the body came to rest on top of it."

Berdie shook her head. "Thank you, Loren."

"The victim's body has given me much more information I think you'll find intriguing," the doctor confided.

"Dr. Meredith," Lillie's voice rang, "how was your drive from Timsley?"

"Go ahead," Berdie urged the pathologist. She acknowledged Lillie's attempt to engage the gentleman in conversation.

"We'll talk later," Loren offered and caught up with the amicable Lillie.

Soon the troupe entered the library where books stood at rapt attention on the dark wooden shelves and light from the waning fire added warmth to the brown leather armchairs. Upon an antique sideboard, a large Christmas tray held all the makings of a holiday afternoon tea. Berdie freshened the pot then poured the brew for each individual from the teapot that was adorned with the jolly Christmas robin. She handed a saucer holding a cup of hot refreshment to Reverend Lewis. Then she gave one to Dr. Meredith.

"Do you usually attend the funerals of your victims, Doctor?" Berdie quipped.

Reverend Gerald Lewis gurgled on a sip of the hot tea and coughed, jiggling his teacup. Some of the liquid toppled into the saucer and several droplets swished over the edge onto the gentleman's trousers.

"Oh, that didn't come out right a'tall, I'm sorry," Berdie offered as she adeptly grabbed a holiday serviette and dabbed at the wet pant leg.

The visiting clergyman, quite sternly, snatched the linen from her hand and went forward with the cleanup.

Dr. Meredith spoke up. "I assure you, Reverend, Mrs. Elliott knows they are victims not of my making. I just care for them once they've become someone else's victim. You see, I'm the pathologist on the Lavender Cottage case."

"Yes, well said, that clears things up," Hugh affirmed.

But the pastor guest still tottered his teacup and seemed genuinely inhospitable.

"And no, Mrs. Elliott, I don't usually attend the funerals of my *corpses*, but I have"— the doctor's eyes took a quick detour to Lillie then returned—"I have a special interest in this case." He had a gentle curve upward at the edges of his mouth. "Don't worry, Reverend Lewis, I'll spare you the details of my professional workings."

The clergyman put aside the serviette. "Thank you," is all he said.

As Berdie gave a full cup to her husband, Hugh chimed in, "Indeed, we've an opportunity to retreat to the pleasure of a holiday table for tea." He looked straight at Berdie. "Let's leave the ordeal of today behind us and enjoy this moment."

"Here, here," Lillie agreed.

Hugh lifted his cup. "To Christmas tea with friends."

All lifted their cups in agreement and sipped.

Berdie felt a tinge of uneasiness. What with the fuss resulting from asking an inappropriate question, and the doctor and Lillie trying to find their proper way with each other, it rather made for a taut dance, she thought.

"Darling?" Hugh almost whispered.

"Oh yes." Berdie popped up and presented the platter laden with food goods. "Really, the women of the parish supplied our treats." She beamed and held out the tray to Reverend Lewis, who helped himself to one of each. "Ginger biscuits baked by Mrs. White." Berdie turned the tray to the doctor. "Chocolate truffles handmade by Mr. and Mrs. Turner, and Christmas *kulich*, still warm, from Mrs. Braunhoff's oven."

"Delights," the doctor raved and took one of each, as did Hugh and Lillie.

"Not quite enough butter in the kulich," the visiting reverend commented while slowly chewing. "A touch heavy on the almandine."

"Um, I think it's grand," Lillie countered and lightly swept her lips for crumbs.

"Indeed," the doctor agreed, swallowing.

"Yes, you would then." Gerald grinned.

"I say," Hugh piped, holding a well-bitten truffle, "well done to the Turners."

Berdie just popped a bit of ginger biscuit in her mouth when a very loud "Glorious Things of Thee Are Spoken" orchestrated from Reverend Lewis's belt satchel. He nearly dropped his treats trying to reach the mobile phone inside.

"Yes?" he rather growled then jumped up. "Excuse me," he offered Hugh, "I'll take this in the hall."

"I must be odd," Berdie spoke. "All I have is bell tones for my mobile phone ring."

"You can download for a custom sound," Dr. Meredith offered with a hint of chocolate on his lip. "I have Elgar as my tone."

"Yes." Lillie smiled at the doctor. "My tone is his breathtaking 'Nimrod.' Doctor, did you know the London Chorus will be performing an Elgar concert in Timsley this Monday next?"

"Yes, I'm going. Say, might you—"

The library door flung open. In haste, Reverend Lewis briskly reentered the study. "Must go. Please excuse me. . .a timely opportunity."

Hugh arose from his chair. "I'll see you to the. . ."

Reverend Lewis was gone before Hugh could finish his sentence.

Elgar's "Nimrod" burst forth from inside the doctor's suit coat. "Breathtaking." He smiled at Lillie and pulled the mobile from an inside pocket. He pursed his lips. "Yes, yes, now?" he spoke into the phone then hung up. "Work emergency. I'm afraid I must go as well." The physician laid his tea and goods aside and stood. "Sorry, please excuse. Thank you for your hospitality." He took in Lillie's visage. "Truly enjoyable."

"Oh." Lillie wore disappointment poorly. "It was a delight."

Berdie invited, "You must come again."

The gentleman tipped his head toward the women. "I gladly accept your invitation."

With that, Hugh escorted Loren Meredith to the door.

"Well. . ." Berdie sat without cheer and a half-eaten ginger biscuit in her hand, steam still rolling from her holiday cup.

"Yes, well," Lillie agreed and gazed at the last red embers in the library fireplace.

CHAPTER SIX

Berdie stared at herself in the undulating mirror of her antique dressing table. Her holiday sleeping gown, a now washed-out red, had a holly-strewn goose strolling across her chest, with a Christmas pudding and broad-brimmed hat. A gift several years ago from her aunt Clara, it was made from gentle fleece and ever-so-comfy soft, but certainly not one of Hugh's favorites. She ran the brush through her red brown hair and observed Hugh's distorted reflection in the antique mirror. Her busy husband had arrived home from congregational house calls just an hour earlier, tired and unusually quiet. Now he stoked the flames in the hearth of the Cotswold stone fireplace, adding warmth to the bedroom from the sizable oak beams across the lime-washed ceiling to the polished wooden floors laden with Scottish wool rugs.

"Ready to retire, my dear husband?" Berdie spoke to the image in the mirror.

"I should almost consider it after the events of today." Hugh exhaled.

"I mean, are you ready to go to bed?" Berdie amended.

"Oh, of course that's what you meant," her exhausted husband responded with gentle laughter.

Berdie turned in her petite dressing chair and faced her robe-wrapped husband.

"What happened today, Hugh, I mean with that odd visitor who turned our world topsy-turvy?"

"I'm all in, love, can we discuss this later?"

"What did he say to you, Hugh?"

Hugh punched the flames with the poker. He withdrew it and, standing the tool erect, pushed the handle against the stone fireplace. "I'm going to bed."

"You've put me off all day. This isn't like you." Berdie watched him toss his robe on the end of the large sleigh bed and ease his way under the snow-white eiderdown that lay across the place of rest.

"I gave my word as a man of the cloth. What transpired in the sacristy stays there."

Berdie was impertinent. "But I'm your wife."

"And I'm a man of my word." Hugh patted the pillow next to him, a familiar beckoning gesture to her.

Berdie spun back to face the looking glass and stayed fastened to the dressing chair, brushing her hair with rapid sweeps. This reminded her of the many times he couldn't speak of his intelligence work when in the military.

Hugh raised himself up on an elbow. "Thank you for handling things well today, Berdie, including the impromptu tea."

"For what it was worth." Berdie felt sure her hairbrush would soon catch fire. "Reverend Lewis was certainly unappreciative, and exactly why has he decided to visit Aidan Kirkwood?"

"He saw the advert about rental of the church grounds for

special events that our parish counsel put on the Net. His church is searching for a spring retreat site and heaven knows our counsel needs funds."

"Well he's hiding something, Hugh." Berdie spit it out.

"Yes. It seems most clergymen are keeping something under wraps." Her tired husband patted the vacant pillow again.

"Well, we know what you're keeping mum on." Berdie twirled in the chair and vigorously pointed her hairbrush in her husband's direction. "You'll go round the houses all you want, but I'm going to get to the bottom of this murder—mystery man and all."

Hugh settled on his back, hands resting under his head on the goose-down pillow. "I wish you would," he spoke almost a whisper.

Berdie put the hairbrush down. "You what?" She stepped lightly over to the bed where Hugh stared at the large wooden ceiling beam above him. Placing herself carefully on the mattress edge, she saw clearly Hugh's knitted brow, the weary droop to his otherwise sure lips. "You really do?" Berdie threw back the eiderdown and nestled herself beneath it. She laid her hand upon her husband's chest. She felt it rise and fall as Hugh drew a heavy breath.

"Constable Goodnight has asked the church to clean up and clear out Lavender Cottage on Saturday."

Berdie's pulse tripped. "And I'm the person for the job."

"Mind you, you must promise—"

"To fulfill my church duties," she finished.

"Mind you," Hugh went on, "you must promise not to take any unnecessary chances, and keep Goodnight in the loop."

Everything within Berdie wanted to protest. Goodnight! His investigative line of reason was better suited at the end of a fishing rod. And she never, well rarely, took unnecessary chances. But she didn't fuss. Instead she reached, turned the bedside lamp off, and laid her head on the sturdy shoulder that was a devoted part of her life. "On my honor as the wife who irons the cloth of the churchman."

Saturday morning, Berdie arose, exercised, did morning devotion prayers, wrote three thank-you notes for holiday treats, cooked Hugh a full English breakfast, and cleaned up after a leaking dishwasher, all before half eight. By eight thirty-five, she was at Lavender Cottage, Lillie in tow, where she met Constable Goodnight at the front doorstep. He held two electric lanterns, and the yellow crime tape still draped the door. The policeman unlatched the door and lifted the ribbon.

"House is officially cleared but I don't want any dolts nosing round," he grunted.

Oh, I'm up a rung on Goodnight's respect ladder, Berdie thought to herself.

The constable lit the lanterns and handed them over to the women. "Edsel Butz will be by later to fix the electric." The man stepped toward the garden gate. "I'll leave you to it then." He patted his rotund stomach. "I'll be taking sustenance at the Upland Arms."

Before Berdie could call out that they would ring him when finished, he was out the gate.

The women gingerly entered the front hall. Though full of

tumbled goods, the cottage held a profound emptiness. Both women shivered. Berdie shut the door against the cold, but the moist English morning permeated throughout.

"Where do we start?" Lillie was bewildered.

"Sitting room," Berdie determined. Several large boxes were stacked high in the hall. The two carefully pulled a couple of them out. Berdie deposited one at the sitting room door. "Rubbish in this one," she directed, "and undamaged goods in the other one, to start."

"Maybe things of distinct value we can place on the dining table," Lillie offered and placed the goods box near the fireplace.

Though Lillie was just helping a friend, Berdie saw every mite as an opportunity to unravel the truths hidden amid the rubble.

"Go carefully," Berdie urged. "If you come upon anything that strikes you odd, give a word."

Lillie set to and gathered upholstery stuffing strewn across the floor while Berdie went straight to the Advent wreath. Carefully she picked up the large pillar Christ candle; it felt almost wooden. She examined its sides, top, and bottom then quizzed Lillie.

"If you saw this candle, say, sitting on a dining table, would you identify it as a Christ candle for an Advent wreath?"

Lillie glanced at the candle. "No."

"Because?"

"Obviously, it's yellow, and Christ candles are snow white."

"Quite right." Berdie nodded and placed it in the undamaged goods box. "Does the word *Bridgestones* mean anything to you?"

"No." Lillie stopped. "Maybe. We had a Bridgestones Department Store in Timsley, but it went out of business." She continued to pick up the stuffing. "I think in the late seventies."

Berdie removed the three weekly Advent candles from the holders. She laid them down across the hearth, bottoms facing her. She nosed closer to them and squinted. "These candles have designs carved on the bottom."

Lillie looked at them. "Odd."

"They're trying to tell us something," Berdie spoke her thoughts.

"I wonder where the fourth candle is." Lillie looked across the floor.

"Ah yes, the fourth candle." Berdie nodded. "I daresay it's in the bedroom."

The helper looked perplexed. "What's it doing in the bedroom?"

"When we answer that, my dear, we shall have the key to unlock this mystery." In sleuth mode, Berdie sounded profoundly certain.

Both women stared at the sticks of wax.

"Do you think the murderer made these marks?" Lillie asked.

"Hardly likely. No. They would have to inscribe them and put them back perfectly to hide them. And why do that?" Berdie tipped her head. "Yes, and why do that?"

She lifted the decorative lavender and evergreen wreath with silver berries that beautifully disguised the circular wire containing the candleholders underneath. She eased the florals carefully into the box.

"So many people have been taken with Miss Livingston's idea to weave lavender into the evergreen for the Advent wreath."

"The White Window Box can't keep up with the demand

for them, and with Miriam the sole supplier," Lillie informed, "they're quite dear, close to forty pounds each."

Berdie examined the golden wreath ring. "She must have been making a small fortune."

"And she was sleeping on it," Lillie added.

Berdie brought the Advent ring near the lantern. "Usually there's a fair bit of wax in the candleholders, but these have none," she observed. She caught her breath. "There's something etched on the inside bottom of the metal."

Lillie stepped lively to Berdie. "Something incriminating?" she almost cooed.

"It looks like single numbers."

"Oh." Lillie sounded a bit letdown. "Like one, two, three, four, for each candle?"

"No." Berdie wiped the lenses of her glasses with the sleeve of her coat. "Seven." She turned the ring. "Four." She turned the ring again. "Three." She peered so closely to find the next number that she bumped her glasses on the candle ring. Taken by surprise, she reared back and the glasses slid clear of her nose. What started as a yip of surprise became a howl of laughter as the two women scrambled to retrieve the errant pair of tortoiseshell glasses. "I think the last number's a three," Berdie chortled while her best friend found the escapee.

Lillie replaced the glasses on Berdie's nose. "There! And in the case of this wreath wire,"—Lillie took it from Berdie's hands—"in the box it goes." Lillie tucked it away safely.

"Remember those numbers Lillie; they could lead us to something." Berdie mulled. "Hiding indeed."

"Seven, four, three, three," the friend recited.

"A pin number?" Berdie puzzled. "The last four letters of an account? A birth date?"

"The phone number of a long-lost lover," Lillie dreamed.

"A long-lost love," Berdie whispered then set to on the task at hand, that of cleaning. "Maybe there's something else here that can shed some light." She picked up a sea of old LP record albums and covers littering the rug. "You don't see many of these anymore." She scooped them up two and three at a time, matching record to jacket.

"They can be valuable, at least to collectors," Lillie assessed.

"Miss Livingston was a true classical fan." Berdie read the covers aloud, "Claude Debussy, Sans-Saëns, Bizet, Puccini, several are Ravel."

"Oh yes." Lillie paused, cotton batting in her hand. "Ravel was her favorite. She would often hum when working among her lavender, that haunting rhythm from *Boléro* you know, that starts out humbly then ends up exploding. Dum de de de de *dum*." She lifted the volume of the syncopated beats. "Dum de de de de *dum*."

"Not one Bach," Berdie interrupted.

"What?" Lillie still hummed her dum de de's.

"Don't all classical fans fancy Bach? And where's Beethoven?"

"Maybe the perp took it," Lillie chided. "Perhaps he favors Beethoven's Ninth." The choirmaster thundered into song. "Da da da d–a–a–a–a."

"Everyone has an accounting of taste I suppose." Berdie shuffled the albums. "See here, intact, an Elgar." Berdie held it up for her friend to view, one of the few unmolested items.

Instantly, Lillie snatched the album from Berdie's hand. "That goes on the dining table," she declared and placed it there like a sacred relic on the otherwise empty surface. "That's a treasure."

"Take it," Berdie offered.

"Do you think?" Lillie picked it back up.

"I'll bet Miriam would have wanted you to have it," Berdie encouraged. "Besides, it's just going into a jumble shop. If it's special to you, 'the labourer is worthy of [her] hire.' "

"I believe you're right, my dear vicar's wife."

Berdie picked up an overturned basket only to discover a sachet pocket clinging to the weave. She opened the scented fabric.

"Lavender, of course." Berdie sniffed. "What are these?" She pulled several index cards from the envelope-shaped pocket. She read a card. "One part water, one part lemon juice, a squeeze of honey." She waved the card toward Lillie. "Odd recipe holder."

Lillie, busy arranging a box, offered barely a glance. "Not recipes, really. . .well, not for dishes. Miss Livingston swore by her home remedies, said modern medicine had run amok. She had one for skin care that worked quite well—kept her looking fairly youthful. The one you just read was her prescriptive for a clear singing voice."

"There are enough remedies here to render the whole village a perfect bill of health," Berdie observed. "I'll put the pouch in the box with the wreath," she quipped.

Thirty minutes into the cleanup, and the chaos of the sitting room gave way to a more orderly, though gaunt, appearance.

Lillie gathered books from the floor, some flung open, and

others just toppled. "*Le Petit Prince*," she said, admiring a small book, "one of my favorites as a child. My parents insisted I learn French, but I'm afraid it was a bit of a disappointment for them." She continued collecting the stray hardbacks. "I never quite got the grammar, although I loved that story."

Berdie added three books to the pile in Lillie's arms. "Two of three novels I've picked up have French titles," she noted to Lillie. "Did Miriam speak French?"

"A bit or bob. My parents, rest their souls, said she didn't speak at all the first five years she lived in Aidan Kirkwood. She just stayed in her cottage and worked in her garden, never spoke to anyone."

Berdie placed more books on the stack Lillie held. "The human soul can tolerate isolation only a limited time."

"Batty Natty moved in next door." Lillie's arms were straining to hold the volumes. "They started attending Evensong at church." The choirmaster looked wistful. "She won't be caroling with us tomorrow evening, will she?"

"No," Berdie replied, "if indeed any of us will."

The space where they stood suddenly felt utterly vacant.

Bong. The chime of the sitting room clock abruptly filled the place, and Lillie shuddered and hurled the books into the air, rivaling Christmas fireworks. *Bong.*

"Wretched clock!" Berdie roared. *Bong.*

"What did you say?" Lillie all but screamed. The musician placed her hands over her ears.

The bongs continued until it finished declaring the arrival of the nine o'clock hour.

"Miss Livingston must have wanted to know when teatime arrived while working in the back garden," Lillie declared.

"I forgot about that fiendish thing." Berdie thought back to the first time she heard the bell in the dark, disheveled sitting room. She regathered the books.

Lillie had just placed a handful of reading materials in a box when there was a decisive knock on the front door. She got to her feet and peered out the window. "Edsel," she announced.

Berdie was in the hall, door opened wide to let the workman in. He fumbled about with a worn toolbox.

"Mornin'," he greeted.

"Edsel." Berdie smiled.

Entering, his toolbox caught the edge of the half-moon table pressed against the hallway wall. The whole affair went up over end, spilling the drawer out with its entire contents of candles rolling across the floor. "Silly place for a table." Edsel scowled. "There're enough candles here to light the entire village." The candles rolled everywhere.

Lillie was jolly on the spot.

Edsel bent down to pick up a few, clanging his toolbox against the fallen table. "Old dears sometimes keep these 'practical candles' they call them, in droves, a leave over from the war blackouts and all." He grunted as he dipped lower.

"It's all right Edsel, Lillie and I can get them. You go about your work—we can use the light."

"If you're sure." The man stood upright and took a breath.

"We'll have this cleaned up in no time," Lillie chimed in while gathering.

"Sorry," Edsel Butz said sheepishly. "I'll just go to the back garden then." He tried to step diligently but cracked some candles underfoot. He kept moving until he was out the back door, leaving a trail of wax.

"How could she think in a lifetime these would all be used?" Lillie mused out loud. "It is an odd place to keep them."

"Not at all," said Berdie. "Look." Berdie acted it out. "Step into the hallway from the door. Turn the switch, no lights, pull out the drawer, light the candle, and Bob's your uncle."

"I see what you mean, yes."

By the time the women had replaced the table and had all the candles collected and placed in a box, the electrician returned.

"Need to go get the taller ladder at the shop. Be back presently," he assured. And he was gone without incident.

"Lantern light it is for a while longer." Berdie was getting restless. "Not so easy in half shadows, is it, Lillie?"

"I admit I'd love the heat on," she replied.

It couldn't have been four minutes, when there was another knock at the door.

"That was fast." Lillie's brows shot up.

Not waiting for an invitation, Ivy Butz sprang in the door, holding a takeout tray full of Styrofoam cups in one hand, little Duncan on her hip, and daughter Lila behind. "Isn't it a lovely morning? Tea anyone?"

"Ivy." Berdie was surprised to see the woman. "How kind."

"Lila's got the scones."

Only a year younger than Lucy, Lila Butz looked like she might be twelve. A miniature Ivy physically, plus glasses, but her personality was a polar opposite of her mother's. Shyly, Lila lifted the scones bag without making any verbal acknowledgments.

When Ivy put her wee Duncan on the floor, he made his presence known with a coo and an overwhelming smell that only babies in nappies can conjure.

"Has Duncan been in the peanut butter?" Berdie squinted against the aroma. At the same moment she was glad all the furniture was upright, that the room was certainly more safe and orderly for a wee one. "Here." Berdie took the tray from Ivy and sat it on an end table near the fireplace.

"Thought you might need a bit of a warm-up." Ivy's eyes roamed the room, apparently unaffected by Duncan's offenses. "We were on our way to see Dr. Huntington. Lila's got a cold, out stargazing in the deep of night again."

"The aurora borealis are coming active, mother." Lila wiped her nose with a tissue.

Ivy bent forward to see into the kitchen. "Is"—she paused—"my husband about?"

"You just missed him," Lillie answered and removed the finger from in front of her nose, "but he promised a quick return."

Ivy's cheerful visage now looked as if someone had stolen her colorful Christmas cracker from off her plate.

"He'll be back before you can finish a scone," Berdie offered. Truthfully, a scone didn't sound appetizing at the moment, but Berdie could see those familiar wells of tears coming to the disappointed woman's eyes.

"We've this whole lot for the jumble shop." Lillie pointed to the boxes of goods, making a poor attempt to redirect Ivy's focus, acting as if the entire village didn't know Edsel had temporarily moved from home. The choirmaster grabbed a wall plaque from a box and took it to Ivy. "Isn't this lovely?"

Lila stepped the bag of scones to Berdie, who was adding cream to the hot teas. The young lady was taken in by something on the mantel. In fact, she became almost animated. She laid the scones aside and stood at the fireplace, rolled one of the Advent candles a half twist, and smiled. "Look! The phases of the moon."

Berdie and Lillie both came close.

"See," she said and pointed, "waxing, full, and waning."

Berdie thought a moment. "If there was a fourth candle, Lila, what would follow?"

"Nothing. It's the new moon you see, the dark face of the moon."

Berdie's eyes snapped open. "The dark side."

Ivy stood upright. She held the plaque close to her chest. "I want this plaque." The woman sounded almost desperate. "How much?" She rummaged through her coat pocket. "Here's a pound." Tears started to tumble down her cheeks.

"A pound?" Berdie's head was not in the conversation with Ivy. "Lillie, I need to go upstairs. Can you aid Ivy?"

Lillie breathed through her mouth and tried to answer all at once, "But how?"

Berdie was out of the room, running up the stairs, Ivy's daughter Lila behind her. They stopped on the landing.

"Two pounds then," Ivy bellowed up the stairs.

"You shouldn't come in, Lila, the room's not sorted. Stay here," Berdie urged. "But may I borrow your tissue?"

The inquisitive teen frowned and handed over the tissue.

Berdie entered the room and, using the tissue, picked up the candle. She peered at the bottom. "Dark side indeed," she breathed.

Berdie heard steps race up the stairs, and Lillie's agitated voice sounded on the landing. "Lila, come."

"Unhand me! What are you doing?" Lila's voice was elevated.

Berdie put the candle down and returned to the landing. "What's going on, Lillie?"

"Ivy's left, and in such a state. She scooped up Duncan but has forgotten her daughter."

"Let go," Lila reiterated.

From the bottom of the stairs, Berdie could hear a distressed Ivy screech, "Lila!" But now she heard another voice, a man's.

"Get out of the house!" It was Mr. Raheem.

"My daughter!" Ivy sounded panicked. "Lila!"

"I'll get your daughter. Please stay outside!"

Berdie watched the man leap the stairs two at a time.

"You must get out!" he yelled. He grabbed both Lillie and Lila tightly by their arms. "You, too, Mrs. Elliott, now."

Berdie took one step and an odor seized her nostrils, but it wasn't Duncan. The scent jolted through her body. Smoke!

Lillie could keep up with Mr. Raheem's descent, but stout Lila slipped. The teen screamed. Mr. Raheem stopped. Berdie was at the young girl's side. "Go ahead, Mr. Raheem, take Lillie. I've got Lila." While he went on, Berdie lifted the tearful girl to her feet. "It's okay, Lila. We're okay."

"Ouch!" Lila grabbed her ankle. "It hurts." She grimaced.

"One step at a time." Berdie coaxed the frightened child. Lila took one stair then collapsed.

"I can't," she yelled, and began to cry.

Haze like a December morning fog began making its presence known near the ceiling.

"Cover your mouth with your coat collar," Berdie commanded. *Dear God of tender mercies*, Berdie prayed silently. She tried to hoist Lila up with her shoulder, but the youngster screamed. She grabbed Berdie with both arms. Berdie could feel the weight of the girl pull her downward.

"I can't get up." Desperation filled Lila's voice as she clung to Berdie.

"Lila, let go of Mrs. Elliott and put your arms around my neck." It was Mr. Raheem. "Mrs. Elliott, outside now."

Berdie hesitated.

"Now!" he screamed.

Berdie all but flew down the stairs. Once out the door, she took a deep breath of the moist air and coughed.

She could hear Lillie's shaky voice utter, "Are you okay?" Her friend pointed to the roofline. "Look."

Berdie saw flames lapping up from the back garden.

"My daughter!" Ivy screamed.

The beleaguered Hardeep Raheem appeared at the door, Lila in his arms. He struggled with his burden to the gate. The winded greengrocer barked, "Mrs. Butz, open your car door. Ladies, move away, in the street quickly."

Berdie and Lillie followed orders. A crowd had started gathering in the road. Mr. Clark gave the rescuer an assist to get

Lila safely settled in the backseat of Ivy's car. "Can you take her to Dr. Huntington?" Mr. Raheem could see Ivy's tender state. The frightened Duncan's wail added to the fray.

As if scripted, Edsel Butz drove up in his work lorry. He lowered the driver's side window. "Love?" the man called out to his wife.

"Lila's hurt," Mrs. Butz blurted.

Like a shot he leaped from the vehicle and was at her side. He spied the smoke wrapped around the roofline. "What were you doing here?"

"Looking for you," Ivy bawled.

"I could have lost you." Edsel closed his eyes tightly and reopened them. "Get in the car, I'm driving."

Without hesitation the Butz family was packed up. Edsel drove off so quickly he almost hit the fire brigade lorry that rounded the corner along with Constable Goodnight. Horns blared and sirens split the chilly air. Everyone moved aside so the emergency vehicles could park in front of the cottage. The firefighters set to on the blaze; in a blur of ordered chaos, they worked to tame the dancing flames.

Goodnight barked commands, which no one really listened to. "Back, move along you lot." He stood in front of Berdie. "Well, here we are again." He glared. "Seems disaster follows you like hounds on a rabbit."

Before Berdie could respond to Goodnight, Cara Graystone stepped in between them.

"Is everything in there?" The woman was trying to catch her breath and question Berdie at the same time. In running gear, her shoulders heaved up and down. "Did you take anything out of there?"

Berdie's mind was dizzy. "Yes, no."

"Well, what is it?" Cara's face was flushed.

Now Goodnight moved between the two women. "Hang about. I'm talking to Mrs. Elliott. You move along home," he boomed at Cara loud enough the whole street heard it.

She took in both Goodnight and Berdie. "Well, you'll both be talking to me," she said and thrust her thumb to her chest, "tomorrow, at my father's solicitor's office."

"What you trying to say?" Goodnight's bushy brows met.

Preston Graystone stepped into the ring, directly in Goodnight's space. "Hear now, it's to everyone's good if that blasted cottage burns to a cinder." Graystone leaned into Goodnight's face. "But you address my daughter with respect," the lawyer demanded, "or I'll have your badge."

"Oh you will?" Goodnight growled.

"Gentlemen. . ." Berdie used the word loosely.

"I'll see the both of you at two o'clock at my office on the morrow," Graystone demanded, addressing Berdie and the Constable. He refocused on Berdie. "And your husband should come as well."

"But it's the Sabbath tomorrow," Berdie protested after she found her voice.

"Perhaps for you, Mrs. Elliott." Mr. Graystone sounded cool as the morning frost. "But not for the law."

CHAPTER SEVEN

Berdie adjusted her woolen dress hat with one hand and tried to button her suit coat with the other, all while swiftly moving across Oak Leaf's front garden to Saint Aidan of the Wood Parish Church, only yards away. She was losing the battle against the clock, having slept past the alarm this morning.

The church stood stalwart against the morning spray of fog. When almost there, she saw a sight she'd never seen in the three months of Sunday mornings her husband had preached here in the quaint little church. A crowd milled in the front garden, people Berdie had never seen before along with a few familiar faces. She couldn't help but ask herself why. She excused her way through the crowd to enter the front door. Immediately she understood the cause of the dilemma. The church was full to the brim. People in pews were squeezed together like Christmas shoppers at Debenhams. Still, not everyone was seated. Berdie spotted Hugh up front shaking hands with a couple, smiling gently, then urging those in the first pew to make room for the two. Berdie went to his side. "Hugh?" she asked, catching her breath.

"Curiosity is a powerful force," Hugh spoke quietly.

"We should make a habit of canceling funerals," Berdie whispered. "And why didn't you wake me this morning?"

Hugh took her hand and gave it a tender squeeze. "You need rest, love."

Edsel Butz's voice bounced across the stone chapel. "Ready, Vicar." Having set chairs along the side aisles, he finished up the last chairs along the back wall.

Hugh went to join the candle acolytes, and the garden crowd filed in, taking the impromptu seats.

Lillie had chosen "A Safe Stronghold Our God Is Still" for the processional hymn. The body of worshippers stood and the organ boomed, signaling all to join in.

Berdie's voice felt small amid the crowd. "A safe stronghold our God is still, a trusty shield and weapon. He'll help us clear from all the ill, that hath us now o'ertaken."

Perfectly fitting. Good choice, Lillie, Berdie reasoned inside. "But for us fights the proper Man." Even though Mrs. Plinkerton's elbow hit Berdie in the ribs with every swell of the music, Berdie was pleased with the full house. "Ask ye who is this same? Christ Jesus is His name, the Lord Sabaoth's Son; He and no other one, shall conquer in the battle."

The prayers and scripture reading went well, although Lila Butz let go a whopping sneeze at the end of the reading from the Gospels that sounded like an exclamation mark.

By the time Hugh took his place for the sermon, the church was hot enough to roast a holiday fowl. The ancient erratic heating system plus the large crowd combined to create the Bahamas feel. Children were starting to move about. The people in the back seats uncomfortably squirmed. Many elderly heads were drooped and bobbing, falling prey to the warmth of the bodies around them. But when Hugh's voice spoke the first syllable, the place went quiet.

"With the difficult events of this week, I know many of you are here hoping to hear an explanation of why Miss Livingston's funeral was canceled." Hugh got straight to the point and a quiet buzz wove through the congregation. "But I've given my promise to keep confidences concerning the matter." The buzz became a ripple of voices. Hugh held his palm up to quiet the congregation. Berdie was sure Hugh would say the appropriate thing. "Just as you would expect me to keep a confidence given in trust on a matter, I'm sure you would not want trust broken, particularly from the pulpit." There was another round of murmurs, though most sounded positive. "I can't speak on the matters surrounding the canceling of the funeral, but I can tell you this. Though we can't control all the events that come our way in this life, we are only a whisper of prayer away from He who can give us peace and faith in even the bleakest of times. Just as our Lord stood in faith in His deepest hour, we, too, can stand. He cares for each one here and we can trust, as indeed the psalmist did, that we shall see the goodness of the Lord in the land of the living. Let us unite in the words of the apostle Paul, 'Be not overcome of evil, but overcome evil with good.' " Hugh took a deep breath. "Now, with that said, I shall move forward on the topic for today's Advent sermon, 'Waiting for the Light of Christmas.' "

Hugh could wax eloquently. But Berdie was glad that, though very well done, the sermon was brief. By the time the church service was over, Berdie noted that the morning fog had lifted outside. A rarely seen December sun pronounced its glory as the sea of humanity exited the church and made its way home.

Berdie entered the sacristy where Hugh was hanging up his liturgical garments.

"Well done, Reverend Elliott." She smiled.

Hugh planted a kiss on her cheek. "I'm glad there's at least one person who thinks so." He grinned.

"I'm afraid a defrosting shepherd's pie is all I have to offer for lunch. I should have brought it to church today; it would be cooked through."

Hugh laughed. He put his hands on Berdie's waist. "I'm afraid lunch must wait. I told Ivy we'd be round after church. She's in a state, poor thing, eyes red, tear stains." Hugh beguiled her with his brilliant blue eyes. "You understand, love."

"Of course." Berdie was tired, but she knew Ivy needed encouragement. Besides, she became besotted whenever her spouse looked at her that way. "Do you hold hope for reconciliation in that family?"

"With every prayer I breathe," Hugh answered.

The walk to the Butz home was pleasant—the sunshine saw to that.

Berdie and Hugh arrived at the house and knocked several times at the door decorated with one of Miss Livingston's wreaths. Finally, the door cracked opened. Lila Butz balanced herself on one crutch and pushed the door wide open with the other, gingerly protecting her bandaged ankle. "Mum says you're to go to the drawing room." Lila spoke the best she could with her stuffed nose.

Hugh caught the door. "Let me help, Lila."

"How's the ankle?" Berdie questioned.

"Okay." Lila gave a weak smile. "Excuse me, please." With that, the ailing youth began hobbling off.

The Elliotts stepped into the hall. "Lila," Berdie called, "can I speak to you for a moment?"

The girl stopped and looked toward Berdie.

"Go on in the drawing room, Hugh. I'll be there in a moment."

Berdie smiled and came close to Lila. "A sprain?"

"Yes, three weeks on crutches anyway." Lila ran a tissue over her red nose.

"That long?" Berdie paused. "I wanted to ask, Lila, you seem so well versed in the activity of the night heavens, do you belong to an area club or society for stargazers?"

Lila perked up a bit. "I belong to the National Society for Amateur Astronomers, but there's no local chapter." The girl repositioned her wrapped ankle. "Why, do you want to join, Mrs. Elliott?"

"Me? Oh no. I mean, I'm sure it's a fine group." Berdie continued, "No I was just curious if Miss Livingston may have been a member or ever talked to you about such things."

Lila scrunched her nose. "Miss Livingston? She's hardly the type."

"What do you mean?"

"The society is for scientists, people who study heavenly bodies, not carve them into wax." She shifted her leg again. "More an old mystic if you ask me."

Berdie was pensive. "Yes."

The teen returned the wadded tissue to her nose while precariously balanced on her crutch. "Is there anything else, Mrs. Elliott?"

Berdie jumped. "Oh no, no Lila, thank you. You've been a great help. Now, have you tried eucalyptus oil for your congestion? And keep that foot elevated, yes?"

Lila nodded an affirmative and trundled down the hallway.

When Berdie came in and sat herself down in the drawing room, Hugh was reading the Sunday edition of the *Timsley Beacon*.

"I hope Ivy's not too long," Berdie spoke to her husband. "We need to be at Graystone's office by two o'clock."

"Mmm," was Hugh's reply. Berdie knew, after many years of being married to this man, that sound meant precisely the same thing as "be quiet."

Berdie looked around the space. How could a drawing room repel so? Some bright damask pillows would add a little warmth . . .perhaps a cheerful painting, she speculated. Then something caught her eye. She spied a small plaque on the wall near the front window. It hadn't been there last week when they visited. She stood and stepped closer for a good look. She recognized it as the plaque Ivy had so desperately wanted from the goods at Lavender Cottage. It was very simple in design with an imprinted motto.

Berdie read aloud, "I believe in the sun, even when it doesn't shine. I believe in love, even when I feel it not. I believe in God, even when He is silent."

"World War II," Hugh quipped, his eyes not leaving the paper.

Berdie turned. "What?"

"That was penned during World War II," Hugh mumbled, "on a concentration camp wall."

Hugh's response was curtailed by a horrible screeching sound out in the front road. It was akin to several hundred pairs of sharp fingernails dragging across a school blackboard.

"I say!" Hugh was at the window with his wife.

BUTZ & SONS ELECTRIC read in large blue letters on the white work lorry that pulled into the drive. It wasn't until it came to a complete stop there that the racket subsided.

"That's certainly one way to announce your arrival," Hugh remarked. "Isn't that Jamie Donovan's work lorry?"

"But that's certainly not Jamie, it's Edsel."

"Right." Hugh smiled. "And look who's with him. Lucy."

The scramble of children's feet sounded in the hallway. Before you could say, "God bless us one and all," the Elliotts watched Milton and Martha sprint to the vehicle with little Duncan between them, the tiny tot holding on to their hands for precious life, his baby feet only occasionally hit the ground.

"Daddy, Da'!" The excited voices carried through the window glass where Berdie and Hugh took it all in. "Lucy!" Milty squeezed his sister's waist and Martha hoisted Duncan into Edsel's arms then grabbed hold of her father's leg.

A ragged *bump-scoot* moved hurriedly down the hallway. Lila soon joined the celebration. Lucy embraced her sister so tightly Milty got caught in the hug. He squeezed his head out from between them to catch air and finally broke free.

Another distant shuffle, and the mother of the family stood

next to her husband. Berdie had to look twice at Ivy. It was no longer a tearful nose and eyes that were red. It was her smart frock and the crimson silk ribbon in her hair. Mrs. Butz was radiant. Her husband gave her a peck on the cheek, his eyes admiring his beloved. Lucy, still with an arm around her sister, greeted her mother courteously. Ivy smiled nervously.

"That relationship still needs some sorting," Berdie pointed out.

"In time," Hugh assured.

"Are we being voyeuristic, standing at the window like this?"

Hugh pointed to houses across the road where eyes were discreetly peeking around curtains. "At least we've been invited in."

Lila's eye caught Berdie, then Hugh. She pointed to the window where they stood and said something to her mother. Ivy Butz put her hand to her mouth and rushed for the door.

"Let's meet her," Hugh suggested.

The hallway rang with Ivy's excited words, "I'd forget to stir the Christmas pudding but not for my hinnies!" Now her face matched the dress. "Vicar, Mrs. Elliott, I'm sorry."

"It's fine," Hugh assured her.

"We're just happy to see you're doing well," Berdie added.

Ivy giggled. "My Edsel called right after church. He's taking us out to tea in Timsley. And he's invited the Raheems, a thank-you, you know." She paused. "Oh, would you like to come?" It was obviously an afterthought.

"Thank you, but we have a two o'clock appointment." Hugh put his arm around Berdie's back.

"Of course. Well, thank you ever so for coming." She motioned. "Outside then?"

With the door latched and locked by Ivy's hand, the Elliotts stood in the sunny drive sharing hellos and good-byes in the same moment with the entire Butz family. The lot piled into the work lorry, waving as they drove past Berdie and Hugh, who had begun walking.

Berdie took her husband's hand. Even though dashing about, she cherished time with her Hugh. "The Butz family appears to be well in order." Berdie could sense relief in her husband's swift gait. She continued, "Yesterday's dreadful events prompted a change of priorities with those dear ones, I would say."

Hugh was bright. "Ashes to beauty, my love. Literally, ashes to beauty."

Berdie's stomach growled. "Down, girl," she said, patting her tum.

"Now there's a declaration for lunch," Hugh teased. "I say, let's stop for takeaway at The Copper Kettle."

"Mmm, one of their tasty minced-ham sandwiches." Berdie's mouth watered.

Vibrations buzzed in Hugh's suit pocket. He pulled the mobile out and answered, "Reverend Elliott."

Berdie observed his left eyebrow arch. *Not good*, she thought to herself.

"Yes,"—he paused—"yes, quite. Just a moment, please." Hugh directed his eyes to Berdie with an apologetic look. "Can you manage this afternoon without me?" he whispered.

Berdie knew her disappointment displayed itself unashamedly across her face. "Hugh."

He placed his hand over the mouthpiece. "I wouldn't ask if it wasn't important." His voice was hushed.

"I just haven't the bottle to go head-to-head with Graystone alone today," she whispered back.

"What about Lillie? Can she join you for the meeting?"

"Well, I suppose. If some parishioner can't live another moment without you." Berdie's voice was brisk.

"Berdie, I'm sorry, I—"

"Oh, I'll call Lillie."

Hugh spoke into the phone, "I'll be there in ten minutes."

When Berdie exited The Copper Kettle alone, sandwich in hand, the sun decided to take a hiatus behind a rather large cloud bank. One quick ring up, and within moments, her best friend met her at the Grade Two listed building that was Graystone's office. It was small, but the oldy-worldy look and feel gave it much grace.

Lillie, a market bag slung over her arm, greeted Berdie with a hug then pointed to a note taped to the lovely Georgian door. "Clients for the two o'clock meeting, please enter and be seated in the outer office."

"What's this all about anyway?" Lillie gurgled.

"We'll find out"—Berdie glanced at the large clock above the White Window Box—"in fifteen minutes." She lifted her takeaway bag. "Meanwhile, I'm famished."

Once inside, it became apparent that the outer office had a former life as a sitting room. A sizable lavender and evergreen wreath that decorated the mirror above the fireplace had little white berries that matched the white marble mantel. Flames barely flickered in the hearth; a small lamp on an end table gave the only light. Lillie took her ease in a large brocade armchair while Berdie sank onto a grand dark velvet couch that echoed the drapery fabric of the only window.

"Elegant," Lillie whispered in deference to the quiet room.

"Money," Berdie answered and ran her hand across the rich fabric.

At the other end of the room, beyond the Turkish rug that set off the hardwood floors, sat a small desk. "Graystone's?" Berdie asked in hushed tones.

"Oh my no. The clerk's. Graystone's is much more pretentious."

Berdie grinned. "Do you think he would refuse me a mini-picnic and a zonk on this expansive couch?"

"I'll just tell him you never learned proper manners," Lillie joked.

Berdie laid her head on the back of the sofa and took in the scent of lavender and evergreen. She was really looking forward to that first bite of minced-ham sandwich. In the quiet she became aware of barely audible voices.

Lillie started to murmur, "Oh yes, I brought—"

"Shh," Berdie interrupted. "Listen." She pointed to a barely open door, surely Graystone's office.

"Cheers, ol' boy, it's all yours now, top to bottom," Mr. Graystone's baritone voice carried. "Here's to no more bank on your back."

"Thank you, Mr. Graystone." It was Mr. Raheem.

There was a *clink* of glasses.

"Hardeep Raheem is supposed to be with the Butz family in Timsley," Berdie informed Lillie. Then her eyes flashed the same time Lillie's widened. " 'It's all yours now,' " Berdie whispered.

" 'Top to bottom,' " Lillie breathed. "He's not only paid off his mortgage past due, he's paid it all."

Elgars' "Nimrod"—Lillie's mobile bell tone—broke through the reverie of the quiet room like the high note of a Christmas aria. Lillie scrambled to turn it off.

"Someone there?" Preston Graystone marched from the office. "How long have you been here?" he demanded.

"We just arrived. Sorry to interrupt," Berdie responded while Lillie silenced the offending phone.

The *plunk* of a glass hitting a table sounded from the office and Mr. Raheem stepped past Mr. Graystone.

"Mrs. Elliott, Miss Foxworth." Mr. Raheem gave a smile and a slight bow. "Please indulge me; I'm late for an appointment with friends. I must go." He shook Mr. Graystone's hand. "Thank you again, sir." A brief acknowldgment again to Berdie was followed by his quick exit.

"I had no idea we were intruding," Berdie explained. "The note on the door—"

"Never mind," Graystone interrupted, clearly peeved. "You're early," he barked.

Berdie felt hunger and little rest push her capacity for politeness. She stood. "We can leave until the meeting starts if it suits you." Her voice was crusty.

"Please sit down." The solicitor made it sound like a command. He cleared his throat then softened his voice. "No, please, take your ease, Mrs. Elliott." He nodded to Lillie.

Berdie recognized his words as a polite and reasonable apology. Peckish or not, propriety dictated her response. "Thank you, Mr.

Graystone." Berdie sat squarely on the sofa.

Graystone lifted his pointed chin. "What transpires between myself and my clients is of the highest confidence."

"Of course." Berdie looked at Lillie, who agreed with a quick nod. *But we can't help what we heard*, Berdie thought to herself. And Lillie's eyes said the same.

Mr. Graystone remained standing. His gray suit added no distinction to his pallid skin. His salt-and-pepper hair was decidedly more *salt*.

The solicitor ran his hand over his stylish tie. "I'm afraid this business about Miss Livingston's will has been somewhat unpleasant. That old Livingston made a right dog's dish of it."

"Her will?" Berdie questioned, and Lillie lifted her brows.

"Exactly." Graystone relished their surprise. "Highly uncharacteristic. She had a gag on it until six days postdeath. Today's the sixth day." The man's narrow eyes went pensive. "Just the daft thing that one would do. On paper the old girl didn't even exist, you know. No birth certificate, no christening records, no family, no accounts, cash for everything. No wonder she and Natty got on so well."

"Not wholly reasonable then?" Berdie mined.

"Humph," he said with a scowl, "she was balmy and not by halves. Nearly did in my Cara."

Lillie shot a glance to Berdie.

"How's that then?" Berdie was boring for more.

"See here, where's my manners? Join me in my office," the man invited.

"Hugh had business, so Lillie has graciously accompanied me.

I hope you don't mind."

The man observed the coy and quiet Lillie. He shrugged. "Don't see any harm. By the way, I'm Cara's proxy today; she won't be in as she's wrestling with a flu bug."

Graystone's office, with three top-to-bottom walls of books and a desk that rivaled a pool table for size, was slightly intimidating. But Berdie found the large leather armchairs he offered them to be comfortable. They sat a bit apprehensively while Mr. Graystone cleared the half-full glasses and finally landed on his padded pivotal desk chair to tidy some papers on his desk.

"I hired Livingston as nanny for my daughter when we first moved to Aidan Kirkwood, you know." His angular nose flared as he tipped back in his fluid chair. "Had to give her the push." The solicitor ran his fingers across a file sitting on the desk and sat upright, folding his bony hands. "She was turning my lovely girl bohemian, peddling lavender in open-air markets, running barefoot all about the village, no discipline, no proper manners." He grabbed a pen from a handsome desk set and turned it end over end. "When it was time to send Cara to boarding school, she refused to go."

"Oh yes, I remember," Lillie said.

"Miss Livingston had long since been removed as nanny, but the dye was cast. I had to settle for five years of summer finishing school in Dublin."

"If memory serves me, it was the late Mrs. Graystone's sister who owned the school." Lillie smiled.

Graystone nodded.

"Cara's a lovely girl. She seems none the worse by it," Berdie encouraged.

Graystone spread his hands, his eyes alight, and lifted his skinny finger toward Berdie. "None the worse?" Preston Graystone flung open a desk drawer and pulled out several papers that he held high, turning his index finger upon them, thumping as he spoke. "Durham University, accepted." He slapped the paper down on the desk. "Cornell University in New York, accepted." He threw the papers across his desk like seeds to the wind. "But my daughter wanted to stay here and work in lavender with that wretched woman." When Graystone snarled, his angular features likened him to a medieval gargoyle. "Now, with her inheriting the lot, well but for a few bits, all hope of finer education is dashed." He blew a heavy sigh. "And of course now. . ." He looked away and dropped his head momentarily. He brought it upright, as if remembering why they were gathered, and gazed at Berdie. "Any word on Goodnight's whereabouts?"

Berdie tried to adjust to the sudden change in conversation. "No, I haven't spoken to him since yesterday."

"I'll ring him up." Graystone was almost woozy. "Excuse me, I'll make my call in the lounge." He politely nodded and left the room.

"Cara inherits!" Lillie blurted.

"Keep your voice down, Lillie." Berdie quietly scooted her chair closer to Lillie. "Indeed, and what are the bits she doesn't get, and to whom do they go, and just exactly why did he want me here?"

"Elgar." Lillie looked gravely at Berdie and went pink. "When Preston was so adamant yesterday about not touching anything in the house. . ." The woman caught her breath and brought her hand to her cheek. "I'm in possession of stolen goods."

"What are you going on about?" Berdie watched her friend pull the market bag from her shoulder. She thrust her hand inside. "The LP I took from Lavender Cottage. . .I brought it with me." Lillie zipped the album out of the bag with such exuberance, it went flying across the floor. "Oh no!" she cried. The precious record came to rest against one of the lower bookshelves, with the jacket landing astutely on a corner of Graystone's massive desk. But it was what fluttered out of the cover that caught Berdie's eye.

"Oh I hope it's not damaged." Lillie erupted from the chair and was on her hands and knees, rescuing the disk, while Berdie picked up a photo that had escaped from inside the cover. She went to Lillie's side and knelt down.

"Look," she said and prodded Lillie on the shoulder. "Isn't that. . ."

Her cohort looked closely. "A young Miss Livingston? Who are the females with her?" Lillie's love for Elgar was being challenged by her delight in intrigue.

Berdie pointed to a wild sea background where a rugged mound topped by an ancient castle jutted upward. "Holy Island," she whispered in recognition.

"It is," Lillie confirmed.

"The farm in Northumberland." Berdie nodded. "Of course, when I told Natty that Miriam was in a place of peace, she mentioned a farm in Northumberland." Berdie turned the picture over. There was scribbled writing.

"Can you read it, Berdie?" Lillie squeezed her head next to

Berdie, who squinted and adjusted her glasses lower on her nose. "To our cherished"—she tilted the photo so the light hit from a different angle—"sister Miri!"

"Sister?" Lillie shouted.

The door swung wide. "What's going on?" Graystone's entry into the office gave the women such a startle that Berdie dropped the picture and the women bumped heads. "Two grown women on the floor and one a vicar's wife!"

Graystone bent down to help them up, but Berdie sprung to her feet while Lillie rubbed the side of her head. "We lost an earring." Berdie knew it was a lame excuse but she decided to try it on.

"We?" Graystone asked Berdie while standing upright again.

"That is, it's found."

"Ah," Graystone pronounced. "All right then, are we, ladies?"

Lillie stood awkwardly. "Fine."

He espied the record in Lillie's hand. "And what's this?"

"It's Cara's." Lillie smiled.

"The record is in very good condition." Berdie nodded her head while Lillie slipped it back into the cover. Berdie eyed the floor. The photo had disappeared.

Graystone grabbed the album from Lillie. "Something from Lavender Cottage, no doubt."

Berdie smiled.

"You know not to touch anything there—nothing. Have I made myself clear?"

"Indeed." Berdie wanted to say barrels more.

"Right. Well, you can run along then. Goodnight's

professionally detained. It seems the fire yesterday was deemed arson and he's on the investigation as we speak."

"Arson?" Lillie went white.

"I was afraid of that," Berdie said under her breath.

Graystone shook his head. "Even the reading of her will has gone pear-shaped." He waved his finger in the direction of the front door. "Good afternoon, then, ladies."

"Good afternoon." With as much polish as she could muster, her friend in tow, Berdie left the solicitor's building.

Once outside she nearly exploded. "Where's the photo, Lillie?"

Her comrade-in-arms pulled it out from under her armpit inside her coat. "Oh look, it's our earring."

"Snap!" Berdie's pulse kicked up. "Photos are earrings. I've been going about this investigation all wrong. I've been seeking out the identity of the criminal. I must first establish the identity of the victim." Berdie took the photo. "Miss Livingston's a wool puller." She smiled at Lillie. "Work to do, my dear Holmes. Work to do."

CHAPTER EIGHT

Berdie was draped perpendicular across the comfortable sleigh bed in the peaceful manse bedroom, her comfy nightshirt soft against her skin. Hugh sat on the bed edge, his strong fingers making circular movements across Berdie's throbbing temples.

"This is what comes of no rest and poor nourishment," Hugh gently scolded.

"I know, love." Berdie's words were sincere but barely formed.

"Lillie did a lovely job of rallying the troops for tonight's second Sunday of Advent caroling, don't you think?"

"Mmm," she moaned, her lids getting heavy.

"Making it a tribute to our fallen chorister was a brilliant idea." Hugh continued the easy motion down Berdie's neck.

"And discreetly canceling the party after," Berdie murmured.

"Indeed." There was a smile in Hugh's voice as he moved his fingers up into the edge of her scalp. "Lillie was quite chipper this evening."

"Dr. Meredith. . .mobile voice message. . .this afternoon." Berdie had trouble stringing her words together. "Elgar concert tomorrow night. . .they have a date."

"Ah, he seems a fine chap, good for her."

Berdie drifted toward the sandman's domain.

Hugh's voice sounded distant, ". . .parish council. . .and the anonymous benefactor. . .Miss Livingston's photo."

Those last words made Berdie's eyes pop open. "Wha'?" she slurred and pulled her head upward. Hugh's fingers stopped.

"Can you sit up, love?" Hugh's voice was now clear and distinct.

Berdie lifted her torso and rolled her legs across the bed to a sitting position, distinctly close to her husband. He took her hands.

"About Miss Livingston's photo," Hugh started.

Berdie almost forgot she had told him about it earlier. Was he going to ask her to return it, give it to Goodnight? She was too relaxed to protest. At least his left eyebrow wasn't arching.

"Since the parish council has granted three days' leave, well four, but I have New Believers' class Wednesday evening—"

"When did that happen?"

"I just told you, darling, this afternoon at the council meeting. I thought we'd holiday at Nethpool House."

"In Northumberland." Berdie was awake. "Oh Hugh."

"Now,"—her husband's voice was firm—"this is a holiday with a mingle of fact-finding. It doesn't mean hours of endless investigating, it means a considerable rest with a touch of unearthing."

"Of course." Berdie shook her fully loosened-up and now pain-free head.

"Room's reserved. We take the 9:30 train tomorrow morning from Timsley."

"Oh Hugh!" Berdie threw her arms around her husband and hugged him tightly. This was exactly what was needed, on both accounts.

While they relaxed their embrace, a noise hit their eardrums that neither wanted to acknowledge. The phone. *Ring, ring.* Pause. *Ring, ring.* The couple sat motionless, neither of them speaking, just staring at each other. Finally, Hugh reached across the bedside nightstand and answered, "Vicar."

Berdie wanted to yank that contraption from the wall.

Hugh handed the mouthpiece to his wife. "It's for you," he whispered. "It's Lillie and she sounds horrible."

Berdie spoke into the phone, "Lillie?" She looked at Hugh and shook her head, acknowledging that Lillie indeed was low. "Oh rough luck. Called out of town for work then, was he?"

Understanding registered in Hugh's eyes.

"Did he say anything about getting together on another occasion?" Berdie hoped she was encouraging, as knackered as she was. "Oh Lillie, this has been a difficult week. Being exhausted always makes disappointment larger than life."

Hugh signaled for Berdie's attention.

"Can you hold just a moment dear?" Berdie gripped her hand over the mouthpiece.

Hugh asked, "Are you canny to taking Lillie with us?"

"Are you?" Berdie countered. "She has been a massive help through everything and it would do her such good."

Hugh paused, smiled broadly, and winked. "I'll book a second room."

"Lillie," Berdie said, resuming her conversation, "what would you say to a couple days with Hugh and me at Nethpool House in Northumbria?"

—

The next morning, what with excited packing, errands, and locking up, the threesome nearly missed the train. But once aboard, everyone relaxed. There was little conversation but a great deal of reading, zonking, and watching the world zip past out the window. The countryside was refreshing. Yorkshire was picturesque, and when they rode past the berns that kiss the North Sea beaches, they were entranced. The sea was restless, and Berdie thought of the all those who called this part of England wild, ragged, or untamed. Those were the very qualities that drew her into the heartbeat of its wonder.

Departing the train, all three inhaled the sea air with vigor. The wind was brisk and they scrambled to their hired vehicle. Hugh took the wheel while Berdie and Lillie drank in the stone fences, hedgerows, roaming sheep, and occasional homes that edged the narrow road to Nethpool House.

Upon approach, Berdie observed the baronial Arts and Crafts Hall with its plentiful turrets and private valley. She and Hugh had been here several times, but it was a first for Lillie.

The moment Hugh brought the vehicle to a stop in front of the hall-now-inn, no one had to be coaxed from the car.

"I'm gob smacked," Lillie confessed and turned a slow spin. "I'm in a fairy tale."

"And you're the princess," Hugh offered, unpacking the bags.

Once inside, Mr. and Mrs. Alfred Peach, the colorful owners, welcomed them.

"What's on offer in the dining room this evening?" Hugh asked.

"Our specialty." Mr. Peach smiled. "Tweed salmon and fresh grouse."

"Sounds wonderful." Berdie beamed and turned to Lillie. "People come from all round to dine at Nethpool, and it's Michelin rated."

"Just last night several people motored in from Edinburough," Mr. Peach boasted.

Hugh hoisted a suitcase. "Well done. What say tea to the room in about twenty minutes?"

"I have fresh border cake with that, Reverend Elliott, and still warm." Mrs. Peach was a perfect hostess.

Lillie insisted that she wanted the afternoon for a quiet lie in. But Berdie knew it was Lillie's way of giving Hugh and Berdie time alone together, and she loved her friend all the more for it. They all agreed to meet in the dining room at half seven for the evening meal.

Hugh and Berdie arrived at the threesome's reserved table a few moments early. It was easily spotted from the dining room entrance.

Pinecones woven into evergreen and holly wreaths scented the air. Polished red apples sprinkled with nuts in the shell exuded holiday cheer. The arrangements were accented with red and green tartan ribbons and bows. Large hurricane lamps brought a warm gleam to the polished wood that lined the walls. It came together to create a festive holiday touch to the rustic elegance of the room.

Berdie pulled the mysterious Livingston photo from her beaded evening bag that delightfully offset her midnight-blue dinner dress. She handed the snap to her husband.

"Yes, that's no doubt Holy Island," he affirmed. "Of the four girls, Miriam looks oldest by far, midtwenties perhaps. The youngest could be eleven, twelve."

Berdie admired her spouse sitting across from her at the well-set table. The candlelight cast a merry glow on the stemmed glassware and complemented Hugh's dark tweed jacket. It gave him an air of distinction, even without his collar. The gentleman laid the picture on the table.

"Ah, there's our Lillie," Hugh announced.

Lillie Foxworth floated into the room wearing a cream-colored lamb's wool sweater that enhanced her hazel eyes and deep brunette hair. The matching straight skirt flattered her slender figure.

Hugh stood and pulled out her chair.

"Thanks, Hugh." She was radiant.

Berdie squeezed Lillie's hand. "You look beautiful." She leaned closer to her dearest friend. "You never know in a place like this. A highland baron may come seeking dinner and leave with a bride."

Lillie laughed. "Indeed! There's an air here that fairy tales come true."

Hugh lifted a liter of Kilwillee Highland Sparkling Spring Water out of an icy bucket and filled their glasses. "I propose a toast," he said, lifting his glass.

Berdie and Lillie followed suit.

"In God's good grace, blessings upon this house, upon this

table with friends old and new, and blessings"—he looked at Berdie—"on our pilgrimage into truth."

"Here, here," Lillie chanted.

"Cheers," Berdie added.

The *clink* of stemware glasses sounded like chimes declaring cherished friendship and renewed spirits.

Berdie sipped the sparkling water and enjoyed its fizzy refreshment. She relished a second sip and noticed that though Hugh was already refilling his glass, Lillie hadn't taken any in. Instead the woman stared straight ahead, hand to her chest, eyes larger than the charger plates that adorned the table.

"Lillie?" Berdie tried to read her friend's expression. It was a mix of shock, panic, and delirium. At the same moment Berdie turned to look in the direction of Lillie's gaze, Hugh put a voice to the affair.

"I say, look. Isn't that Dr. Meredith? How remarkable."

Berdie returned her gaze to Lillie, who now drank the frosty water in gulps.

Immediately Hugh stood and went to the doctor who was chatting with Mr. Peach at the dining entrance. Astonished, Loren Meredith greeted Hugh with a bright smile. The gentlemen shook hands, then Hugh waved his hand toward the table. The coroner's astonishment turned to enchantment upon espying the table's occupants. Hugh continued to speak, but Dr. Meredith's eyes were upon Lillie. The men moved toward the table.

"Here he comes," Lillie breathed.

"Baroness, you look smashing," Berdie assured her dearest ally. "No, you *are* smashing."

The men arrived. "Even on an off chance, who'd have thought," Hugh declared.

"Mrs. Elliott." The doctor tipped his well-groomed head. "Miss Foxworth." He spoke straight to Lillie. "How fortuitous, and you look. . ." The handsome man searched for the words. "What an unexpected turn. . ." He stumbled over his sentiments, captured by Lillie's glow. "Indeed."

"It's a grand evening, and all the more for seeing you," Lillie responded regally.

Hugh broke into the momentary dazzle. "Our good doctor is seeing to a business matter here in the area. He's lodging in Berwick," he informed.

Loren adjusted the lapel of his dark sport coat that covered a black turtleneck sweater. The slimming colors couldn't hide his broad shoulders. "I understand you're here on holiday."

"Well, on holiday and fact-finding," Berdie had to add. "The opportunity just came up last evening, a rather quick push."

"Yes." The coroner glanced at Lillie. "My call to do a consultation came quickly as well, as Miss Foxworth can avow." He was a handsome figure, still, not as tall as Hugh.

"The coroner for this area is on emergency leave, and the lead crime scene investigator, an old university chum, called on my district for help." He spread his arms. "And here I am."

"Please dine with us," Hugh invited.

"Ah," the man replied, sounding apologetic, "well, you see, I'm meeting my colleague here for dinner tonight and a wrap-up report, an arduous task made less so by salmon fillet."

Everyone enjoyed his easy rapport.

"Otherwise, baying wolves couldn't keep me away," he finished.

The gild of Lillie's radiance took on a bit of tarnish.

Berdie spoke up. "Perhaps you'd be interested in joining us tomorrow for our small adventure."

"Adventure?"

"Splendid idea," Hugh agreed.

Berdie handed the Livingston photo to Dr. Meredith. "Lillie stumbled upon this concealed photo while doing a clear-out at Lavender Cottage. It would appear the lone Miss Livingston had family after all, and in this area. We mean to get to the bottom of it."

"As time allows," Hugh added.

The doctor studied the photo. "This case gets more and more interesting."

"How's that?" Berdie asked.

He put the photo down. "Livingston's autopsy revealed distinct oddities." The doctor looked toward the entryway and paused. "I see my colleague has arrived."

"Don't let us keep you." Hugh smiled.

Berdie turned to see a tall, thin woman with yellow hair, a briefcase, and years of tangling with the seedy side of humanity upon her face. Her smile revealed the habit of heavy smoking.

"So what time do we leave for our adventure tomorrow then?" Dr. Meredith asked.

"Capitol!" Hugh delighted.

"You're coming then?" Lillie broke into a blinding smile.

"Wouldn't miss," Dr. Meredith said and returned the smile.

"Here, around half past nine." Hugh shook the gentleman's hand.

"Berdie's adventures are surprises in the making," Lillie informed.

"I look forward to it. Well. . ." He looked to the waiting friend. "Please excuse me."

"Of course," Lillie proffered.

With that, Loren Meredith left to greet his coworker. They were seated on the far side of the dining area but still in plain view of the threesome.

Berdie was pleased both for Lillie and her own sake. The coroner could be of great assistance in searching out clues.

Hugh looked like he was reading her mind. "Jolly well he's aboard; he'll be a wonderful asset." He stopped. "And, Lillie, a fine day's companion as well of course."

Menus arrived then meals were ordered and served by an attentive staff. It was a slow and leisurely meal wherein Berdie relished every taste of gourmand delight, as did her hungry husband. She noticed Lillie seemed to just pick at her food. The "Recipe Corner" contributor couldn't believe her friend was snubbing a superb meal.

"It's not to your liking?" Berdie asked.

"Well, look at them." Lillie almost scoffed. "A quiet table for two, that's hardly business."

"Oh my." Berdie leaned closer. "I'm talking about the food, dear heart. Do you like it?"

"Oh. . .the food." Lillie ran her fork over her creamed pheasant. "Yes, it's some of the best I've had."

"Do I detect a greenish tint about your halo, Lillie?" Hugh prodded.

"Of course not," she declared, her face gone crimson.

"She may have his attention, but you have his esteem," Hugh offered.

Berdie observed Dr. Meredith coming their way. She gave her husband a gentle tap with her foot under the table.

"Sorry to bother," the doctor spoke. "Mrs. Elliott, may I see that picture again? I'd like to show it to my colleague. Perhaps she can shed some light on the matter, seeing she's native to Northumberland."

"Certainly." Berdie pulled the photo from her bag and gave it to Dr. Meredith.

Now both women, trying desperately to be unobtrusive, watched him return to his table. "He's showing it to her. She's nodding her head," Berdie gleefully observed.

"A bit too close to his, may I point out," Lillie added.

"She's pointing at something. This could crack it." Berdie stretched her neck. "She's examining the back." She ducked her head.

"He's on his way back." She put a forkful of buttered winter potatoes in her mouth. Lillie adjusted an errant curl of hair.

Loren returned the photo as his dining partner arose and waited for him at the entrance. "We have a bit more work back at the lab, but I think Roz—Rosalyn—may have given us some helpful information," he volunteered and put the photograph down. "Must push through."

"Half nine then," Hugh reminded.

But the doctor focused on Lillie. "It can't come quickly enough. Good evening."

Berdie tried her best to gulp down the mouthful of potatoes. She dabbed her mouth with the linen napkin. "I wonder what his colleague knows?"

She spoke too late. The doctor and his friend were out the door.

"Splendid man," Hugh commented.

"Go after him, Hugh," Berdie urged.

"What on earth for?" Hugh chewed. "We'll have the word in the morning, love. Nothing we can do with it tonight anyway." Hugh was intent on his meal.

"He called her Roz," Lillie murmured.

Hugh swallowed. "Yes, and well he should. They've known each other for years. Quite familiar, I should think."

Hugh looked from Lillie to Berdie. "What?" he asked.

Berdie's glance to him was meant to convey far more than any words.

"No pudding then?" Hugh put his fork down and hailed the waiter. "Bill, please."

❧

The Northumberland winter marked itself with force winds and heavy rain all through the night. By morning the landscape dripped, rousing only enough warmth to totter above freezing.

The heavy clouds didn't dampen anyone's enthusiasm that Berdie could see. After she tried to urge Lillie, to no avail, to wear more sturdy shoes for the border weather, the foursome was in the car and traveling the splashy lane ten minutes after the doctor's arrival.

"Now tell us again, Dr. Meredith, how your friend knows of the Livingstons," Berdie compelled.

"Please call me Loren," he corrected, "all way round."

Hugh, who drove, and Berdie, nodded, but Lillie smiled at the gentleman next to her.

"Well then, you must call me Lillie."

"Settled then," Hugh pronounced.

Loren continued, "Roz didn't know the Livingstons, but she knew of a Livingston Farm. Her father was district coroner and required to make a call there. Indeed, it was the first time Roz attended her father on a job. Mr. Livingston didn't have a suspicious death, but swine flu was rearing its ugly head and Roz's father autopsied as a precaution. When flu was confirmed, he went to the farm to inform the family. The Livingstons had two pigs that were put down on the spot."

"Difficult for a child," Hugh commented.

"Indeed. That's why she remembered the event. To help ease his daughter, the coroner stopped in Alnmouth after, to get her a sweetie and fizzy pop."

"So, that's why we're off to Alnmouth," Berdie stated.

The doctor shook his head. "She couldn't remember where the farm was, but she knew it was somewhere near that village."

"What do we do when we get there?" Lillie asked.

"Ah, well," Hugh responded, "that's where my wife's nose for the scent comes to play."

Berdie couldn't help but smile.

"Alnmouth, ho!" Hugh charged.

The drive to the seaside village was a pleasant one. Once in town, Hugh parked the car on the ancient cobbled main street. The stone shops and cottages ran to the winter beach where a deserted golf course looked forward to spring.

Berdie wasted no time in getting her plan into action. While she and Hugh went to the post office, Lillie and Loren were dispatched to the town hall.

"How many residents here do you suppose?" Hugh asked Berdie, stepping into the postage stamp–size space that was postal headquarters.

"Round three hundred," the keen-eared young woman behind the tiny counter answered. Her youthful countenance lacked charm. "Tourists then?"

"Of sorts," Berdie answered. "We're seeking the location of the Livingston Farm. We understand it's in the area."

The woman paused. "No, no Livingston Farm round here."

"Could have been here many years past, actually," Hugh prompted.

Berdie showed the aged photo to the young woman. "Anyone familiar?"

She elevated it closer to her face. "Older than dirt," she observed and handed it back.

"Yes, the photo is not recent." Berdie tried to be kind.

"Nor the people by now." The girl popped her gum. "That's my gran's expertise. Delivered mail here most her life." She shifted a stack of magazines. "She may know something."

"Grand." Berdie was hopeful.

"I tried to ring her not five minutes ago though. No answer. Never home; always playing about since becoming a pensioner."

"There are so few delights in aging." Berdie couldn't help herself.

Hugh took his wife by the arm. "Thank you," he spoke to the clerk. "You've been helpful, and our best to your grandmother."

Outside the shop, Berdie pulled her arm from Hugh's grasp. "I could have gotten more information, you know."

"Perhaps, but I'm not fond of brawls."

Berdie recognized Lillie and Loren walking toward her. The gentleman took Lillie's elbow as they crossed the street. "Maybe they'll have something."

"Town hall is a vacated church, locked tight as a drum," Loren related upon arrival. "Lillie rang the posted 'emergency' number on her mobile."

"Not even a voice mail or answering machine," she remarked.

The doctor added, "Thumbed through the directory at a phone box. No Livingstons."

The foursome took in the salty sea air and courted disappointment all at once.

"Perhaps we should take our ease and play a few rounds of golf," was Hugh's attempt at levity.

Lillie shivered against the cold.

"What say a hot cuppa, my treat," Loren countered. He eased Lillie closer to his side.

Directly across the street a door flung open and two people departed. The din of voices sprang from the opened portal.

"Grand idea," Berdie agreed. "I should say." She read the hanging plaque above the door and pointed. "There at the Shoreline Inn."

"It looks to be the local," Hugh observed, but Berdie was already halfway across. She had much more than tea on her mind. *My dear Lord*, she thought her prayer as she crossed the road, *I can't believe this photo would fall to us at an opportune time only to be of no purpose.* She stepped lively, expectantly into the beachfront of the Shoreline Inn.

CHAPTER NINE

The public house smelled of pipe smoke, last night's pub grub and spirits, and decades of hearth fires. After the foursome was seated at a small corner table, Berdie accompanied Loren to the counter.

"Four teas, please," he ordered.

"Any border cake on offer?" Berdie asked.

The giant man behind the counter ran his huge fingers across his rough-shaved face. "No deary. . .a few crumpets," he mumbled.

"Include them with the teas, please," Loren instructed, then looked at Berdie. "I'm sorry, it seems I've put us on a wild-goose chase."

"Don't apologize yet, Doctor. Pubs can be store-holds of everyone's business." Berdie winked. She laid the photo out on the counter and spoke to the man pouring the teas. "Excuse me, does anyone in this snap look familiar?"

The middle-aged man stopped pouring and looked closely at the photo. He squinted. "Who wants to know?" he asked.

"It's a legal matter," Loren responded.

The publican turned an ogle to the two. "You don't look like the bill."

"Oh, I assure you, we're not police. I'm a vicar's wife," Berdie solidly stated.

The man squinted again and took in the doctor. "Right."

"Fergus, gimme another one," a ragged voice yelled, and a small glass slid down the counter like a sled on a slope.

"Ah Maude," the large man shouted. "How many times have I asked ya' not to do that?"

A small woman, not more than twenty inches taller than the counter, shook her silver-haired head so that her spectacles nearly took flight. "How else can I get you to serve me then?"

Berdie wondered how such a bawdy voice came from one so petite.

"Your taste for lemon shandies has severely cut into my stock," the man loudly informed, then growled to Berdie, "It bites into my offerings for the kiddies. Better for that one to get back in her postal buggy, idling all hours in here."

"Postal buggy?" Berdie twinkled. "Her granddaughter works the shop right across the way?"

"You've met the charming girl then."

The fierce oldster down the counter waddled to Berdie's side and gawked at the photo. She turned it right way round. "Look here, it's the Livingston girls." This time her head shook with remembering. "Now that takes one back."

"You know them?" Loren Meredith, who hadn't any inkling of the significance of "Maude," now was piqued.

"Knew them? Not really. Livingston Farm was on my delivery. Nice folk. Kept to themselves."

"Where is the farm?" Berdie asked.

"Oh, no farm, not no more. Sold that off when the father passed." The oldster pushed the photo aside. "And where's my shandy, Fergus?"

"Are any of the sisters still round?" Loren questioned.

The woman stretched her stubby finger to the youngest in the photo. "That one. That would be Bossy. . .Bessy? Betty. Yes, Betty. Married an Oglesby from Henley Road." The woman squinted. "Right, they were the farm with the converted barn, no drive mind you, eight kilometers east of the A-1. Isolated. But that was several years back."

Fergus placed the lemon shandy on the counter.

"Let me get that for you," the doctor insisted.

"Ta'." The small woman grinned.

He handed the publican a twenty-pound note and nodded toward the shandy lover. "Keep her supplied."

"And make our teas takeaway, please." Berdie shot a glance at Dr. Meredith.

He smiled then addressed the innkeeper. "We're motoring on."

—

A task that Berdie thought would take thirty minutes stretched into two hours.

"Do you get the sense we're going in circles?" Lillie asked.

"This is the area," Berdie reaffirmed.

"She said it was isolated." Lillie stared out the window of the car at the rows of identical newly built homes. "Far from isolated." She stated the obvious.

"To be fair, love, it was several years back." Hugh addressed Berdie.

"Farmland with a converted barn." She was not giving up yet. "But maybe they had to sell some of the land, perhaps to developers. So many do these days." She looked ahead. "Hugh, please pull the car over." Berdie spotted an old gentleman slogging through the winter mud, his welly boots covered with the muck. "Did he come from the building on the far end of that muddy field?" Just as Hugh stopped, the figure entered a vehicle on the edge of the road and drove off.

"Aha," Berdie all but yelled. "Isn't that a barn conversion?" She pointed to the distant building beyond a row of new homes.

"That's almost an acre back from the road," Loren observed.

"And all of it mud." Lillie looked at her espadrilles. Her stylishly small feet almost made them seem like ballet slippers.

"No apparent pavement or path to the place," Hugh observed.

"Oh come you lot." Berdie was charged with energy. "The other side of that mud holds a wealth of possibility, a key perhaps to solving Miriam's case."

"Or a possible dead end," Hugh warned. He pulled his liturgical collar from out of his jacket interior pocket.

"What are you doing?" Berdie quizzed.

"My badge of office may put them at their ease."

"Good thought," Loren approved, "we being inquisitive strangers and all."

Berdie thought momentarily. "Put them at their ease, yes."

"They won't care about attire, they'll just observe the sludge we flog about their hall." Lillie sounded edgy.

"You really dislike that mud." The corners of Loren's mouth turned upward.

"Hugh?" Berdie opened the car door.

"Off we trudge then," Hugh said.

"In for a penny in for a pound," the doctor agreed and eyed the lovely dissenter.

"Oh very well then." Lillie's determined eyes said she was hardly going to let them venture on without her.

Hugh and Berdie were, what seemed, knee-deep in Northumberland mud and several yards ahead of Lillie and Loren. Lillie had a difficult time negotiating the hike, but Loren Meredith was a strong help and Berdie could hear ripples of occasional laughter. Just a few short meters from the door, a horrible yelp accompanied by a great *splat* sounded from the rear guard. Berdie spun to see the dear Lillie face-first in the mud, the doctor trying to position himself to make a valiant rescue.

"I say!" Hugh beheld the sight.

Berdie's first instinct was to run to her friend's aid, although she was undeniably sure she would laugh without control. And that just wouldn't do. Indeed, she was biting her lip to keep from it now.

Loren got Lillie to her feet. She put Berdie in mind of a raccoon. Lillie blinked, and the white orbs were one of the few spots on her not black with mire. Loren held her steady with one hand and used the thumb of his other hand to remove the mud smears from her lips and cheeks.

"My dear woman," his said in a gentle voice, "if you wanted a mud bath, you could have said and I'd have taken you to Leamington Spa."

Lillie, eyes misty with humiliation, chuckled. "Thank you,

Doctor, but I've always preferred rose-fragranced salts and bubble baths."

"Can we assist?" Hugh called.

"A towel would be splendid," the doctor responded.

"Lillie?" Berdie called.

The choirmaster scraped her hands across her winter coat, down her sleeves, and the length of her slender legs, throwing the mud to the ground. "I just wanted to make a lasting impression on the hostess," Lillie called.

Now Dr. Meredith laughed and rearranged the woman's dark curls away from her face.

Hugh was at the door and knocked firmly. A woman in a blue pinny and print headscarf answered, wiping her hands on a tea towel. But she looked right past Hugh to the pitiful Lillie.

"Oh my lovely," she empathized and handed the towel to Hugh. "Get it to her now," she coaxed.

Berdie trudged to the door and apologized to the gracious woman. She tried briefly to explain it was a personal matter that had brought them to her door. But the farm wife's concern for Lillie hardly allowed her to be attentive to Berdie. She insisted the muddy woman avail herself of the shower room and had the kettle to the boil almost instantly. After depositing Lillie in the bathroom, she served hot tea all round at the large wooden table in the kitchen.

"Whenever I have an unexpected vicar at my door, I reason 'tisn't good news." The woman's weathered face was kind.

"Yes, possibly so," Hugh spoke quietly.

"Possibly so?" She looked puzzled.

"First we must ask if you have a sister living in Aidan Kirkwood—a Miriam Livingston." Berdie placed the yellowed picture next to Mrs. Oglesby's chaffed hand.

The woman took a deep breath. "Miri." She stared out the tiny window above the kitchen sink that revealed voluminous gray clouds and patches of wild winter grasses. "Dear, dear Miri. I s'pose she's gone on then?"

Everyone was silent. Berdie nodded in the affirmative. She wanted to take the woman's hand but decided it could be intrusive.

"So you found us." Betty Livingston Oglesby had a quiet relief. A mist started forming across her aged eyes. She used the corner of her pinny to dab at the moisture. "How?"

"We found this picture among her goods," Berdie explained. "We came upon information that led us here to your farm."

Hugh checked his pockets. "I'm sorry, I can't find a tissue."

"It's all right, Vicar, sir." Betty Oglesby used her pinny to dab both eyes. She sniffed then straightened her back. "She tweren't a blood sister, but she were a sister sure enough. Sad it were."

"We really don't know a great deal about Miriam," Hugh explained.

"No, you wouldn't then." The woman bit her thin lip. "Not even my Robert knew the truth of it." She put her hands in her lap. "Well, she's gone now, God rest her soul. I s'pose it's time the truth be known." Betty looked squarely at her guests. "My parents took her in near the end of World War II. They were a part of the war resettlement scheme. Very hush-hush. We told folks round here she were a cousin come to stay. Poor dear hardly knew English."

"She was French," Berdie spoke up.

Betty nodded her head. "She worked hard to learn English, got it near perfect. Still, she didn't go out."

"You called her Mary?" Berdie asked.

"Miri. Never knew her surname, just Miri. Many nights she woke from dreams, frightened, shakylike." The woman sighed. "As an adult, I realized she were probably part of the war resistance over there." The woman swallowed hard. "The longer she were here, the more we cared for her and she for us." A smile crept across her small mouth. "She had a way with lavender, and basil, and lemon balm."

"Lavender was her trade," Hugh commented.

"She grew that lavender where others dared not and it were lovely."

"When did she leave your family?" Dr. Meredith asked.

The woman put her eyes back to the window. "She was just gettin' stronger, both outside and insidelike, when this man come, dark. Never seen one quite like him, kitted out for a circus seemed. Came right near the house in a horse cart, spoke to Miri, and left as fast as he come. It were like a darkness fell." She returned her eyes to her guests. "And that night she told us she had to go and wouldn't ever see us again. Miri said this because she loved us. And at dawn, her bed were empty. We never laid eyes on her after."

The woman abruptly stood and ran a finger across her nose. "Excuse me while I sort out the wet one." Betty left the kitchen and disappeared into another room.

"I say, far more than I expected." Hugh sounded mystified.

"It all falls into place now." Berdie was demystified.

"How did you know she was French?" Loren asked.

"I had an idea in the clear-out, packing away her goods. Most of her library was in the French language and yet, by all accounts, she seldom if ever spoke French. And there was her love of lavender, in itself not notable. A casual look at her gardens that few truly viewed behind the fence wasn't notable either. But a closer look revealed English lavender in the front garden, French lavender in the back. Which was it that won the prize at the flower show?"

"Her French lavender," Hugh said.

Berdie went on, "Better cultivated, more time, more love, yet it was hidden in the back garden. Then there was her great love of music. Most of her music LPs were by French composers; in fact Lillie noted that Miriam's favorite was Ravel. Again, not notable in itself, yet she had only one English composer, Elgar. But what I couldn't sort out was why hide her nationality? When we found this snap," Berdie said, her head in the direction of the photo, "tucked up inside the Elgar album, the whole identity issue became complex and at the same moment more assured."

"Well, we've certainly made strides in uncovering that issue," Hugh encouraged.

"But there's more, there's more," Berdie asserted.

"Indeed there is," Dr. Meredith agreed.

"Our wet one's drying," Mrs. Oglesby announced. "She'll be kitted out soon."

"Thank you for the lend." Berdie was grateful. "We'll send the clothes back by post."

"Not to worry, they're hers." Betty poured more tea. "I have something to ask ya,"

"Something we can do?" Hugh said promptly.

She placed a tiny red enameled box by Hugh's hand and opened it. "Seeds of her labor. I harvested her lavender when she were off. Tried my hand but 'tweren't the same." She fumbled one of the seeds. "A child needs somethin' of the one gone." She paused. "Could you see your way to plant these where she lay?"

"Where she lay?" Berdie asked, hoping it didn't mean what she supposed it did.

"At her grave, like."

Berdie and Loren looked expectantly at Hugh.

He thought for a moment, closed the lid, and put the tiny treasure in his pocket. "By God's grace, I'll move heaven and earth to grant your wish, Mrs. Oglesby."

"Right then." The woman smiled.

In the doorway, the "wet one" appeared. If it weren't for the fact that Lillie had just experienced a most embarrassing and humiliating event, you'd think she had dressed for a stroll of a warm summer's eve in Donostia. The full multitiered red skirt fell in gathers from her small waist. The white peasant-style blouse with full sleeves was laced with red ribbons. And a colorful-patterned scarf showed off her graceful neck. But it was her smile that made Lillie truly beautiful—it radiated all the grace and warmth the woman possessed. Berdie watched Loren Meredith soak in the glow of this incredible woman who turned disaster into a jolly good romp.

"Time for a serenade then?" Lillie snapped her fingers in a castanet motion and made a little twirl. Even her damp, dark hair formed ringlets that invited a dance.

"Bravo," Dr. Meredith cheered, and clapped.

"The real applause of course goes to Mrs. Oglesby." Lillie bowed to the farmer's wife.

Gone red, Betty just grinned and nervously flipped the hem of her pinny.

"Wherever did you find such colorful clothes?" Berdie was curious since they were far too small to fit Mrs. Oglesby.

"Four girls meant hand-me-downs," Betty replied. "They were Miri's, then my sister May's, and so on, until I, number four, grew big enough to inherit them. But that's the problem ya' see." She stretched both hands forward in front of her stomach. "I grew big."

The foursome had to smile.

"As far as I can see, Mrs. Oglesby," Hugh voiced, strong and sincere, "it was your hospitality that grew large. We can't thank you enough for your kindness. We must move along then."

"Oh do take care for the sludge," Betty offered.

Hugh smiled. "Yes. And we'll offer prayers for you and Robert this week at Matins."

"Bless ya' then," Mrs. Oglesby said in a hoarse whisper.

After farewells and best wishes, the foursome made their way to the road's edge, the doctor carrying the delighted señorita to the car. In no time at all the travelers were on the road back to Nethpool House.

In the backseat of the car, Loren spoke under his voice to Lillie. "When you said last evening Berdie's adventures were full of surprises, it wasn't far off the mark."

Lillie gave a wink and a smile.

"Who knew I'd be returning from the escapade with a lovely gypsy troubadour next to me?"

By the time the hardworking detectives returned to Nethpool House, Hugh announced his plan to have a nice lie down then nestle into a good read. Berdie said she had every intention of joining in with her husband's plan. Loren, by mobile, arranged tea for himself and Lillie at the quiet winter lodge in Nethpool's west garden, a plan that delighted Lillie.

Trying to scrape the dark mire from off their footwear at the front steps of Nethpool House was a chilly business. The warmth of the front hall felt like a beloved eiderdown had wrapped itself around them, and Mrs. Peach was at their call. In good humor she demanded that they remove the muddy shoes and give them to her.

"I shall get these shoes back to you in double time. And well polished," she promised. "Now, you'll need these." She handed everyone a pair of fresh guest slippers that they handily fitted into.

"Well, to the room then." Hugh eyed Berdie.

"Go on, love, I'm going to peruse the gift cove. I'll be up presently."

"The gypsy troubadour must return to her choirmaster attire." Lillie was already on the stairway with Hugh right behind.

Loren spoke to Berdie. "Actually, I'm glad we have a moment together—do you mind?" The doctor was keen.

"What is it?" Berdie asked.

Loren measured his words. "I prefer not to talk about my work when someone of particular interest is present."

"Ah, yes." Berdie nodded her comprehension.

"Somehow, talk of wounds and body scars can be off-putting." He recognized Berdie's understanding. "And of course there is professional etiquette as well."

Berdie was pleased that Dr. Meredith considered her one with whom professional etiquette could be shared.

"I thought you would be interested in Miss Livingston's autopsy results, or should I say our female victim in the case. But first may I ask you a question?"

"Yes." Berdie was attentive.

"I understand arson is suspected concerning the blaze at Lavender Cottage."

Berdie nodded her head.

"Do you think it was intended toward you?" Loren came right to it.

"One always wonders, but at the moment I would say no, it wasn't an intention toward me or Lillie." Berdie knew where his concern really lay. "It was the night before that Goodnight assigned the duty of the clear-out to Hugh, who gave it to me. Up until that point, I had avoided investigating the affair, by my husband's coaxing, of course."

"I see."

Berdie could see the concern of Loren Meredith's brow ease.

"Now, moving on, about the autopsy." The doctor spoke eagerly, in a discreet volume. "I discovered several things of interest. First, concerning her demise, it was a swift passing, no signs of struggle. In fact, she had a widely used prescriptive sleeping aid in her bloodstream. Mind you, it was a bit more than required for a woman of her stature, but nothing abusive. Her singular fatal wound was one swift blow done with military precision."

"Are you saying the perpetrator has a military background?" Berdie took in the information.

"Well-trained skill, at any rate. They placed one blow at an exact angle to cause death."

"Go on," Berdie urged.

"The facial scars."

"Ah yes, from a childhood disease," Berdie recalled.

"Is that what she told people? No, they were burns—small circular burns. Well scarred over, as they occurred decades ago."

"Oh my, poor dear." Berdie was processing the information.

"There was also scar tissue on her lower right arm. I would say our victim attempted to remove a tattoo."

"Miriam always wore long sleeves. That explains that then."

"Perhaps this information will help put you on the scent." Loren Meredith continued, confiding, "I haven't much faith in Goodnight."

"Quite frankly, Doctor Meredith, I shouldn't think Constable Goodnight could catch a Christmas snowflake with an upturned umbrella," Berdie agreed.

Mr. Peach approached the pair. "Tea's on, Dr. Meredith. Miss Foxworth rang to say she would be down presently." The host grinned. "The winter lodge is quite charming. There's a cozy hearth with a well-tended fire. You'll find the gracious overstuffed chairs have removable cushions if you fancy sitting on the rug in front of the fireplace. The stereo system has a wide collection of CDs, and the view over the west garden runs all way down the valley. Mrs.

Peach has laid a marvelous winter tea that includes fondue. You'll have to share the pot, of course, with your fine lady." Mr. Peach winked. "I think you'll find the lodge comfortable and well-suited for a twosome tea."

"Grand!" The doctor tendered only one word, but the anticipation and delight in his eyes spoke volumes.

"Well, I'll just excuse myself." Berdie smiled at the gentlemen. "And thank you, Dr. Meredith, for the information." She laid her finger aside her head. "Collected and stored." Her eyes twinkled. "And enjoy tea with your person of interest. I know she certainly will."

With that, Berdie entered the gift cove. *What a golden opportunity*, she thought, *for Lillie and Loren to share uninterrupted time together and grow in appreciation and understanding of each other.* She prayed the best for her dear friend and the wonderful new man in her life.

After a quick look at local handcrafted work in the Nethpool House gift cove, Berdie moved on in her thoughts and up the stairwell. With the update of Miriam's identity and fresh details from Dr. Meredith, along with renewed vitality, Berdie's brain buzzed, her investigator's nose twitched, and she knew her sleuthing of the case was in full swing.

CHAPTER ⛧ TEN

The train ride back to Aidan Kirkwood seemed to take far less time than going. But then Berdie often thought that was the way when returning from a holiday, even a working holiday. Hugh promised her that he would contact Sergeant Major Andrew Busby, still working in the intelligence community, to search out more delicate historical information concerning Miri. As for Lillie, she still hadn't awakened from her dream.

The Timsley train station hummed, tooted, and clanged with rush-hour arrivals and departures. More and more urbanites were opting to up-sticks and move to rural areas, living with arduous commutes. The Timsley train station was a testament to that fact.

Disembarking was a mad rush, but tall Hugh blazed a trail, with Berdie and Lillie in his wake.

In the central station, shops were lively and the cafés were deceptively inviting. Lillie stopped, jolted back to everyday life, and stood near the entrance of The Daily Grind.

"I could go a hot cuppa," Lillie suggested when her suitcase was bumped by a fast-paced gentleman.

Hugh and Berdie paused, bags in hand.

"I've found these station cafés offer a fine grade of motor oil and call it tea." Hugh was not interested.

Berdie glanced through a large sheet of glass to the space inside. "It's quite crowded that." She peered at a corner table where she saw three men seated together. She pressed her head forward. "Isn't that Preston Graystone?"

Lillie strained to peek. "Yes, and with him is Reverend Lewis, I believe."

Berdie could see Mathew Reese's profile clearly. "What is Mathew doing here? Is it Christmas break at university already?"

"It's Wednesday. . .maybe a long weekend?" Both women stood in puzzlement.

"What an odd lot," Lillie observed.

"Isn't it just," Berdie agreed.

"Ladies, we haven't time for tea or speculation." Hugh was nearly assaulted by a woman using her mobile phone who lunged for the restaurant entryway. "I don't fancy being late to my New Believers' class." Hugh turned and pushed on, waving Berdie and Lillie to follow.

"We better keep up." Berdie pulled herself away from the glass and took Lillie's hand. "Or we could be thrashed forever in the sea of modern civilization. I'll fix a nice cup at home." But Berdie wasn't intent on tea while she stored a mental snapshot of the peculiar gathering in The Daily Grind.

Hugh made his New Believers' class with time to spare while Berdie and Lillie made plans to meet the next morning to sort their to-do lists, which had grown over the holiday. Since Hugh needed the Elliotts' vehicle for calls, the women opted for the coach to Timsley in the morning.

The December air made Berdie glad to board the toasty warm coach. The public transport into Timsley was direct, timely, and certainly adequate.

Lillie chose a seat next to a window and Berdie took the aisle seat next to her. The coach came to its regular stop just down from Mr. Raheem's shop to accept waiting riders.

"Oh my, what's going on?" Lillie viewed the produce store out her window. "Half the village is at the greengrocer's."

Berdie bent forward to see. "It's Thursday. Whatever is the draw?"

"Mrs. Elliott, Miss Foxworth, oh my, you're missing it." Mrs. Plinkerton, who had just boarded the vehicle, sank into the seat cross the aisle, holding a large market bag of produce. She spoke as the vehicle lurched forward on its route. "I must say, whyever didn't you come? Oh yes, you've been away. Right." The woman continued. "Mr. Raheem is giving a wee basket of nuts and assorted dried fruit to everyone who buys five kilograms of produce." The woman held up a tiny straw basket with the goods enclosed and a bright red bow tied to the handle. Mrs. Plinkerton looked quite smart in her Sunday hat and fur-collared coat. "It's to celebrate your well-being, you know."

"My what?" Berdie blinked.

"Your rescue," the woman puffed. "It's a bit of a do to celebrate Mr. Raheem's rescue of you both—oh, and Lila Butz—from that wretched fire. Isn't he ever so clever?"

Lillie stared at the woman. "We weren't aware."

"Of course you weren't, darling, off on holiday. No, the whole village is very proud of Mr. Raheem, you know. Quite frankly I hadn't been to the shop since it was taken over by the gentleman. But I daresay he has certainly proved himself." She dipped her chin as if making her point perfectly clear. "And isn't it the cutest little basket?" Mrs. Plinkerton patted the item and replaced it in her market bag. She pushed the bell signal to alert the driver to halt at the next drop-off. "Here's my stop." The well-coiffed lady rose to her feet. "Do take in his little market later. I think you'll find it quite tidy. Cheerio, then."

"See you at church Sunday?" Berdie called after the exiting woman.

"Well," Lillie breathed.

"On our return home, I believe a stop at the greengrocer is in order," Berdie offered.

"Following our nose are we?" Lillie chirped.

Berdie smiled. "Well, it's not every day one is so boldly rescued."

The ride to Timsley went quickly. The coach traveled the road several kilometers, making occasional halts at the indicated coach stops, picking up and depositing the riders.

In Timsley proper, Berdie and Lillie disembarked at the newly opened women's surgery.

Berdie took in the new large structure. "I must say, National Health has splashed out on this one. I read the specialty here is in pre- and postnatal care. Now remind me, what is it we're doing here?"

"Making a delivery," Lillie quipped.

"Well it certainly isn't mine," Berdie joked.

Lillie laughed. "I should have gotten this sheet music to Dr. Avery last week. She's new to the choir, well. . .new to the church for that matter. . .wonderful mezzo you know."

"Good, get her connected."

"Speaking of connected." Lillie pulled the folder of sheet music from her market bag. "I think I've sorted what the three men were doing together at The Daily Grind yesterday."

"Have you then? Well, let's hear it." Berdie was attentive.

Both women entered the automatic doors into the lobby.

"They were planning Mathew and Cara's wedding. Graystone was consulting with Reverend Lewis on procedural matters and they met Mathew, just in from school, at the train station." Lillie looked pleased with herself.

"One vital element is missing, dear Watson. The bride."

"I've thought of that. She's sick, remember? Preston told us Sunday she had a flu bug." Lillie looked delighted to demonstrate her reasonality.

"Granted, but flu or not, can you imagine Cara Graystone to be the kind of woman who would let three men plan even a hair's breadth of her wedding?"

Lillie stopped and looked at Berdie. "About the same chance as you not flying to the nut of the matter like a homing pigeon."

The lobby held several women, many of whom were obviously with child. Wee ones played in a reading corner designed for the very purpose of entertaining them. How many books had she read to her own Nick and Clare when they were small?

Berdie followed Lillie to the receiving desk where an energetic young woman managed chaotic reception duties with a smile and amazing success.

"I'm here to give this to Dr. Avery. It's a folder of sheet music," Lillie informed.

"You must be Miss Foxworth, the choirmaster. Dr. Avery will be very pleased to get this. She's been expecting it."

Among the din of children playing and mothers in conversation, the sound of a woman sobbing came to Berdie's ear. It seemed dire, and she wondered what grief or difficulty stirred the person to such sadness. She turned round just in time to see a young woman with honey-colored hair and a pleasing figure step from the doorway of a doctor's office.

"Is that. . . ?" Berdie stopped.

"I should say. Divine timing!" Lillie whispered and took in the woman.

Cara Graystone held a tissue to her nose then lifted it to wipe her eyes. She stepped forward, trying to move as unobtrusively as possible toward the clinic exit, but already several eyes peaked over the tops of magazines.

"Cara?" Berdie heard herself say it in a quiet tone.

The village beauty came up short at the sound of her name. She closed her eyes as if trying to escape the recognition of her person. Slowly she reopened the red orbs, cleared her throat, and wiped her wet cheeks. Without any acknowledgment to Berdie, Cara moved forward to the automatic door.

"Cara," Berdie called again.

The young woman stopped, lifted her chin, and turned to acknowledge Berdie's beckoning.

"Oh, Mrs. Elliott, it's you." The girl found her voice when she realized it was Berdie. A sense of relief played across Cara's face while at the same time she gripped her handbag fiercely. A single tear ran down the red cheek.

Berdie was at the girl's side. "I was just thinking a hot tea would go down well. Do you want to join us then?"

Lillie discreetly handed Cara a fresh tissue.

A humble nod of honey-gold hair and a "Very much so" meant Berdie's day had just taken an abrupt turn.

The three women were the first customers of the day at the café straight cross from the surgery. They settled into a cozy wooden snug where high-back benches assured privacy. The tea was fresh although Berdie couldn't say the same of poor Cara's countenance.

The distressed beauty looked at the table then into the women's faces.

"I'm in a difficult situation that should be a considerable joy."

"Yes, dear." Berdie wasn't entirely shocked after Cara's display at the surgery.

"But I wouldn't have you think ill of me, Mrs. Elliott."

"Is Mathew aware of your difficult situation?" Berdie tried to be tactful.

"Mathew." Cara stared at her tea. "No."

"You must tell him. He's entitled as your fiancé," Lillie said quietly.

Cara dabbed a tissue to her nose. "No, he's not my fiancé. I don't believe he ever was, really."

Berdie was pensive. "Then what are we talking about, Cara?"

Cara opened her handbag and drew something out. She guarded it in her clenched hand like an unfathomable secret then laid it out, in the light of day, on the bare table. The glint of shine caught Berdie's eye while it caught Lillie's breath. It was a simple silver band.

The young woman sighed as if an unbearable tempest was releasing its strength.

"Thursday next I'll be married three months now." Cara slipped the perfectly fitted band on her left ring finger. "I'm Mrs. Jamie Donovan."

A shock wave shot through Berdie like a string of Christmas fairy lights. She found it difficult to contain her amazement, but as the wife to Cara's parish priest, she felt she must retain some professional bearing. But Lillie was completely unabashed.

"My dear girl, how ever did that happen?" Lillie's voice was three pitches higher than normal. "And why carry on with Mathew?"

"It's all a bit complicated." Cara took a deep breath and looked at Berdie. "You deserve an explanation." The girl began, "I spent several summers at my aunt's finishing school in Dublin."

"Yes." Berdie remembered Mr. Graystone mentioning it Sunday in his office.

"My first summer there I met Jamie on an evening river stroll. It was love's first blush in the beginning, but five summers later we were desperately in love. My aunt was horrified, my father determined to crush it, although he never met Jamie. But love's star had set to glowing. In our innocence, we made a pledge to true love." Cara went still.

"A youthful oath is as disparate from the commitment of marriage as shoes in the store window are to the wearing of them."

Berdie sipped her tea.

"Yes." Cara shook her head. "My last summer in Dublin, I discovered Jamie had made a stupid mistake that spring. A brush with the law. His violation was joyriding. He was given several months' imprisonment."

"Whyever for?" Berdie knew the punishment was harsh for the crime.

"The auto belonged to a government official."

"Ah," was all Berdie need say.

"And so," Cara continued, "I plundered his shame and imprudence by telling him his recklessness had ruined any chance for our future together. I am my father's child." Cara wiped the moisture at the corner of her eye. "I told him he needn't bother with me until he had gotten things right way round, including a real career. The next day when I realized what I had done and tried for reconciliation, Jamie begged off. He was shattered. I had lost him forever."

"That's when Mathew came into the picture," Lillie spoke.

"My relationship with Mathew was an attempt to dull the pain. I see that now. My father thought Mathew well suited. Mr. and Mrs. Reese encouraged the relationship, and poor Mathew worked so hard to please them, to win their affections."

"I should say that the pleasing them bit has changed." Berdie thought of the argument he had with his mother and father at the Advent party.

"He's found his way to his own person. Going off to university certainly helped." Cara stirred her tea. "His first summer home, things were different with us. But it was easier to pretend all was well and just move through our lives."

"You appeared compatible," Lillie added.

"Didn't we just." Cara brought the teacup to her lips and took a swallow. "But I never stopped loving Jamie just as sure as Mathew grew into a new man." Cara sat the cup down. "And then, by some gracious miracle and three years to grow up, Jamie was on my doorstep in September, hat in hand, offering a promising future as Edsel's apprentice and a simple silver band."

Berdie tipped her head. "But why hide the marriage, why the charade?"

"My father would never accept Jamie as my husband. He forbade the very thought. But Jamie and I knew it to be right. We belonged together. So we married in secret with the hopes that my father would get to know Jamie in his own right and come to respect him."

"And?" Lillie asked.

Cara just shook her head and took another sip. "I thought by now. . ." The bride looked at the ring.

"Have you told anyone else about the marriage?" Berdie asked.

"Mathew. He took it splendidly, and though he didn't get on with Jamie, he agreed to the ruse. I just told my father this past Tuesday. That went horribly. And I also told Miriam—Miss Livingston."

"Miss Livingston!" Berdie was hearing the sound of trumpeting elephants. "Her response?"

"I thought she'd be happy for me, but she cursed the day my father sent me to Dublin." Cara's eyes filled with wet hurt. "She said, 'Heartache and despair are handmaids to marriage with Jamie.' " Quiet tears escaped and dripped from the young wife's chin. "And then the party, and all this horrible. . ." Cara buried her face in her hands and cried.

Berdie slipped closer to the woman and put her arm around her.

Lillie was to the rescue with a tissue. "I'll just get you a warm-up," she said and took Cara's cup to the counter.

Cara gazed back to her new confidant. "Mrs. Elliott, help Jamie please."

Berdie nodded. "I must ask, Cara, did you lie to Goodnight about seeing a tall, light-haired man in the woods the day of the murder?"

Cara swallowed. "Yes."

"To protect your husband," Berdie added. "Natty said she saw someone that fit that description."

"Natty?" Cara pleaded, "You've got to clear Jamie. He's innocent, I swear he's innocent."

"Yes, Cara, yes." Berdie was not only comforting Cara but also stating what she believed to be true. The word *framed* ran through her mind. But would public knowledge of the marriage help or hinder Jamie's cause?

"Now you must take care of yourself, despite all the difficulties," Berdie exhorted.

"These nine weeks I've had stomach upset, but the doctor said all seems to be developing normally."

"And Jamie knows?"

"Yes. And he's over the moon," she said. "At least he was until all this mess."

Lillie returned with the steaming cup. "You know, I think I saw Mathew standing cross the road."

"Mathew?" Cara wiped her face and stood to her feet. "He's given me a ride, such a dear through all this. I must go. And please, Mrs. Elliott, clear my Jamie."

The young woman rushed out the door to Mathew.

"Well." Lillie looked as if she had been on the bumper cars at Blackpool. "Quite the revelation."

"Lillie," Berdie asked, "how far is the Timsley Detention Center? I think it's time to pay Jamie Donovan a visit."

When Berdie and Lillie entered the police station, Berdie made straight for the reception desk as Lillie gazed about, trying not to be too obvious that it was her first visit to the "old bill."

"May I help you ladies?" The new recruit behind the desk looked quite smart in his fresh uniform.

"We're here to visit James Donovan," came Berdie's quick reply.

"In what capacity do you wish to see the accused?" asked the young man, word for word nicely memorized from his training manual.

Berdie hesitated. "I'm his clergyman."

Lillie's eyes widened.

"And this is my assistant."

The assistant awkwardly smiled and pushed the market bag on her shoulder to her back.

"As quickly as possible, please?" Berdie added.

The young man showed them toward the visitors' room.

The two women sat in uncomfortable chairs at a small steel table.

"Well now, here we are," Berdie quipped.

"I can't believe you told a policeman you were clergy," Lillie hoarsely whispered.

Berdie leaned closely. "Technicalities. Besides, all the pastoral papers I edited and typed for Hugh in seminary, I could have a Master of Divinity myself."

The door swung open and the suspect was escorted into the room. Jamie expressed surprise when he saw Lillie and Berdie at the table. He nodded to the guard and sat down.

"I didn't expect to see *you*," he said in a low voice.

Berdie saw deep anguish in Jamie's weary eyes. "Jamie, I'm here because I may be able to help you out of this mess, but you've got to tell me the truth. All of it." Berdie spoke softly, "Lillie and I just spent the last hour with Cara. We happened to see her at the women's surgery."

Jamie sat forward in his chair. "She's okay?"

"Mrs. Donovan is fine and everything's developing normally," Berdie replied.

"So you know." Jamie put his head in his hands. "I know this looks bad, Mrs. Elliot." He lifted his head and sprawled his hands across the table. "We never—" He paused. "I didn't touch Cara, in that way, until she was my bride. I love her, and she loves me."

"I understand *that*," Berdie annunciated.

Jamie's jaw set. "I didn't kill Miss Livingston. I was spittin' angry, but I would never kill her. I swear."

The young man checked Berdie's eyes, as though searching

for a reason to trust her. Instinctively, she grasped Jamie's hand and gave it a quick squeeze.

"The truth then," Berdie said.

The young man glanced at the guard on duty. "The day before Miss Livingston was killed, I had been working on her dodgy electric, when Edsel called and asked me to attend another customer." His whisper was nearly inaudible. "I excused myself and said the earliest I could come back was the next morning to finish the job. Miss Livingston told me she was doing the early shift at the holiday jumble sale, wouldn't be home, and in the same breath demanded the work be done. So, as much as it chafed her, she gave me her spare key, said to come in and take care of the problem. I stopped on the way into work the next morning, near seven." The young man swallowed. "The door was ajar. I knocked, but she didn't answer, so I went in." Jamie hesitated and wagged his head. "And the place was thrashed. I knew something was wrong. I heard a noise. 'Miss Livingston,' I called, but she didn't answer. I went upstairs and looked into her bedroom. There she lay." Jamie dropped his head. "I knew she was gone." He shut and opened his dark eyes. He clenched his fist. "I panicked. Mrs. Elliott, once you've been banged up, the ol' bill never trusts you. Any trouble and you're the first accused." Jamie swallowed hard. "I didn't want Cara to be alone with the baby, and me banged up, so I bolted. I just needed some time to think."

"Did anyone actually see you at the scene?" Berdie quizzed.

"That balmy woman maybe."

"Batty Natty." Berdie remembered Natty telling Goodnight she had seen someone short and dark.

"Have you tried telling the law the real story?" Berdie asked. "You've got to try, for everybody's sake: Cara, the baby, and your own. You've got to take the chance they'll believe you. And Jamie, God's mercies are new every morning."

"But is the justice system's?" A prolonged sigh left Jamie's lips. "I came to Aidan Kirkwood to start over. I got a good job and married the only woman I've ever loved. Cara's the best thing that's ever happened to me. For the first time in my entire existence I saw my life going somewhere. Now I'm banged up in here for something I didn't do."

It was difficult to watch Jamie's face contort and flush as he tried to hold back the tears.

"Jamie, can you think of anyone who may want to frame you?" Berdie asked carefully.

Jamie shook his head. "Why would anyone want to do that?"

"Just think. Who knew you had Miriam's key?"

The lad shrugged. "Edsel, Cara." He paused. "Well the whole village practically."

"What?" Berdie bent forward.

"I went late that Saturday night to the Upland Arms. Filled to the rafters. I had a lemon shandy with Mat Reese and Reverend Lewis. When I went up to order another round, I jammed my hand into my cash-carrying pocket and the key flung out, skipped across the floor, and landed on Dudley Horn's shoe. When I retrieved it, I made some comment like, 'Livingston would have my head if I lost it.' The whole place broke into laughter. Seemed funny at the time. Now I wish I'd never seen that key."

Berdie took in every word.

The lad shook his head. "No, the people I know here really seem to care. Edsel Butz, he knows about my marriage and has visited several times, trying to help. Reverend Lewis as well, but what can they really do?"

"Reverend Lewis?" Berdie's territorial instinct flared.

"He came just Tuesday with some scheme to help hire a private solicitor. What I really need is a miracle."

"That's what we'll ask for and that's what we'll work for, but you must start the process by telling the truth."

Jamie took Berdie in. She thought she saw a flicker of hope in those cheerless eyes. "Can you keep Cara's name out of this, I mean as much as possible? I want to be a good husband, and I want to be a proper father for my child, Mrs. Elliott. Do you really think you can help me out of this mess?"

"By God's grace I'll do my best," Berdie assured him.

Jamie nodded.

"She's a brilliant investigator," Lillie assured.

"I'll ask Hugh to come by. He's a tower of strength that one."

Jamie let go a sigh deeper than Jacob's well. Atlas was no longer holding the world on his shoulders. It fell and rolled into the capable hands of his "clergyman" sleuth.

Berdie gave Jamie's hand another squeeze.

"Move your hand away from the prisoner," the guard growled. "Visit's over."

Lillie started. The prisoner stood and the guard nodded. "Tell Cara I love her." With those words, Jamie was led from the room.

Berdie and Lillie stood.

"What now?" Lillie asked.

Bernadine Elliott gave her determined answer. "I'm going to find the real killer!"

CHAPTER ELEVEN

Getting errands done in Timsley took the rest of the afternoon, so visiting Mr. Raheem was postponed until the following day. Berdie and Lillie decided they would meet at Mr. Raheem's shop Friday noon. Lillie's morning was booked with teaching voice lessons, and Berdie promised Mrs. Braunhoff to help prepare the Nativity figures for the Christmas Eve service.

That Friday morning, the gray December clouds hung low with the burden of their contents as if waiting for the right moment to shower all of creation. Umbrella close by, Mrs. Braunhoff met Berdie at the aged outbuilding on the far back of the church property near the woods.

It took both women to force the down-at-heel door that opened to a dark, damp interior. The sturdy Mrs. Braunhoff wore her wool-lined denim work jacket and a dark headscarf that was tied neat as a pin at her chin.

"Are you the official keeper of the Nativity?" Berdie asked.

"My husband and I, yes." She grinned.

Barbara Braunhoff wielded a battery-operated torch about that flashed its way over a water-spotted Joseph, a very pale Mary, several muddy shepherds, and a sheep that had lost its tail altogether. It lighted on the crèche where a soft-smiling baby Jesus lay on His side.

"First thing is to wash them up," Mrs. Braunhoff explained. "We need to move them to the lot near the church, on the south terrace, where we can scour them and get them safe inside."

Berdie stood to the side as the woman handily lifted a water-spotted male by the waist. "It looks like our blessed Joseph was baptized by the heavenly waters themselves."

Both women espied the roof where a spot of daylight showed itself.

"Mr. Braunhoff will see to that," Barbara Braunhoff declared. The robust woman snuggled Joseph tightly on her hip. "An hour's time and a lick of paint, my husband will have all tidy." The woman shone her torch on the Mary figure. "Can you manage the Virgin?" she asked Berdie.

Berdie saw the figure was somewhat smaller. "I should think so, and the baby as well."

Berdie cradled the baby Jesus in her arm, and with the other arm pulled Mary close, grasping her by the elbow. "No newborn wants to be far from mum." Berdie laughed as they stepped into the light of the back garden.

Not more than a few meters away Berdie saw Reverend Lewis speaking into a small handheld digital recorder. Both women stopped.

"Ah, Mrs. Elliott, would you say this area could hold a standard-size marquee tent?" he called and came near.

"I would think." Berdie knitted her brow.

Mrs. Braunhoff assessed the vicar in one glance. "He criticized my kulich."

"We would need it for our final banquet, if this venue is my congregation's choice." The man smiled awkwardly. He nodded toward Berdie's cargo. "Quite pale, that one." He vainly snickered. "Looks like she's seen a ghost."

"I daresay we would as well had we given birth on a cold porch," Berdie spouted.

Mrs. Braunhoff smothered a chuckle and made off with her Joseph in tow.

"In good holiday cheer, are we?" Reverend Lewis sniffed and put his hands on his hips.

"Did my husband suggest you come here today?" Berdie squeezed the baby Jesus in her arm a bit tighter.

"Do I need permission to be in a church garden?" The man narrowed his blue eyes that were just visible below the rim of his dark homburg.

"Perhaps not, but I should say you have taken liberties." Berdie was politely direct.

"What are you talking about?"

Berdie took a breath. "Visiting Jamie Donovan in jail, for one."

"Visiting?" The man paused. "Oh no. You're not going to disparage me for doing a good turn."

"Very well. I'll just say thank you and ask you to keep your distance from him. Jamie is Hugh's parishioner; it's not your job to attend to our church body." Berdie discreetly tipped her head to the man and took a step toward the terrace.

"Mrs. Elliott," Reverend Lewis cried, "your husband left that poor lad sitting in the clink while you and he puttered about on holiday."

Berdie turned on her heel, nearly pulling the Virgin Mother's elbow from the socket. "What?"

"I was there for the boy in his hour of need." Reverend Lewis stepped closer to Berdie. "And what has your dear husband done to help his case?"

Berdie pulled the baby Jesus to her heart. "My husband has soothed and nourished the people of this village." Berdie felt her face go red despite the cool weather. "Furthermore, it was a working holiday, and at this moment Hugh has his fingers in the pie of sensitive intelligence concerning the victim's background and shadowed history, which could go a long way on Jamie's behalf." Berdie's voice almost became a trumpet. "So I suggest you let Hugh tend to things."

Reverend Lewis lunged toward her, his eyes flared and his back stiff. She stepped backward, almost tripping over the holy mother's hem.

The angry man drew a shallow breath. "You tell me what I can and cannot do? You stick your nose in where it's not wanted and call it charity because your husband is in the church. It's just an excuse to be a meddlesome busybody."

As if in a moment of inspiration, the three men sitting in The Daily Grind together popped into Berdie's head while Jamie's voice rang in her ears. *"He came. . .with some scheme to help hire a private solicitor."* Her eyes flickered. "You're trying to get Graystone to represent Jamie Donovan."

The man's face flushed. "Whatever business it is of yours, Graystone would move heaven and earth to keep his son—" He caught himself. "To keep Jamie out of jail. He has a vested interest to defend him."

"Does he really? From what I can see of the situation, that's like saying King Herod has a vested interest to defend the crèche."

"Why, you silly cow!" Reverend Lewis thrust his forefinger toward her and hurled his voice at her like a winter gale. "From now on stay out of my way. I'll talk to the organ-grinder, not his monkey."

"My dear sir!" Mrs. Braunhoff stepped her sturdy body next to Berdie.

Reverend Gerald Lewis raised his chin and took a deep breath. As if having done battle, the reverend marched off from the garden.

Barbara Braunhoff put her hands to her hips. "If ever a man were ill-suited for the cloth, it would be that one." She took the Virgin Mother from Berdie's grasp. "Let's get on with the scrub-up then."

Berdie transferred her dislike for Reverend Lewis's comments into scrubbing power. That, plus Mrs. Braunhoff's skillful scouring, and it took no longer than an hour to get the figures prepared for their upcoming fix-ups and command performance. Not two minutes after sudsing the last sheep, the laden clouds let go their cascade. Dashing madly, the Holy Family and friends were tucked safely inside the church. Berdie and Barbara offered cordial farewells and scooped up their umbrellas.

—

After freshening up, it was a sloshy walk to Mr. Raheem's store. Berdie prayed as she went and it calmed her considerably. Umbrellas bounced and weaved all along the High Street, and at last Lillie's came into view.

"Are you okay?" was Lillie's greeting as she took in her friend's visage.

"I'm much better now, but I had a considerable head-butt with Gerald Lewis."

"That man and fish. . ." Lillie quoted her late father. "Both go off after three days."

Berdie nodded. "And he's been here for weeks. I'll tell you what happened later. Right now I need some Jerusalem artichokes, red potatoes, and a boatload of answers."

Three people exited the store as Berdie and Lillie entered. The jolly bells danced and the threesome admired their little fruit baskets while trying to manage full produce bags and popped umbrellas.

"Ah, my dear women," Mr. Raheem greeted from across the shop and quickly made his way past Mrs. Horn, who was fingering the cranberries. "Welcome! And how was your holiday?"

"Delightful," Berdie responded. "Thank you for asking. It looks like your wee baskets are quite popular."

"Even as you say," the man replied, grinning. "It was my dear wife's idea, a celebration gift of sorts."

"And what is it exactly that you're celebrating?" Lillie asked.

"Your well-being, for one."

"Very kind, Mr. Raheem, thank you. And there's another reason?" Berdie quizzed.

The man espied Villette Horn at the checkout. "Let me tend to my customer and then I can tell you." The grocer went to the counter.

"Very wise man—get the town crier out the door before you say anything you don't want marched up and down the High Street." Lillie smiled as she spoke.

While Mr. Raheem calculated the merchandise, Villette turned toward the two women. "Isn't it wonderful? The three of you reunited after that dramatic rescue. You must be so grateful."

Berdie just bobbed her head while Lillie kept her pasted smile. She spoke to Berdie through her teeth, "Keep the story growing and Mr. Raheem will have rescued hundreds from a blazing inferno while single-handedly putting the fire out himself."

With business settled and the crier out the door, the happy man returned to Berdie's side.

"Mrs. Raheem and I have a praise to God to celebrate." He leaned his head closer and whispered as if Mrs. Horn were listening from outside. "My brother in London bought out my half of the business our father left us. I have put the money into the business here. It's all ours—Sharday and Hardeep Raheem, greengrocers. A dream come true." Mr. Raheem's face was lit like a Christmas candle. "All goodness from God."

"Congratulations! Would you like Hugh to come do a shop blessing of sorts?" Berdie offered.

"Oh, for now we want to keep the good news mum. If the village knew, well, perhaps they wouldn't be so eager to buy. But I would be delighted with a private blessing—a grand idea."

"It's your recognition as a hero, it would seem, that keeps the people of Aidan Kirkwood eager to buy." Berdie made the point clearly.

"I only did what any Christian would do." The grocer smiled.

"It is others who, how you say, toot the horn." The gentleman pointed to a bin. "Look," he said.

Berdie spied the almost empty structure.

"You're running low on red potatoes." Lillie spoke her observation.

"Exactly!" Mr. Raheem beamed.

"Ah." Berdie smiled.

"I don't say I am pleased a home caught on fire, or that you were in danger, God forbid! But I am pleased that I had an opportunity to do something good, and the community took note. Now, is there something I can get you?"

"Some Jerusalem artichokes," Berdie answered.

Mr. Raheem directed the women to the bin holding the delectable vegetable. "Just unearthed this week." The grocer held one up. "Decidedly fresh. How many do you wish?"

"Let's start with four of them." Berdie moved seamlessly on to her question while Mr. Raheem inspected the artichokes. "You know we never discussed how it was you were at Lavender Cottage the day of the blaze."

The man held up a lovely green plant for Berdie's approval. She nodded.

"I wasn't actually at the cottage. I was looking in on Mrs. Bell's home."

"Natty's?" Lillie asked.

The man plied the artichokes for the largest ones. "Mrs. Bell's family hired me to care for her home while she's away. That's when I spotted the fire. I used to make produce deliveries to Miss Livingston, too, you know."

The vegetable connoisseur held up two more plump delights. Berdie nodded again. "Often?" Berdie asked.

"My best customer, every week, sometimes twice a week. She would always pay with hundred-pound notes. I could seldom break them so she carried over the extra to the next purchase. An act of trust. She could be quite rude, but Miss Livingston possessed keen understanding. . .of being a stranger in a new place."

"Yes, I believe she would understand that clearly," Berdie agreed.

The man added one more artichoke to the stash in his arms. "Can I get you anything else?"

"What's left of your red potatoes, please," Berdie requested, "and an answer to another question."

The grocer put the artichokes in a plastic bag.

"You saw Jamie Donovan at the train station the morning Miss Livingston left us."

"I will never forget that day, never." The man went solemn. "A very sad day. Yes, I saw the young man run to catch the train to Holyhead, very distressed. I didn't know he was suspect at the time, but as soon as I heard, I called Mr. Goodnight."

Mr. Raheem had the potatoes to the last one in a bag. He took a breath and his countenance brightened again. "It seemed all of Aidan Kirkwood was at the station that morning."

"Oh yes?" Berdie's ears were finely tuned.

"There was Mathew Reese, going back to school perhaps, Miss Graystone—she brought her fiancé to the station, I would think."

Berdie and Lillie's eyes locked momentarily.

"And Reverend Lewis, who was going to inspect a property for his church's retreat. I saw Mr. Graystone's auto in the car park, but I didn't see him."

"My, it was a busy morning for several people," Lillie commented.

"The holiday season can bring more than usual dashing about it seems. A time perhaps that should better suit peace and gratitude." Mr. Raheem handed the bag of potatoes to Berdie.

"You must not forget a little container of dried fruit." He pointed to a display that held several of the merry baskets.

"Thank you, Mr. Raheem."

"Yes, thank you," Lillie reiterated.

"And the vegetables are on the home," he added.

"House?" Lillie corrected.

"How very kind, Mr. Raheem." Berdie held the goods in her arms. "You and your wife must come for dinner before the holiday passes."

"We would be delighted." The man tipped his head and the two women were back out in the rain, laden with bags and opened umbrellas.

"Our Mr. Raheem is either a most sincere and genuine Christian as ever could be," Berdie announced, "or a complete and utter fake of the worst kind. And I believe the former rather than latter."

"Here, here," Lillie agreed.

"Any play we've given to Mr. Raheem being the perpetrator of any horrid crime can be laid to rest, I should think. Wolves in sheep's clothing I've seen time and again, but Mr. Raheem is definitely one of the sheepfold. Yes. . .definitely."

The two women parted. Berdie felt most confident about the visit to the kind greengrocer who, in a week's time and one strategic divine appointment, moved from dog-paddler in the Aidan Kirkwood goldfish bowl to strident freestyle swimmer.

Soggy but keen, Berdie was home fixing tea for herself and her husband. She prepared one of the artichokes with dipping sauce and poached some fresh salmon with herbs. It was a light meal, but she looked to the evening for a sturdy repast. When she and her husband finished eating, Berdie prepared to break the news of her standoff with Reverend Lewis.

"By the way," she began while removing the plates from the small table, "you are looking at a cowky."

"What are you on about?" Hugh asked in between gathering the used tableware.

"I came upon Reverend Lewis in the church back garden today, measuring something. And when I asked him to leave off and let you do your parish care, first he called me a cow, then the organ-grinder's monkey. You see, a cowky."

The generously patient Hugh clattered the forks and knives into the ample kitchen sink, making Berdie blink. "That is the last straw." Hugh turned the tap on to rinse the silverware. "He has name-called, bullied, and overstepped once too often. And never, under any circumstances, call your host vicar's wife names. Not ever." Hugh leaned against the sink and let out a long, slow breath.

"Hugh." Berdie moved to her husband and touched his

shoulder. "You've shown only generosity of spirit toward a visiting clergyman."

"And when that clergyman brings dishonor to the collar, things have to change." He crossed his arms. "You know I've never been able to pin him down to what parish he serves." Hugh shook his head. "Yes, I know what I need to do." The vicar moved swiftly to the kitchen door.

"Hugh?" Berdie knew her husband would do the wise thing.

"I'm calling Canon Fraser. This situation will soon be sorted."

Berdie stacked the old dishwasher with the dirty dishes and made a wee prayer for both her husband and the archaic machine. "Please work." She pushed the START button and had to admit the kitchen floor was shiny clean for wiping up after the leaking vessel. On it came, swishing like a lulling Christmas cradlesong.

"Thank You, Lord." Berdie smiled as she whipped her bright green holiday dishcloth over the oak-wood counters. She hummed "God Bless Ye Merry, Gentlemen" as she worked. About half done with giving the fridge door a go, a definite *clunk* sounded from the dishwasher, which was followed by complete silence.

"Really," Berdie moaned and went to collect her husband, who had just finished his call in the library.

Hugh spoke. "Canon Fraser is on it. He'll telephone back soon."

"I'm sure it will all work out well." Berdie exhaled. "However, Hugh, our dear old dishwasher is another story. It has finally run its course. I think we need to give it a decent burial and look for another."

"Oh." Hugh had an eyebrow arched. He arose and walked with

her back to the kitchen. The lovely swishing noise wafted through the warm room. Berdie stopped in her tracks. "It's washing."

"Of course, love, that's what washing machines do."

"No, I mean it had stopped, completely."

"Perhaps it was just between cycles," Hugh suggested and left the room.

Berdie crossed her arms and addressed the fickle electronic gadget. "You and I are going to go round."

Hugh popped his head through the doorway. "Oh, and I must let you know that. . ." Before the vicar could finish his sentence, a rather loud *clank* made itself known, as happened before, then a sad whimper that faded to silence.

"Aha," Berdie proclaimed, "there you see."

Almost as if the appliance heard every word and was set on spite, a thunderous splashing noise throttled the silence. The loud sound settled into its sloshing lullaby rhythm once more. Then *clunk*.

"You see? The thing's gone daft!" Berdie declared.

Hugh eyed the dishwasher as if a personal affront had been committed, and lifted his left brow. His jaw set and the muscles of his upper body tensed as if suiting up to joust.

"We'll sort this then. Where's my tool kit?"

—

Only minutes into it, bits and bobs of the dishwasher were already prostrate on the floor.

"Are you sure you know what you're doing?" Berdie swallowed. Hugh was masterful at many things, but fixing electrical appliances was not one of them.

"Can you hand me the small screwdriver?" Hugh asked.

Berdie looked through the maze of tools. "This one?" she asked and held it out.

A masculine hand reached forward from the back side of the machine and grabbed it.

"You said earlier you had something to tell me?" Berdie queried.

"Right. Andrew Busby called earlier. He found some information about our 'Miss Livingston.' "

"Oh yes?" Berdie heard a smothered grunt.

"Is there a smaller screwdriver, love?" Hugh rolled the unacceptable one toward Berdie as she fingered her way through the tools.

Hugh spoke on, "Miriam Livingston was actually Miri Avent. Well, Avent was her married name."

Berdie handed the smallest screwdriver she could locate to Hugh. "Do we know who her husband was?"

"Indeed." Another grunt. "Marquis Avent, member of the French Resistance, by all accounts quite the hero." The vicar let go a long exhale. "Got it," he said. "Can you take this, love?"

Berdie received the metal piece from Hugh and turned it over, ogling it. She thought to herself, *Oh my dear Hugh, whatever is this? Oh well, the old machine has served its purpose. It's finished off anyway.*

"How did Miri and this man meet?" Berdie spoke.

Hugh stuck his head out from around the ailing vessel. "It was a military report, Berdie, not a Barbara Carlton novel."

"Yes, well." Berdie laid the part on the floor.

"It is odd for Romas to marry outside their culture." The "repairman" started to wrestle with another part. "Please hand me the large screwdriver."

Berdie delivered the item. "What do you mean 'outside their culture'?"

"What? Didn't I say? Miss Livingston—Miri—was a registered Roma, a gypsy."

Berdie nodded. "Roma, yes, I thought as much. Yes, but what do you mean by 'registered'?"

"Interned. She was in a German concentration camp in France, registered as a Roma." Hugh stuck his hand out. "Give the part back, please."

Berdie laid it in his hand and Hugh continued. "You know there were hundreds of Romas interned during World War II. That's what happened to those who were seen as different in that regime."

Berdie stared at the floor. "It's all coming together," she said almost to herself.

"Yes, just a bit more with the screwdriver," Hugh called.

Her eyes gave a quick sparkle. "No, I mean Miss Livingston. Giving a child their head to run barefoot through the village, a peculiar Advent wreath, theatrical clothing, mystery men who come and go, phases of the moon, a peddler of lavender, a removed tattoo."

"What are you going on about?" Hugh paused. "Ah," he said with assurance. "Hand me the rest of the parts and the small screwdriver, dear."

Berdie moved in response but her mind was putting facts in

ragged order.

"You see," Hugh mumbled while working, "the dishwasher's timer has gone off. It's not really trying to start up so much as it's trying to finish the job."

"Yes, finish the job," Berdie said absently. "Now what became of her husband?" Berdie asked.

"Say again," Hugh charged.

"What became of Mr. Avent?"

"Things start to get a bit less clear there." Hugh gave a light murmur as he made twisting motions. "He was in the same camp for a short while, was eventually tried, and executed."

"How tragic."

"You know some of those in high rank, camp administrators and such, actually crossed the water in the end, went deep."

"What? You mean they took up here in England?" Berdie was sharp.

"Now dear, they're all gone now, either found out, moved on, or dead."

Hugh arose and wore the look of one who had faced the mountain and won. He wiped his hands back and forth together. "Jolly good."

"There's more to this report of course," Berdie prodded.

Hugh draped his arm around her shoulders. "Of course there is, love, there always is with military intelligence. But if I told you, using today's vernacular," he said, then placed a grease-smudged kiss on her cheek, "I'd have to neutralize you."

"Well tell your Sergeant Major Busby I'll supply the shovel if he'll keep digging." Berdie actually would barely supply the rough, indulgent man the time of day, but she wanted to get as much information as possible. She always treated Hugh's military right-hand man with courtesy, but just.

"Do you remember our agreement we made concerning your working on this case?" Hugh asked.

Berdie nodded. "Don't take any unnecessary chances."

"And?" Hugh tipped his head.

Berdie spoke in a small voice, "Keep Goodnight in the loop."

"Well, have you? Kept Goodnight informed, that is?" Hugh looked into her eyes.

Berdie sighed heavily. "Will do, first thing in the morning," she promised.

Hugh peeked at Berdie's other hand, checking that no fingers were crossed. "There's a dear. Now how's 'bout some tea?"

—

Berdie was up and about, getting her morning exercises of spiritual and physical well-being behind her before she walked to Goodnight's residence. She hoped to return promptly in light of today's church events.

Along the way, Berdie observed the gray sky that allotted just enough sun to peek out and make the frosted rooftops sparkle like holiday tinsel. Her cheeks felt the whip of quick winds that danced around the gardens. She smelled the damp December air and felt her feet couldn't move her quickly enough to Constable Goodnight's residence. When she arrived, she found the policeman bundled in a police-issue overcoat, rushed, and just about to enter his car.

"I've got a call," Goodnight grumbled through his sadly

neglected mustache. "Must push on."

"Yes," Berdie spoke sprightly, "and good morning to you as well. This will only take a moment." She sprung toward the car and stood in front of the driver's door.

"I believe I have some information you may have an interest in concerning the Livingston case," Berdie blurted out and talked straight on, "information that concerns Miss Livingston's true identity. I know it sounds dubious, but it is from a good source."

The policeman gripped his car key and stood straight.

"She's a French gypsy, you see, and a former prisoner of war. Now I believe it ties in with the murder."

Goodnight tried to smother a chuckle. "Oh yes, our Miss Livingston? And your source of information?"

Berdie hesitated. Revealing Hugh's source would create considerable trouble.

"Batty Natty then?" The policeman knitted his thick brows and jerked his head sideways to indicate his desire to see Berdie step aside. "Now please!"

Determined, Berdie pursed her lips and stepped away from the door. Goodnight wrenched it open.

"Give me twenty seconds, that's all, just twenty seconds." Berdie was firm.

"Ten seconds starting right now and not a second more."

"Think about it. The fire and murder are linked. Who started the fire and why? Whoever killed Miriam Livingston was looking for something and it wasn't money. When they couldn't find it they decided to burn the place down to destroy whatever it was. And of course, where was Jamie Donovan when the fire occurred?

Squarely in jail."

Goodnight got into the vehicle.

"The real killer may be tall and light-haired. And the Advent wreath is intrinsic to the situation." Berdie drew a breath. "How much time do I have left?"

"None!" The constable turned the key and started the car. His stomach just cleared the steering wheel. "Oh my, what's that I see rolling round over there?"

Berdie looked in the direction Goodnight pointed.

"Oh, it's one your of marbles," he taunted. "Ta, Mrs. Elliott."

The constable pulled his car away from the verge so quickly Berdie jumped.

"Well!" Berdie looked after the speeding car that held the keeper of the law in Aidan Kirkwood. "My dear constable," she called out after the retreating auto, "the loop has just snapped." She turned her back to the vehicle and began the frosty walk back to the vicarage.

CHAPTER TWELVE

Berdie didn't care about the now gray, dreary sky that signaled the probability of storms somewhere in the day, nor that Goodnight was unresponsive. She was too taken with admiration for the nosegays of holly and ivy tied with lovely gold ribbons that decorated the pew ends of the central aisle of the church. This central aisle of the nave had been built in the twelfth century, the side aisles added a bit later. And it was known throughout the area that the present church site was where a simple wooden structure had been established in the centuries earlier after a humble traveling monk, Aidan of Lindesfarne, brought the gospel to the people in the wooded hamlet. Berdie marveled at the thought that for over a thousand years the faithful had gathered in this place to hear God's Word, to be in community together and pray. Marriages, births, baptisms, and memorials were etched into the very atmosphere of the sacred space. And today, in just under an hour, another christening would take place at the ancient carved stone font, Hugh's first at Saint Aidan of the Wood Parish Church.

Yes, the altar guild had done a fine job adorning the pews. Now Berdie was set to move on to her next task. She entered the half-open sacristy door to ask her husband what tasks he still needed done in preparation. Hugh was just hanging up the church telephone.

"Flowers are done, and they're really quite. . ." Berdie hushed. Hugh's left eyebrow was not only arched, its next landing site was the moon. "Hugh, who is it?"

"Mistcome Greene police."

"What then?"

"There's been a murder in a traveler caravan site near the woods there."

Berdie knew a traveler site was just a modern way of saying a gypsy camp. "Hugh, this is no coincidence." Berdie spoke what she could see in her husband's face, and now the thought enwrapped her mind like a swathing cloth.

"No, it's not," he stated flatly.

"But why call you? Isn't that Winston Wainwright's parish?"

"Indeed," Hugh assured his wife, "but they found our church calling card on the body of the victim and they want to speak with me immediately."

"What's happening, Hugh?" Berdie quizzed.

"I have my suspicions." Hugh stopped his statement at that defining point. He shook his head. "But clearly, my duty is here."

"The christening." Berdie became conscious once again of the most important event that was to take place shortly. "It can't go on without you." She stepped closer to her husband.

"That's why I need you to go to Mistcome Greene for me, Berdie, and sort the situation."

As a former investigator, she reasoned she couldn't help the thrust of energy she felt shoot through her being.

Hugh put his hand on her shoulder. "The police are there, you'll be safe, but nonetheless take Lillie with you. Things are in hand here."

"I should think Lillie could spare me a few hours from the ardent preparation for her dinner date with the good doctor this evening. And I can be out the door in three minutes," Berdie promised as she felt her pulse quicken.

"Be careful, Berdie," Hugh said, his vivid blue eyes sending his message keenly, "and get your instincts into top gear."

"Just as you say."

———

The time flew nearly as fast as the little Citron down the narrow country lanes that led to Mistcome Greene. The car was not known to be fast, but with Berdie on a mission to ferret out truth, it became a Mazarati. And Lillie was along for the joyride.

They arrived at the edge of the Mistcome wood where the large green lea spread out like a velvet blanket. But the reverie of the rural scene was despoiled by police tape strewn across the area where several travel caravans were parked tightly together as if huddled against the cold. Police milled around searching the vegetated grounds with long poles, looking for evidence and clues.

Berdie and Lillie got out of the car, and a young constable approached them.

"There is a proper investigation being carried out here. I suggest you move along." The young woman's stern voice and appearance reiterated her words.

"We've been summoned to speak to the officer in charge of this investigation," Berdie asserted.

"Who are you then?"

"I'm Berdie Elliott. I've come in Hugh Elliott's stead as he's currently performing a christening. He's my husband—I'm the vicar's wife."

A crackled voice jumped into the conversation. "Now that's one I've not heard you use before, Berdie Elliott, creative I have to admit."

Berdie knew that oddly familiar voice. She blinked. "Chief Inspector Kent!"

Jasper Kent, the forty-something agent for Scotland Yard, already stood with a slight stoop forward, his eyes set in a permanent droop. He sported his ever-present tan overcoat that hung on his medium frame like an oversized Father Christmas robe. "When was the last time I saw you? The Chilton art heist, I believe?"

Berdie cleared her throat. "Good to see you, Chief Inspector."

"And what was it you told the investigating team that time? Ah yes, you were an art agent representing a duke or some such."

Berdie looked toward the female constable and back to the inspector. "That was a technical misunderstanding."

Lillie's eyes widened. "She really is a vicar's wife," she asserted.

"And who's this?" The man looked in Lillie's direction.

"My assistant," Berdie replied.

"Lillie Foxworth," said the "assistant" in a light, easy manner and stretched out her hand.

Bypassing the hand, a quick once-over was all he offered Lillie and turned his attention back to Berdie. "Now Elliott, tell me why you're really here." The inspector sniffed.

Lillie was indolent. "She's already told you."

Berdie gave her friend a slight nudge with her elbow.

"Okay, Chief Inspector Kent, there's been a murder in Aidan Kirkwood. I think it could be connected to this one here."

"Aidan Kirkwood?" The inspector grinned. "That's Albert Goodnight's patch."

The young female constable tried to smother a chuckle. "Sorry, sir," she said and put her hands behind her back, "but Albert Goodnight couldn't catch a cold in flu season."

"Ah, yes. . .well." Inspector Kent tried to erase his half smile. "We don't cast aspersions on a fellow officer of the law in the presence of the public, do we?"

"No sir, certainly not." The woman grinned and looked at the ground.

A man attired in constable gear approached Kent with a plastic bag that held a barely used cigarette. "We found this, sir."

"Ah, well done," the inspector acknowledged. "We'll collect DNA samples from this gaggle of goers, see what we come up with."

"Yes, sir." The constable tipped his head and moved along.

Kent looked at Berdie. "The murderer always makes a mistake, right, Mrs. Elliott?"

"Usually several," Berdie offered then went right into it. "Tell me now, Inspector. . .I should say the cause of death was one precisely landed fatal wound, the home of the deceased was on its head, nook and cranny, and"—Berdie took a deep whiff of air—

"judging by the smell of things the caravan was set ablaze. How am I doing so far?"

The man shifted his weight. He addressed the policewoman. "Constable, get on the horn and call our friend, Goodnight, and find out about the case over there."

The chief inspector nodded and moved toward a police vehicle.

Jasper Kent peered steadily at Berdie. "There's never been any doubt about your professionalism or your ability to sniff out trouble, but this case is strictly on a need-to-know basis."

"This has got to be sorted before anyone else gets hurt," Berdie asserted.

"Oh, is someone else going to get hurt?"

"Could be," Berdie said with a bit of hesitation.

"In respect to your concern, Mrs. Elliott, I'll pass the information I feel is pertinent on to Goodnight," the constable said.

Berdie frowned. "That's tantamount to saying you'll stir up the Christmas pudding but never put it in the oven."

"Take it or leave it."

Berdie knew if Kent was on the case there would be a concerted effort made to get to the truth, and she had to settle with that for now. She reluctantly nodded.

A group of travelers exited the caravan closest to the inspector and stood watching the law enforcement workers prod the ground. The Roma women's long skirts displayed colorful ribbons and the men wore dark hats. Motionless, they huddled together like their small caravans.

"Can I at least speak to the families?" Berdie asked.

"Would to God you could," the man clucked. "These are not

our usual crowd; this lot's from France. Can't understand nor speak a single word of English."

Berdie scanned the faces. Her eyes locked upon a gentleman who took a quick step backward. His eyes were just visible beneath his wide-brimmed hat.

I know those eyes, Berdie thought to herself. *Yes, indeed I do!*

"Can't speak a word of English, you say?" Berdie spoke to Kent but looked directly at the smoky-eyed gypsy male.

Lillie piped up, "Oh perhaps I can help, as I speak. . ."

Berdie gave another careful nudge to her assistant.

"Yes?" Inspector Kent crackled.

"She speaks English quite slowly and clearly," Berdie finished the sentence.

Lillie looked at Berdie then at the inspector. "Yes—I—do."

The inspector squinted at Lillie as if she were a roll short of a dozen. "Right." He then turned back to Berdie. "We're getting a translator in from the home office. But have a go if you want." The lawman looked at the silent Romas. "It's a waste of time and energy."

"Sir, you may want to come take a look at this," a young man in plainclothes called out.

Jasper Kent ran his tongue across his upper teeth, making a whisking sound. "Ladies." He tipped his head and moved across the lea.

Berdie and Lillie edged closer to the bohemian group.

"All right then," Berdie spoke to the man she recognized, "I didn't divulge your English capabilities and now you can return the favor by giving me the truth."

Lillie stood straight. *"Maintenant, je ne. . ."*

Berdie interrupted, "Needn't do Lillie, there's at least one who speaks English, and I should think others as well."

"Oh," Lillie said in surprise.

"This gentleman"—Berdie looked at Lillie and flashed her eyes in the direction of the hesitant Roma man—"is the fellow who called on Hugh at the church, and minutes thereafter Miss Livingston's funeral was canceled."

"Is he now?" Lillie eyed him carefully.

"And I daresay my husband gave him our church calling card, which he then passed on to the person against whom the crime has been committed."

The travelers turned to the fellow in their midst, a sense of foreboding written in their eyes.

"I need some answers," Berdie stated firmly but calmly. The group stood utterly silent.

"Here now." She stood her full height. "I don't want anyone else to get hurt and I trust you would agree. I may be able to help find whoever perpetrated this crime."

The dark man of interest opened the door of the caravan and jerked his head in its direction. All but he filed back into the tiny space as if they were hiding themselves far away from the world.

"You should not speak to us." He closed the door then uttered in shadowed tones, "And we should not speak to you."

His thick French accent required Berdie's full concentration.

"We are ze family of my father's father, Bavol Nav." The man looked at the ground. "We are now, for a time, ze impure."

"I see." Berdie was respectful. "In my faith we're taught to love all, impure or clean. I have no reason not to talk to you if you are willing to talk to me, for the good of everyone."

The man studied Berdie's face as though searching for the sincerity she offered. "What do you want from us?"

"Bavol Nav was the victim?"

Drawing his head back quickly, the Roma eyes narrowed. "We never speak of death—it brings evil."

Berdie thought for a moment. "I see, so let's speak of life," she offered. "Tell me about your grandfather's life."

"I'm sure your relative was dear to you, *tres cher*, no?" Lillie's voice was tender.

The man cast his eyes about to be sure no one watched. "My grandfather is an old man, but a man of courage. He and his horse, long ago, save many people. He is a man of strength, of promises to keep."

"He sent you to retrieve Miri, didn't he?" Berdie comprehended. "The obits, Miri subscribed him to our little paper."

"Promises to keep," the man repeated.

"She was a relative, *famille*?" Lillie asked what Berdie hoped to know.

"La cousine au mon grand-père."

"Miri was his grandfather's cousin," Lillie translated.

The wanderer's eyes became steeled. "We honor her, as is our custom, just as we honor my grandfather in ze soil of our country."

"France," Lillie confirmed.

Having sorted the identity issue, Berdie proceeded to question events around the murders themselves. "Who would want to kill

Miri and your grandfather?"

"No one." The man frowned.

"Have you noticed anyone unusual around the green or in the woods, anyone that appeared edgy or suspicious-looking?"

The gentleman's square chin tightened. "Unusual, suspicious? Zat's ze way I and my people are seen by your people."

He lifted his chin, his eyes coming to rest on Chief Inspector Kent, who trumpeted across the lea. "Mrs. Elliott!"

The Roma's face skewed, his nostrils enlarged as his lips pulled downward, watching the law enforcer cross the turf. He spat on the ground.

"Tell ze priest I give to him *la circle d'Avent*." He pulled open the trailer door and disappeared inside, slamming it behind him with such force the small caravan shook.

Along with the arrival of the Scotland Yard officer at her side, Berdie felt the gentle tap of rain droplets, announcing the need to soon seek cover.

"Goodnight says he has the murder case over there stitched up tighter than his trousers after Christmas lunch."

Berdie pursed her lips. "But he has the trousers on the wrong man!"

"Humph," the lawman muttered, but Berdie watched his eyes go off to the wood as if he looked at it but saw something else in his own mind. The orbs came squarely back to her. "Goodnight's a bulldog about his patch. I should think you need to watch yourself, but if for some reason—"

"I'll keep you informed," Berdie assured.

The lawman tipped his head in politeness. "Well then ladies, time you two move along. Have a safe journey."

By the time she and Lillie were at the car, the rain began to steadily descend upon the green, sending the two promptly on the road. But this time the Citron moved at a more cautious pace. Berdie turned the windshield wipers to a steady quick rhythm.

"It's all adding up, isn't it?" Lillie observed. "The picture that led us to Northumbria, that then led us to the Roma heritage, that now has brought us to the caravan camp. But why kill an old man? How does he play in?"

"The perpetrator needs something, Lillie, is searching for something they believed was in Miss Livingston's ownership, and then somehow connected it to this fellow."

"What would an aging Roma have that someone would want or need?"

Berdie was having more difficulty seeing clearly as the rain intensified. "What do aging people, in general, have that's valuable?"

Lillie thought for a moment. "Generally? Wisdom."

"And experience," Berdie added. "They both had knowledge of someone, something, and that information was stored, secreted, by use of a material object as is obvious from the search through both Bavol Nav's and Miss Livingston's personal goods. That's my take."

"How do you know Mr. Nav's goods were gone through?" Lillie asked.

"Did you see Inspector Kent's reaction when I said the victim's home was upended, along with the other characteristics I see as the M.O. of the murderer?"

Lillie's eyes brightened with understanding. "That's when he had the constable call Goodnight. So, what you're saying is that the murderer was aware of Miriam's background when no one else was, but how and why?"

"That's what we need to figure out, my dear. And I believe we're getting closer."

The rain now descended in sheets.

"Betty Oglesby told us of a stranger that rode into the Livingston farm on a buggy, spoke to Miss Livingston, and left as quickly as he came. I should say that was likely Bavol Nav, coming to warn her off. Yes, I daresay. Their lives touched there, and we know they must have been together earlier, being in the same family, and I should say the same camp."

"So do you think this Mr. Nav was involved in the French War Resistance?"

"The Roma hold family very, very dear so it's quite likely, simply by association if nothing else."

"So Miss Livingston's name was Miri Nav?"

"Oh, didn't I tell you? Her married name was Miri Avent."

Lillie's eyes sparked with a twinkle of her own. "*Avent* is how you say *advent* in French."

"Is it now?" Berdie's mind clicked with such ferocity she just managed to steer the car.

"The Advent wreath!" Lillie spoke, stunned with admiration for Berdie. "You suspected from the start that it held something important. Oh yes, the gypsy fellow, back there, he told me in French to give the Advent wreath to the priest."

"To Hugh?" Berdie became conscious of the fact her acceleration increased with her intrigue. "My dear wonderful husband is now inexplicitly tied into solving this case, Lillie." Berdie glanced in her rearview mirror to spot an approaching large dark car through the rivulets of water coursing down the back windscreen. "We're a hair's breath away from putting this case in the done file my dear Lil—"

Berdie felt the blood drain from her face.

"What?" Lillie questioned.

"Oh dear," Berdie almost screamed, "brace yourself, Lillie!"

At the same moment the words left Berdie's mouth, a thunderous *crash* assaulted the little Citron from behind, sending it into a headlong skid that all but sent it off the road.

Berdie gripped the steering wheel. She held fast with every ounce of strength she had to stay in the lane.

"What's happening?" Lillie screamed while trying to keep her body low.

"Pray and hold on tight," Berdie yelled. She barely caught sight of the luxury black sedan sweep up to the back corner on the driver's side of the Citron. The swift-moving car slammed into the side of the Citron, sending the little auto spiraling across the drenched road. With an abrupt twist, it flew across the lane, skidded off the pavement, jostled and jumped through a shallow ditch, soared over a half breach in the hedgerow, and came to rest in an open rain-soaked lea only inches from two very startled sheep.

Even though Berdie sensed her body adrenalin carrying out its God-given purpose in a matter such as this, her consciousness grew dim until the world went completely black.

Berdie tried to arouse herself when she thought she heard someone shouting. She had no idea how much time had passed since they had made their safe landing.

"Mrs. Elliott, are you all right?"

The voice was accompanied by a heavy knock to her window.

"Mrs. Elliott, can you hear me?"

Berdie willed her eyes open where the light of the gray stormy afternoon brought back the awareness of what had occurred. She felt one stubborn ear wire of her glasses clinging on for dear life and managed the glasses back in their proper spot. She turned her head toward the rain-covered window to see a bright yellow McIntosh, the hood of it encircling a man's face.

"She's conscious," he said and turned away. "Get the first-aid kit, Gustava. She has a passenger."

Berdie tried to make out the details of the man's face. She opened the window, breathed in, and met with splashes of heavenly outpouring. "Dr. Meredith?"

Loren Meredith gently put his hand on her head and leaned closely. "You've got a small cut on your forehead, Berdie, but it's going to be fine I should think. Are you hurt otherwise?"

"Lillie!" Berdie was remembering what had happened now. The doctor left the window and moved to the other side of the car.

"Berdie?" Lillie was almost inaudible.

Berdie could see the tiny slits that were Lillie's eyes trying to open.

"Are we in heaven?" Lillie mumbled. "Oh," she said with twilight-sleep delight, glimpsing the view out her window, "I always said heaven would look like the English countryside."

"Look closer my dear. I should say heaven doesn't look like the interior of a purple Citron." Even though it hurt a bit, Berdie couldn't help but chuckle.

Lillie's eyes were now open but heavy-lidded. "Where are we then?"

Suddenly, the passenger-side car door flew open and Berdie saw Lillie's eyelids now flutter against the frosty wetness.

"Lillie, love, are you okay?"

"Loren?" Lillie looked into the face of her rain-soaked rescuer, professional yet obviously alarmed with concern. "Loren!"

The doctor took her hand. "I'm here and I'm not going anywhere. Tell me what hurts, Lillie."

"Well. . ." She tried moving. "Everything."

"I daresay you've sustained manifold bumps and bruises, despite fastened seat belts. Gustava has gone back to the lorry to get the first-aid kit. Do stay calm." His voice roared against the torrential rain. "It's going to take some work to get your door open, Berdie, but help should be arriving shortly." He put his arm across the back of the car seat in which Lillie sat. "The Lord was surely looking after you two."

Berdie asked the inevitable question. "How is it you're here, Doctor?"

"Actually, we saw the whole thing happen, from a distance mind you."

"We?" Berdie asked.

"Gustava Andres, my assistant, and I were on our way to a stand-in call for an investigation in Mistcome Greene."

Berdie felt a twitch of pain in her right thigh. "Did you see the car, the plate? Did you see a face?"

"I'm afraid not. Between the curtains of rain and trying to keep our vehicle aright to avoid our own misfortune, the only thing I can tell you is that it was a black sedan."

Dr. Meredith pulled back and looked across the lea to the road. Berdie recognized the *ee-ou* of approaching emergency vehicles.

"Excellent," the doctor pronounced, "quick response time." Loren Meredith bent close to Lillie. "My darling, if you didn't want to keep our dinner date this evening, you could have done something less drastic you know."

Lillie laid her head back and smiled. "Now who's worming out? Hospital cafeteria, Doctor, eight o'clock sharp."

Dr. Meredith squeezed her hand. "Right. We're getting you two Stig drivers to emergency care."

CHAPTER ✂✂ THIRTEEN

Berdie repositioned the sturdy bed table, waiting for Hugh's promised surprise. Poor Hugh, he really was doing his best to take care of her, but she almost wished he wouldn't try so hard. He felt guilty and she knew it. She tried to assuage his sense of having put her right in it, but it was to no avail. At least it was Sunday morning and he would depart soon for the church where he could devote his energies to the flock and she could have a moment to herself. It was imperative she call Edsel Butz to come repair the still-defiant dishwasher, but on the QT. She didn't fancy adding letdown to Hugh's already active feelings of remorse.

Berdie heard her husband's footsteps on the stairway. He arrived in the bedroom with a fresh tray of tea and scones, the morning paper folded neatly on the side. She smiled to see Reverend Hugh Elliott, who would be feeding spiritual food to his parishioners in a matter of moments, wearing her holiday pinny with little Christmas robins frolicking about on it. He poured her a cup of tea from the holiday teapot that displayed a like bird upon it.

"Careful, quite hot," Hugh cautioned. "Now here's your favorite. Devonshire cream and strawberry jam for your fresh-from-the-oven scones." He presented the feast before her on the bed table.

Berdie observed the little breads that looked rather more like scorched Frisbees. "Thank you," was her only comment.

"Well, tuck in then." Hugh shifted his weight.

After twenty-some-odd years of marriage, Berdie sensed her husband had something on his mind. She took his hand. "Hugh?"

Hugh released a long exhale, sat on the bed's edge, and looked keenly into her face. Sure enough, there went his rascally eyebrow.

"I thought perhaps we'd talk later but I see the opportunity is at hand." He paused. "I'll come right to it then. First, no caroling for you tonight," he stated flatly, "and second, I don't want you to work on this case anymore. It's just far too dangerous."

"What's far too dangerous, Hugh Elliott, is that some mad person is in our midst wreaking havoc. They think they can bully us into leaving off, and I won't have it."

"And must you be the one who stops this madman?" Hugh almost scolded.

Berdie squeezed her husband's hand. "No, I don't have to be the one who stops it. I'm just saying that I, by God's grace, may be well equipped, if you please, to get at the bottom of the matter and bring it to a vigorous halt."

Hugh looked stern. "When Loren told me what he witnessed of the accident, a shiver ran over my spine. Someone purposely forced you off the road." He clenched his jaw.

Even in the pinny, none of Hugh's masculine strength and fortitude was in any way diminished. "We can talk about this later," Berdie offered.

"No we shan't. It's not on, Berdie, and the door to discussion is closed." Hugh stood up military straight. "Now, Mr. Braunhoff has agreed to stand watch in the sitting room while I'm at church."

Berdie gaped. "What?"

"You need to rest, Berdie, and he'll intercept visitors." Hugh lifted his chin. "Now, come, enjoy your scones."

The devout husband kissed her on the forehead, staunchly turned, and left the room. Berdie stared after him. "My dear, wonderful, overprotective husband, a babysitter and all." Berdie folded her arms. "Mr. Braunhoff indeed! And that door to discussion, my love, is soon to come unhinged!"

—

Berdie awoke with the Monday morning light. It was near cloudless and full of the December sun.

Hugh slumbered on next to Berdie and she seized the opportunity to arise and make her way into the kitchen. It did take concerted effort to navigate the stairs what with the large bruise on her thigh and stiff aches all round, but she was sure if she had another day of being bedfast she would go balmy. The bed rest, however, had afforded her the time to think through the possibilities of entrapping Miss Livingston's murderer in a snare so clever he would never see it coming. She also made contact with Edsel, who promised to come tame the mad dish machine this week on an off moment.

But presently she had an overwhelming need for a cup of breakfast tea. Scarcely did she put the kettle on when the phone rang. Berdie tried to move swiftly so the ring wouldn't awake

Hugh. Monday was his day off, if clergymen ever really have a day off, and she didn't want him disturbed.

It was one of the Darbyshire twins, Rosalie, expressing their regret that she and her sister, Roberta, would not be able to clean or do extra computer work at the sacristy today due to business elsewhere. On two Mondays a month the twins performed their services that were deeply appreciated. But Berdie saw their absence today as a Godsend.

"I shouldn't think it's a problem, Miss Darbyshire," Berdie assured.

"Right then. Well, have a speedy recovery," the twin offered and hung up.

Speedy indeed, Berdie thought to herself after the conversation ended. She ascended the stairs to don her old work trousers and a dust pinny.

Dressed, morning prayers finished, and muesli with tea to the fill, Berdie made her way to the church with her husband's approval, especially when Lillie agreed to come help. The like injured friend felt the need as well to escape her flat. Dear Dr. Meredith had hired an off-duty policeman from Timsley to watch over his beloved. He'd have kept watch himself except for the appearance of impropriety and his incredulous work schedule.

Although a large plainclothes policeman sat rather uncomfortably on a pew in the nave, Berdie and Lillie entered the sacristy as if going on holiday.

"Isn't Mr. Finn rather foreboding?" Lillie half chuckled.

Berdie peeked her head out the room's door to inspect the human protector. "Indeed!" She pulled the door half shut and reached for a feather duster while placing a bottle of wood soap in Lillie's hand. "I also think it's frightfully silly."

Lillie embraced the cleaner container and looked a bit dreamy-eyed. "Well I think it's quite romantic. Rather gallant of Dr. Meredith, really."

"See here, Gwenevere, give a hand to the tidying up," Berdie prodded.

The sacristy was not large, thus enhancing coziness. The cream color of the walls possessed a soothing sense of calm, much like the vicar who spent many hours within them. Several framed paintings retold ancient stories of faith, and an oak-wood surround framed the fireplace hearth that beckoned one to stand close, giving chase the chill of winter. The two overstuffed chairs, along with a properly placed console table, an elegant floor lamp, and ample bookshelves, complemented the aged oak vicar's desk. Atop the structure were stacked folders, an inherited pen rest, a cut-glass dish of simple paper clips, the church telephone, and framed pictures of the Elliott children. All was neat as a pin such as befits a man of military bearing.

Berdie clucked. "Who would have thought we'd relish cleaning the sacristy as though having lunch in the garden?" She fluffed the duster across the tops and spines of several books.

"I must admit that my flat, lovely as it is, seems to have dwarfed in size." Lillie dabbed some polish on the wooden shelves of the bookcase followed by long sweeps with a soft cloth. "I wish the murderer would be found out and locked up at the earliest possible moment."

"Agreed," Berdie piped.

"So." Lillie wore an impish grin. "I'm counting on you to get it sorted, confined to quarters or not."

"Well dear," Berdie said and moved her duster along, "we've ruled out Mr. Raheem. Although. . ." She stopped in thought and gave the cleaning tool a couple gentle taps on her hand. "I still need the answer to a very important question from our greengrocer. Yes, I must call him this afternoon."

"And what is that simple question?" Lillie asked.

"When he left Miss Livingston at her home, did he notice anything odd?"

"Ah-ha." Lillie nodded. She moved along to the console table.

"And," Lillie said with another impish tone, "why should I be convinced of Jamie's innocence?"

Berdie ran her finger round the lamp shade's top rim. The cleaner brushed the shade vigorously, sending a dust plume into the air.

"Several things point to his innocence. First, Miss Livingston's murder was very methodic, well planned and well executed: electricity off, laying hold of the key, one quick and accurate blow, a detailed search with no stone unturned and, to boot, a perfect frame." Berdie felt her nose tickle. "Now Jamie, motivated into action because of a dispute with Miriam about his cherished Cara, that would be the reaction of a young man from the streets, an act of passion, a momentary rage that would result in a pummeling with repeated aggression and with no interest in tearing the place apart after." Berdie swatted at the dust in the air.

Lillie fanned the air as well. "Sounds about right."

"And," Berdie continued, "all that evidence pointing to Jamie was too perfect. Is it likely a killer would leave the murder weapon at the scene and not try to dispose of it?" Berdie moved to the mantel and gave it a quick whisk. "Would they drive a vehicle to the scene that identifies who they are simply by shear racket of the thing? Would they commit an atrocity at the very place where they are presently carrying on their work?" She whisked the mantelpiece adeptly. "And would a slayer of life run to his childhood home to be with his father?"

Lillie fluffed a needlework pillow that sat on the welcoming chair. "Then whoever did do the deed must be ever so clever."

"I should say!" Berdie paused. "Jamie was living his dream, though presently incognito. A good job, the love of his life, a family on the way; he wouldn't intentionally destroy all that."

Lillie generously doused the mantel with wood soap, swirling it into cleaning action. "He said as much when we visited him."

"I daresay," Berdie began, then lowered her voice. "I daresay whoever did in Miss Livingston was at the first Advent party right in my home, mind you."

Lillie all but screamed, "I've often wondered that!"

"Shh," Berdie cautioned, "for the sake of the parish keep your voice down."

A red wad of hair followed by a chiseled stern face popped round the sacristy door. "Everything all right here?"

"Oh." Lillie went pink. "Yes, of course, my friend just gave me a surprise." She looked keenly at Berdie and back to the security guardsman. "With some parish news," she said then paused. "Yes, well, more like parish gossip I should say."

Berdie frowned.

"Well, not really parish gossip as such," Lillie finished.

The guardsman nodded. "I'm just here," he said and jerked his head toward the pews, "if you need me." He left the doorway.

Lillie started to name off the guests of that fateful evening, "Preston Graystone."

Berdie shared her skillful thoughts. "He certainly had a motive. His loathing of Miss Livingston for ruining, as he put it, his daughter's life was substantial. Though in the current picture of things, he had no apparent means."

Lillie sat at the edge of the overstuffed chair. "Cara?"

Berdie dusted a painting of a repentant prodigal in the embrace of his father. "Dear, fretful Cara. She had both means and motive, but I believe she truly loved Miss Livingston." With her finger Berdie softly brushed away a dust ball on the top of the prodigal's head. "When you have a new life growing inside you, it's unimaginable that you'd destroy the life of another. No, Cara Graystone Donovan was too busy getting sick to have time to kill someone."

Lillie tipped her head. "We have discussed Mr. Raheem as an unlikely suspect already. Surely not Batty Natty."

"No, she's a nutter but certainly not violent."

Berdie stepped to the desk. "Now, I think she perhaps saw something in Miriam's back garden."

Lillie ran her cloth over the chair's wooden foot. "What about Ivy Butz?"

"No, not Ivy. The woman has displayed higher than usual emotional volatility recently, no doubt. If she were to off someone it would have been her husband."

"True," Lillie agreed.

"Something's afoot with Ivy, but it's not crime."

"Lucy Butz?"

Berdie knitted her brow. "Oh yes, have you not heard? Little Lucy's taken up with a clandestine knife-wielding militia."

Lillie laughed. "Well, she was there, Berdie."

"True enough, and you're absolutely right. A standard in investigative procedure is to leave no stone unturned." She picked up the framed pictures of Nick, smart in his naval uniform, and Clare radiating the smile that wrapped her father keenly around her smallest finger. Berdie held them to her chest. "Yes, I daresay all the Butz children will stand well as long as they have both their parents' support."

"Berdie Elliott, you're thinking what I'm thinking that I've dared not let myself speak out," Lillie confirmed. "Edsel Butz!"

Berdie put the pictures down and sat in the desk chair squarely at attention behind the desk. "Ah yes, Edsel Butz."

"You heard Jamie. Edsel had access to the key."

"That's what is striking. He had access to the key and the truck, he set up the electrical job but didn't attend to it himself, certainly he had the means at his fingertips. And his timely arrival before the cottage fire could spell suspect. But a simple though very public fuss with Miss Livingston isn't a real motive." She paused again. "Unless, of course, there's indeed a stone yet to be upturned. It would be hard on Hugh if so."

Lillie sat back in the chair. "I'm discovering as I accompany you on this elephant hunt that human nature has an array of surprises."

"Saint Paul quoted it, 'There is none righteous, no, not one,'" Berdie said. "Oh!" She widened her eyes as she sat forward. "Speaking of surprises—well, hardly a surprise in a way, really—I haven't said. My dear husband and his cohort in arms, Andrew Busby, have unearthed some vital information about Gerald Lewis."

"The vicar?" Lillie puzzled.

"That's just it, Lillie. He's not a vicar. Gerald Lewis is not even remotely related to the church."

Lillie, who just stated she had discovered how surprising human nature could be, was once again without words.

"Ah, but there's more." The back of Berdie's neck felt crimson red. "He's the CEO of a company that's connected with a worldwide tech industry. And, to put the cherry atop the pudding, when Hugh called the company, he spoke to Lewis's personal assistant. She said her boss was several weeks out of the office, scouting locations for a new branch."

Lillie spit the words, "Of all the gall!"

Berdie shook an affirmative nod. "Remember when we were in Northumbria and about to introduce ourselves to Betty Oglesby?"

Lillie gave the nod this time. "But all I remember is the mud."

"I should think," Berdie said with a grin. "Well, Hugh suggested he put on his collar with the idea that we would appear less threatening to our host, who had no idea who we were. That's when the thought took root in my mind that perhaps Gerald Lewis wasn't who he gave himself to be."

"Of course." Lillie tapped her finger on the chair arm. "Who's going to get royal treatment in a happy rural community, a vicar or a land grabber?"

"Precisely! He's not been about for several days, but if he reappears, my kind but deeply insulted husband has not a few words to share with that snake in the grass."

"I should say," Lillie concurred. "And the police?"

"That's the thing Lillie, Goodnight can give a shout out to the surrounding towns and villages as a courtesy. But even though Lewis behaved abominably and immorally exploited our entire community, he's done nothing illegal." Berdie lifted her brow. "That we know of."

"Well good riddance to that one."

Berdie worked her duster across the desk, and Lillie joined in, following after with splashes of wood soap and generous rubbing.

"The Reeses were at the Advent party—well, only Mathew really."

"Now there." Berdie shook the duster in Lillie's direction. "Yes, there is a true wild card. Mathew, who seems to have simply hung about the edges, is actually intricately involved in the whole affair."

"He has kept a low profile," Lillie recognized.

"The elaborate ruse of still carrying on as if engaged to Cara, how does he really profit from it? There appears to be no payoff for him."

"Unless. . ." Lillie bit her lip.

"Unless he killed Miriam, framed Jamie, and thought he could woo Cara back to his awaiting arms," Berdie finished.

"Or else he didn't do any of those wretched things and simply cares deeply for Cara's welfare." Lillie sighed. "Oh my! What a tangled web we unweave!"

"Look Lillie, journalistic investigation at its simplest." Berdie grabbed several paper clips from the caddy. She held one up. "This is the what. What happened? Miss Livingston, aka Miri Avent, was murdered." She held up another paper clip. "This is the when." She attached it to the first paper clip. "The night, or rather morning after, the party."

Lillie picked up a third. "This is the how?"

"Indeed! Add it on. Now the bulk of this information was established early on." Berdie snapped up another of the shaped wires while Lillie watched. "This is the why. This little fellow has taken much time and effort to establish. Discovering her true identity, which is germane to the whole *why* issue, leads us to recognize that the victim had some possession, some knowledge, something that probably relates to the past and was worth killing for. Though we've a bit more to go as to the exact nature of the why, we'll add him on."

Berdie held the fifth paper clip that completed the chain like a precious diamond.

"Ah." Lillie smiled. "The who."

Berdie laid the small wire implement down on the desk. "The interminable who. Lillie my dear, there is a stone, or stones, that have yet to show their underside. But when we discover them," Berdie said, holding high the insignificant wire that represented so much, "Bob's your uncle!"

When the teacher of the investigative process returned the

paper clips to their home, something caught her eye. She pulled her tortoiseshell glasses down her nose and looked more closely at the cut-glass dish. "What is that doing there?" Berdie plucked the object out of the container.

"What?" Lillie asked without a glance.

Berdie held something that looked similar to a smart silver cigarette lighter. "Hugh's flash drive." She turned the object over in her hand. "He always keeps it in the safe vault. It holds valuable information. How uncharacteristic of him to forget putting it away." Berdie stood and stepped to a leather ottoman sitting peculiarly against a wall. With one ample shove, she scooted the ottoman aside.

"We should get a new safe vault," Lillie offered. "Yes, a new one that doesn't require knee pads."

Berdie knelt down with some trepidation. "Ouch." She lifted the cut square of wood that hid the subterranean floor vault and spun the numbers that made up the combination to open the lock.

"Having floor vaults went out with medieval times," Lillie spouted.

"New vault. Good idea, Lillie. Bring it up to the parish council." Berdie opened the vault door and placed the flash drive in its safe haven. "Now what's this?"

"What's what?" Lillie came a bit closer.

"This," Berdie said. Still on her knees, she turned to show her friend a green metal box that just fit across her hands.

"How odd." Lillie leaned forward to inspect the lock of the solid box. "An alignment lock," she observed. "Best to put it back,

Berdie. It must be something important."

The little box seemed to magnetize itself to her hands. Her pulse raced. "I've seen this box before, the day of the canceled funeral. It was in the hands of Bavol Nav's grandson." Berdie stared at the small piece like a child's first gift of Christmas. "Lillie, I believe we have just upturned a very telling stone."

Several sturdy raps boomed upon the half-open sacristy door.

Both women caught their breath. In a frenzy Berdie dived to get the prize back into the safe vault while Lillie moved in front of her friend, shielding her from view.

The ever-faithful guardsman showed his face. "Just checking all's well. Near done?"

Berdie could hear her friend release a deep breath. Lillie spoke, "Oh, Mr. Finn, you are a fine bodyguard. Jolly on the spot." Lillie feigned laughter. "Fine, yes fine, all's well. Nearly done really."

"You sure?"

Berdie, still on her knees, closed the wooden slat. She could sense the man's eyes upon her, despite Lillie's attempts to shelter and distract. She was also keenly aware that what was on display was *not* her most attractive side.

"She's just spotted a rascally touch of grime." Lillie gave a quick touch to Berdie's back.

"Right," Berdie yelled. She tried to stand but her legs were not cooperating. Berdie decided instead to simply turn round and sit her backside on the floor. When round, she stretched her legs straight as a soldier across the floor in front of her. "The husband's quite prickly about spots of grime."

The young man half smiled. "Be sure you don't do yourself

a mischief down there."

Berdie nodded. "Thank you, Mr. Finn."

When the gentleman was out of hearing range Lillie let her laughter roll.

Berdie, on the other hand, covered her face with her hands. "Not one of my finer moments in the life of the church."

Lillie took her friend's hand and assisted the embarrassed and sore Berdie to her feet.

"Come now, dear thing, let's push on. Finish tidying up, shipshape."

"Shipshape indeed." Berdie worked to regain her composure and wished her thigh to stop aching.

Lillie put the polish cloth in Berdie's hand and took the feather duster in her own. She fluffed over the church telephone. "Oh my," she said despairingly. "There are twenty-seven messages on the answer machine."

"My husband is notorious for keeping his messages for eons of time. He simply forgets to delete." Berdie went to the machine and pressed a button.

"Reverend Elliott, it's Mrs. Plinkerton, and I can't find my little Nesbit. He's not used to being out of the house since being declawed. Could you pray for him? Thanks ever so."

"That was weeks ago," Lillie said. "Nesbit was found at the fish market on the High Street."

"Delete." Berdie poked the button.

Next came the voice of Dudley Horn, the manager of the Upland Arms. "Vicar, thanks for being prompt in responding to my late call tonight. Your help's appreciated."

Berdie observed the time and day stamp. "Two thirty in the morning. That was the night of the party. Dudley called near two in the morning and asked Hugh to come rescue some parishioners from his pub, the night of the darts tournament. Hugh said he popped his head in but saw no parishioners."

Lillie spoke, "Delete?"

"No, keep it. I need to talk to my husband." Berdie went on to the next message.

"Reverend Elliott, sorry I'll be late for our meeting. It's car trouble. It shouldn't be more than twenty minutes until the work's done. I'll be there shortly."

"Delete," Lillie said and started to plunge her finger on the button.

"No, Lillie." Berdie grabbed Lillie's hand. "Look at the time stamp. This was recorded near the time of the murder. Listen, listen."

Berdie hit the replay indicator. The message started again and Berdie asked, "You recognize that voice?" She looked at Lillie.

"Of course, it's—"

"Shh." Berdie was avid. "Listen!"

The message went on. ". . .shouldn't be, *bong*, more than, *bong*, twenty minutes, *bong*."

Berdie hit the STOP button.

"Lavender Cottage," Lillie breathed.

"God bless that blasted clock."

"We've got them. Oh no. Oh no. . ." Lillie swallowed hard.

"Steady on, Lillie. This isn't enough to bring a courtroom conviction. We've overturned a 'who' stone. Now I've got just the plan to nail them."

Berdie took stunned Lillie's hand. "Come now, let's collect Mr. Finn and go cross to the vicarage. I need to speak to my husband immediately. We all need a stout cup of tea."

CHAPTER FOURTEEN

"B ut Hugh, my trap is next to ironclad."

Hugh's voice was firm. "Berdie, *ironclad* almost always sinks at some juncture or another."

"Come, Hugh, it is a clever ruse," Lillie added.

"What do you think, Loren?" Hugh looked to the doctor for support.

"It would nail the coffin shut, but it does involve some risk."

"Very little," Berdie asserted.

The foursome sat comfortably in the vicarage library, Mr. Finn being momentarily dismissed for an early lunch at the doctor's arrival. The couples had just retired to the room following a tea Berdie prepared. She hoped that bacon and Brie toasties garnished with beetroot marmalade and served with Brown Windsor soup might make her gentleman a bit more willing to discuss even delicate topics. At the least, it was "unhinging the door" to discussion with help from a warming fire and the scent of crisped cinnamon almonds.

Berdie passed the holiday nut bowl round accompanied by Christmas napkins.

"I rather think Jasper Kent would take exception to your

thought that it would be risky. I mean, with he and his boys littered about." Berdie popped a hot almond in her mouth.

"Undercover," Hugh reminded, "and that's only if the Yard decides to go along with this charade."

Dr. Meredith spoke up. "In all fairness, Hugh, I believe they would think Berdie's plan quite admirable."

"Even with the one-in-ten chance that the perpetrator should smell a rat, the Yard is jolly on the spot." Lillie demonstrated her newly acquired investigative jargon while making a good point.

"And Goodnight, would he be informed?" Hugh asked.

"If he's available." Lillie smiled.

Dr. Meredith chuckled. "Have you not heard, Hugh? He drew the short straw. He's playing Father Christmas at the Policeman's Charity Youth Party."

"Those dear children will be traumatized," Berdie commented and popped another sweet nut in her mouth.

The somber vicar didn't join the jovial spirit.

"I daresay Kent would see to Goodnight being made aware," the doctor assured.

The three knew Hugh was really as keen as anyone to see the assailant behind bars. But they were also aware that he was certainly resistant to Berdie's plan.

Hugh took a new tack. "Christmas is next week and all. Do we really need to do this now?"

Every eye in the room, even his own if he were honest, answered, "Absolutely."

"What a gift for our community," Lillie put in.

"Closure, yes. . .put the whole affair behind us and move on to wholly celebrating this sacred season." Loren took his beloved's hand and the couple smiled. "I agree with Lillie."

"Closure for our parish," Berdie approved, "and a fresh start for our innocent Jamie and dispirited Cara."

"I hate standing by while that pair suffer so. And our entire parish could do with a bright holiday." Hugh made his first positive comment on the whole issue.

He stood up and went to the mantel. He ran his hand across the wood. It halted at the figurine of a sweet Christmas angel, all white and dusted with soft glow sparkles. It held a banner that read GLORY TO GOD IN THE HIGHEST, PEACE AND GOODWILL TO MEN.

"There are conditions." Hugh pursed his lips.

Berdie observed a slight lift of both eyebrows. "Yes?" She braced herself.

"I make the telephone call. I'm the primary contender, not my wife."

Berdie stiffened a bit.

Hugh continued, "If it goes pear-shaped, I've got excellent defensive skills."

"That's just it, isn't it?" Berdie needed to watch her volume control. "I would use my knowledge of the case to entrap. You'd have them prone on the floor without a confession. No, if you call they'll see through."

The doctor agreed with Hugh. "I don't see the plan any less salable with Hugh as the key element, and I must say I'd do the same if it were Lillie."

The dark-haired chorister took in Dr. Meredith. "I think it's a very gallant gesture."

Berdie flashed a quick scowl at her friend.

"It is best," Loren reiterated.

Her loving husband, Hugh, moved toward her. He put his hand on her shoulder. "Berdie, you are the love of my life and the mother of our children. I won't allow harmful chances."

"Well, since you put it that way. . ." She sighed. "And if we catch the ogre. . ."

The plan was immediately put upon. Berdie was in her element. Law officials were contacted and everyone briefed on their responsibilities. Everything was in order.

Then Hugh made the call that set everything in motion. Berdie was pleased with the way her husband handled the conversation, and it ended cordially.

"The offender has risen to the bait," he reported. "Zero hour is three in the afternoon on Wednesday. May the Lord keep a careful eye and grant us full resolution."

—

After serving her husband a thank-you treat—a grand English roast and all the trimmings—Berdie washed the lunch dishes with a dash of extra vigor. Tomorrow was D-day, and she was more than ready. Although Hugh would be the one smack in the middle of things, she was pleased. She had also invited the women's prayer group to "pray for victory in a delicate matter," which they delighted in doing. All was going according to Hoyle. Well, all but the disgraceful dishwasher. Berdie tried it earlier for the breakfast dishes and the silly thing just sounded some protest grunts and went completely silent. But in the great scheme of things, it was simply an irritant. She had much larger fish to fry.

The warmth of the kitchen stood well against the icy downpour outside. She hoped her husband had remembered to take the umbrella for his call out to Carlisle's farm. The temporary hire car seemed a bit temperamental. She also wondered how Lillie and Loren were doing on a Christmas shopping lunch hour in Timsley. *What a day to be out about*, she thought to herself, *but then when you're in the flush of new love, does weather matter?*

Berdie washed the last of the food utensils and laid them on the drainboard. She fancied a hot cuppa, so she put the kettle on. It would go quite well with the murder mystery novel that was half done.

"I think I'll have a read," she said out loud.

"Oh yes?" a voice responded.

Berdie nearly left her skin. She caught her breath and put her hand to her heart, where she could feel the rapid fire of it. She recognized that dreadful voice. The sound of it now gave rise to an arctic chill. *Dear Lord, my dear Lord*, she prayed silently. Slowly and deliberately she turned to look in the direction from which the voice arose. *Calm down*, she told herself, *and be very careful.*

"My now! A man of the cloth should always knock, Reverend Lewis." She breathed, realizing her unsteady voice betrayed her alarm. She tried to amend her display with a pallid smile.

The man stood silent, observing each succinct detail of Berdie's performance.

"You're just in time for tea," she offered.

"I'm not here for tea, Mrs. Elliott, and you know it. Arrived a bit earlier than you planned?"

Berdie swallowed. "Hugh should be home any moment."

"Oh I think your husband is in a spot of bother, Berdie, fixing a rascally tire on the road to Carlisle's farm." The man sniffed. "You know, even over the telephone, you can smell the edge of falsehood when a vicar tries to stitch you up."

Her eyes searched across the sink to the drainboard. A hint of light caught where the carving knife lay wet, as if bathed in its own perspiration.

Observing her wandering eye, the uninvited guest sneered, an edgy laugh slipping through his lips. "Now, now, remember, you're a vicar's wife. You don't want to do anything rash."

"And you know all about rash!" Berdie tried to keep her voice even.

He stepped toward her and she immediately backed up.

"All you had to do," he said, thrusting a finger toward her face as his voice elevated, "was keep that interfering nose out."

Berdie nearly stumbled taking backward steps. She ogled the man. *Where is his weapon?* Right now his only crime was intimidation.

The man's nostrils flared. "I had the perfect plan, you know."

Berdie could hear Hugh's words in her mind: *"Ironclad almost always sinks at some juncture."*

Dear God, she prayed silently, *my plan is in the drink. Don't let me go with it.* "There is no perfect plan," Berdie spoke firmly.

The man's eyes narrowed. "You question my competence. . . my genius?"

First step in hostage negotiations, Berdie remembered from reporting on a case: Keep the perpetrator talking.

"Your first mistake was using the new moon." Berdie thought back to the missing Advent candle found in Livingston's bedroom.

"New moon?" The violator laughed in low tones. "I'm not guided by celestial bodies."

He doesn't know about the moon symbols! He doesn't know about the numbers in the wreath! He doesn't even have the metal box. I hold all the cards!

Berdie glanced toward the back door, and as quickly as she did, the intruder came squarely between her and the possible escape route.

"You should have listened to Miss Livingston's instruction," Berdie offered.

The man's face went red. "Listen to that gypsy?"

"Yes, Gerhard." Berdie saw the surprise in his eyes. Good, caught off guard.

He spouted, "Uniquely clever of me, telling Mr. Raheem I wanted to walk the ladies home to get our party conversation issues resolved. Raheem's sort is always an easy mark."

"Because you abused the collar." Berdie's voice was loud. *Calm,* she reminded herself. "When Miriam told you to use a candle from her side table in the entry hall, you didn't take heed. Instead you took a candle from the Advent wreath, already anxious to espy the territory for what you were seeking. Impatience, Gerhard. Your first careless mistake in the murder of Miss Livingston."

"Mistake? She's gone, isn't she?" He scowled.

"You see, there were wax drips in the bedroom. Because they were cool, they made body pressure points. That meant the candle found at her bedside was used earlier in the evening. First your farce, later your murder. You were careless, very careless."

He snarled, edging closer.

Berdie stood firm. *Stay calm, old girl.*

The intruder sneered. "You haven't noted the brilliance of my plan to take that nutter woman home last. I kept that Batty Natty with me as a witness, albeit questionable, then I assisted the old things; protected them in the dark, lit candles, soothed nerves, all but tucked them in."

"I daresay. But to give sleeping tablets to an elderly Roma woman who abhorred modern medicine, another mistake."

The man's face contorted. "You ignorant fräulein. I snipped those outside electrical wires so cleanly, just the smallest of clips, no one knew they were altered. I set a cottage ablaze and was above suspicion. And that sniveling Donovon, a smile and a moment's attention, the lad spilled his insides. The fool nearly framed himself!"

Keep talking, you arrogant con, Berdie thought.

He took another step toward her. "With what ease I involved guileless people in the whole affair, oh yes. And Goodnight. He was just a treat on the side, the best friend a methodical assassin could hope for."

The beads of perspiration rose on the assailant's face. Berdie sensed he was on the edge of an eruption, and that often meant carelessness.

"And you," he snarled, "a common little wench, tell me what mistakes I made?"

It was then she saw it, just the smallest shimmer of steel, held in his right palm. *The Lord is my shield!* Berdie plucked up her courage.

"The early morning of Miri's murder you left a message for Hugh that excused you for tardiness to your appointment. A needy car, you said. Set your alibi. But you were reckless. You forgot about the unique earsplitting chime of Miss Livingston's clock. All caught on tape."

Unexpectedly, a brightly whistled "Joy to the World" sounded forth as the back door flew open and a jolly Edsel Butz splashed into the kitchen, toolbox in hand.

"Oh, Mrs. Elliott, didn't know anyone was here. Sorry." The robust man hailed the visitor who spun to face the intrusion. "Reverend Lewis."

Berdie tried to lunge away, but the impersonator slammed his body backward, pinning Berdie to the wall.

"Steady on there, Reverend, you nearly knocked Mrs. Elliott over."

"Well now, the town jester stumbles in." Lewis frowned as he repositioned his body just next to Berdie.

She inhaled as a sharp touch made itself known at her rib.

"I had an odd moment to come repair. . ." Edsel Butz went silent, spotting the obscure shine of steel in Lewis's hand. "What's going on here?"

"The brain of a gnat!" Lewis spewed.

Edsel's eyes narrowed. He took a step forward.

"Ah, ah, stay there, or the harebrained cow gets it." Lewis gave the weapon another purposeful nudge that made Berdie draw air through her clenched teeth.

The charlatan tipped his head. "Did I say harebrained cow? No, that title's reserved for *your* dim wife."

Edsel's face went bullish.

"Don't listen to him, Edsel," Berdie warned. "He's angry because he can't find it."

Lewis balked. "Can't find what?" he growled.

Berdie took a shallow breath. "Livingston and Nav died by your hand."

The intruder smirked.

"An entire community is in chaos," Berdie went on. "The Yard is breathing down your neck, but you still haven't found the evidence that incriminates your family."

Lewis caught his breath. "Where is it? Tell me!" His whole body shook as his face went dark.

As tightly as Lewis gripped his weapon, Berdie clung fast to the truth. "Gerhard!" Her voice was solid. "This isn't going to bring your father back."

Like a beast struck by an unexpected arrow, the man flinched. The pressure at Berdie's rib became unsteady.

As Lewis fought to regain control, Berdie wrenched herself sideward, knocking the old dishwasher with a profound *thud*.

Boom! bang! The roar of a sonic blast ripped through the kitchen. Water erupted like Noah's deluge, spraying the room and its inhabitants with cold moisture. Grinding and scraping assaulted ears like a bad microphone.

Gerald Lewis, unnerved and thrown off balance, dropped the hand holding his knife.

With a mighty shove, Berdie pushed the tyrant's arm farther

aside. One word rushed from her lips, "Toolbox!"

Edsel Butz, with one powerful sideward thrust, swung his toolbox, which dropped Lewis to the floor, unconscious.

"Call me what you like," Edsel pronounced loudly over the man, water dripping from his chin, "but never, ever call my missus a harebrained cow!"

The machine silenced. Berdie, in a mixture of relief and humor, began to laugh and cry at the same time. "God bless you, Edsel Butz, and God bless that beloved machine!"

"Are you okay, Mrs. Elliott?"

Berdie's knees wanted to buckle, but she held steady. It was then she realized, amid all the to-do, it wasn't Edsel speaking those words. There in her kitchen doorway stood Father Christmas, billowing beard and all, with Mr. Finn beside him. She blinked then wiped her glasses.

Father Christmas drew off his beard. "We got a call that a black luxury auto was parked at the church." He looked round the deluged kitchen. "Poor plumbing."

Berdie gaped, a water droplet clinging to her nose. "Goodnight?"

Finn flew to where Lewis lay and snapped a pair of handcuffs on the comatose man.

Edsel thrust his hand toward Lewis. "Charge that man with slander." He raised his chin. "Slander against my wife!"

Finn arose. "Well done, sir," he commended Edsel.

"Oh 'tweren't me done well," he corrected, "'twas our parish priest's brave wife. The courage of ten, that one." He smiled.

Berdie glowed.

Goodnight, hands on hips, shook his raggedy white shoulder-length curls that made his eyebrows and mustache look even wilder than usual. "Fortunate you're alive." He looked at Berdie. "And I should think you've gotten your Christmas gift already. But I must say, is there ever a moment when you're not right in it?"

CHAPTER ⛪ FIFTEEN

The church bell peeled joyfully across the village as Berdie strolled from the church to the vicarage. To her the chimes sang out peace, joy, and redemption for mankind. Not just because it was Christmas Eve, but once again the whole community was moving wonderfully forward.

Just this afternoon the very proper and very public uniting of Jamie and Cara Donovan had taken place at the church. The village had left behind the initial shock of Cara and Mathew's ruse, the clandestine marriage, and news of a little Donovan. It was replaced with simple admiration for the love that Cara and Jamie dearly held for each other through a very deep valley. Although, it must be said, Preston Graystone was having great difficulty in adjusting to the whole affair. Still, the bride was radiant in French lace, and the Irishman, fitted out in tails and tie, smiled with a fresh glint in his eye.

"All so lovely," Berdie spoke to herself. She reflected back on Jamie's release from prison. "A new start on life again," the lad had told Berdie upon his release from the old bill. In a rush of gratitude, he hugged his "clergyman" as a released captive embraces freedom.

"How can I ever thank you, Mrs. Elliott?"

Berdie had looked heavenward then straight into the eyes of a grateful young man. "There's Someone else you need to thank as well," she reminded.

"Oh, have done." Jamie grinned. "Over and over."

"Well then," she continued, "move on to pursue your dreams. And take care to watch over your family. I'll see you both at church soon, yes?"

Jamie had smiled.

"Oh lovely indeed," Berdie said presently. Her attention now turned back to this glorious evening. It seemed to her that the stars shown just a bit brighter tonight. And there, not ten paces ahead was her dear husband. He bid good evening quietly to a couple that walked toward the village.

"Love," he greeted and took his wife's hand.

"Full house tonight," Berdie commented.

"Edsel was kept busy setting up extra chairs again." Hugh smiled.

"You know, one of the things I so enjoyed this evening was the amber glow of the candles," Berdie said.

"Yes," her husband agreed.

"And the lighted Advent wreath," she added.

"And 'While Shepherds Watched Their Flocks' will never be quite the same after Lucy Butz's flute solo." Hugh grinned. "Quite sweet really."

Berdie chuckled. "Oh, but wasn't the newly come Dr. Avery's performance brilliant?" Berdie's smile widened. "I thought for a moment I was in the Albert Hall."

"Indeed," Hugh agreed.

"Too bad about the sheep, however." Berdie broke into great laughter.

Hugh joined her. "From where I was up front, I heard a crash then saw a large white creature skid into the front pews. What exactly happened?"

Berdie caught her breath. "Oh," she said with a chuckle, "the primary youth choir, you know, was dressed as angels."

"Yes," Hugh spoke.

"Just as they gathered at the Nativity tableau to sing 'Away in a Manger,' Milton Butz tripped on his costume only to go headlong into the sheep." Berdie couldn't help but laugh.

Hugh finished, "sending the creature skidding into the front pew. Yes, I get the picture."

"You know Loren Meredith was right." Hugh sighed. "Closure, misdeeds behind us, it all bodes well for a peaceful Christmas."

Berdie placed her head on her husband's shoulder. She thought through the events of the past week. "You saved my life, you know," she spoke softly.

"Me? I'd rather say that was Edsel," Hugh responded.

"If you hadn't fussed with that old machine—"

Hugh interrupted, "And made it worse!"

"I wouldn't have called Edsel to make the repair. You see?"

Hugh chuckled. "My dear and lovely wife." He placed a tender kiss upon her cheek.

When they reached the vicarage, it was abuzz. Lillie, Ivy, and Barbara Braunhoff had arrived immediately after the service to act as hostesses. Many of the villagers attended the post-service

Christmas Eve celebration at Oak Leaf Cottage.

Once inside, Berdie joined in hosting. "Can I top off your tea?" Berdie asked Preston Graystone, who stood alone in the crowded sitting room.

"Quite," was all the father of the bride replied.

Berdie poured cinnamon tea, spiced with oranges and cloves, into the holiday cup held in the thin angular hand of the solicitor.

"It was a genuinely lovely wedding, Preston," Berdie said as Ivy approached with a canapé tray.

"Dead common!" The man didn't smile. "Even the cake was made slapdash."

Ivy Butz smiled. "Oh I thought it beautiful." She put her chubby hand on Graystone's arm. "We give our hinnies roots so they can grow their own wings," she said robustly. "You gave your daughter wonderful roots, Mr. Graystone, wonderful. You can be proud of that." She gave his arm a pat. "Now how about a canapé?" She pointed to a little morsel. "These have little cheesy bits, very moor-ish."

"Moor-ish?" Preston asked.

"Moor-ish—you want to eat more and more." Ivy giggled.

To Berdie's surprise, the gentleman took one. He made the smallest nibble.

"Indeed." He seemed quite sincere. "Thank you, Mrs. Butz."

"Of course." Ivy smiled, making her round cheeks even fuller and set off to find another taker.

Berdie was pleased to see both congregants and those with unfamiliar faces chat, sip, and enjoy being together.

The children delighted in the Nativity set on the mantel and relished the grand Christmas tree erected just for the occasion. Oddly enough, the hanging candy canes scattered about the tree were slowly disappearing while little mouths became sticky.

Berdie became suddenly aware that someone called to her from across the room.

"Mrs. Elliott." It was David Exton, the young aspiring newspaper editor, teacup in hand. He stood. "I was wondering if you could tell me. . .tell *us* just how you went about solving the Livingston case?"

The entire room came to a hush. It was the question the whole village wanted to ask but hadn't for fear of appearing impolite.

"I mean, really, we're all quite impressed."

The brash inquiry reminded Berdie of a young woman who, when first starting out in investigative journalism, may have done the very same sort of thing.

"Martha," Berdie addressed the Butz twin, "do you fancy taking the children to the library and reading them a Christmas story?"

Martha jumped to her feet. "Love to, Mrs. Elliott." Like babes following the little drummer boy, the young ones scrambled to the library behind Miss Butz.

"Come on, Berdie." It was Lillie. She sat down as if preparing for an oration. "She really is quite brilliant," her friend chirped.

"Indeed!" Dr. Meredith agreed and stood expectantly next to Lillie.

"Well, really, all of you helped me solve the mystery."

The room buzzed then quieted.

"Of course we're keenly aware of Edsel's heroics in recent days, and Mr. Raheem as well."

"Here, here," from the crowd brought blood to Edsel's cheeks, while Mr. Raheem's shy demeanor only allowed him to smile at his wife.

Berdie went on. "The whole plan for Miriam's demise was prompted by the photo of her and her prize-winning lavender. She detested having snaps taken of her for the very reason that they could give away her identity and whereabouts. Remember, though we knew her as a simple villager, she was really in hiding. By way of her clandestine past, Miss Livingston—Miri Avent— was the sworn enemy of Luedke, also known as Gerald Lewis. I daresay the London newspaper running the picture fell into his hands."

"So Gerald Lewis—Luedke—came to our village to seek his prey." Preston Graystone flared.

"And in what better guise than a vicar. He took us in," Mr. Raheem asserted.

"Yes, he took us all in," Hugh spoke as people throughout agreed. "He was churlish, many times odd, but then churchmen are mortals, too. I thought our community might do him well."

"We all gave him the benefit of the doubt," Mrs. Braunhoff agreed.

"As did Miss Livingston," Berdie kept on. "We saw her and Natty leave the Advent party with Mr. Raheem, but Luedke intercepted them. The pretender took the women home knowing the darkness there, which he created by nipped wires, would make them needy. He *assisted* Miriam and induced her to take sleep tablets while getting the lay of the land." Berdie crossed her arms. "When he left, he failed to lock the door. So at his return in the wee hours, he let himself in, and, well, we know what he did then."

Now Mr. Graystone had a question. "My Cara was bequeathed all Livingston's goods, save an Advent wreath. It was willed to some Frenchman." He sniffed. "Never came forward. Why single out a wreath? How could it be of import?"

"Ah," Berdie replied, "never underestimate the power of simple evidence. The wreath was key to burrowing out Miss Livingston's identity, to unlocking treasured evidence, and it even pointed to the murderer."

Graystone knit his brow. "How can a wreath do all that?"

"To start with," Berdie enumerated, "the candles were aged, not used, but for one. This drew my attention. And then there was the placement of the candles in the wreath along with odd symbols carved into the wax, but then it was Lila Butz who solved that."

Lila sat on a sofa, stretching her still-bandaged leg. She blinked her magnified eyes. Her face wore both the fright of being singled out in a crowd and the pleasure of being recognized as quite bright.

Berdie beamed toward the girl. "Her knowledge of the movements of heavenly bodies identified the symbols on the Advent candles: phases of the moon. Also, her simple observation of human nature, more a mystic if you ask me, urged me to discover the true identity of who we know now was Miri Avent."

Ivy Butz patted her daughter's shoulder.

Berdie persisted. "Of course when you clear out one's goods, you learn about even the most discreet effects. Most of her books were in French. All but a few music selections were by French composers."

"And not one German composer," Lillie added.

"Add to that the prize-winning French lavender that filled her back garden. Yes, what we read, our music, our passions, all speak to who we really are."

A lovely young woman sitting beside Mathew Reese spoke up. "I can see this puzzle coming together, but how did Northumbria figure in?"

"That's were Lillie's love for Elgar aided us dramatically." Berdie smiled at her friend. "She discovered the snap of Miriam with her Northumberland English family inside Miriam's Elgar album."

"The only English composer in her music collection." Lillie lifted her chin and looked round then did a slight bow. Gentle laughter filtered through. "Love of Elgar always leads to something good." She looked to the gentleman who stood next to her.

Berdie smiled. "We eventually made contact with the family, and the hidden past of our villager came into a clearer focus."

Berdie nodded toward the handsome gentleman standing next to Lillie. "Our fine doctor of pathology, Loren Meredith, did his work with the utmost attention to detail. His examination of scar tissue brought insight concerning our Miss Livingston's concentration camp internment."

"And he's jolly good fun on an adventure," Lillie added.

"Sporting fellow indeed," Berdie agreed.

The gentleman's smile dazzled as he lifted his teacup high in salute to the generous comments.

"So you see, the wreath was the first whisper of truth pointing to the identity of Mrs. Miri Avent."

"Whatever her past, we'll remember the dear old thing as Miss Livingston," Edsel eulogized.

"Won't we though," Graystone muttered.

"It would suit her to do so," Hugh confirmed.

All nodded in agreement.

"But to squeeze all that from a holiday wreath!" Mrs. Braunhoff displayed amazement.

"Oh yes, and motive as well," Berdie confirmed.

David Exton, who had pulled out his small writing tablet and was scribbling madly, tapped his pen. "You said something about"—he paused to check the tablet—"the wreath unlocked 'treasured evidence.' Can you explain?"

"Of course." Berdie sensed the anticipation in the room. "The wreath literally unlocked the motive in this case."

"As well as identity?" Mathew queried.

"Yes." Berdie looked to her husband. "And I daresay, it was my husband and his trusty comrade at arms, Andrew Busby, that unearthed the true line of motive. And this is strictly off the record, David Exton," Berdie cautioned.

The editor clicked his pen closed.

"They discreetly discovered that Gerhard Luedke, who we knew as Lewis, was actually the son of a World War II prison camp commander that lived underground right here in England."

"You don't say," Edsel piped.

Hugh spoke now. "Miss Livingston had been interned as a Roma at Luedke's camp. Hustled off to safe haven in Northumbria after an escape near war's end. Miss Livingston was the last person standing who could indict the old fellow and cast dispersions upon the entire family line. The Luedkes, who were living under the name Lewis, stood to lose their multimillion business empire and be exiled."

There was a collective gasp.

Berdie tipped her head. "But we now know it wasn't just Miss Livingston who Luedke wanted. He was after recorded incriminating evidence that she possessed."

Mrs. Raheem was getting the picture. "That's why the house was turned bottom end up."

"Right," Berdie affirmed. "She had stolen camp files that implicated Helman Luedke, Gerhard Luedke's father, in the most heinous of atrocities."

"*That's* what Luedke wanted," Hugh proclaimed. "And nothing was too great of cost to get it. Not the life of our friend, not the life of her elderly Roma cousin, nor the automotive attempt on Berdie and Lillie's lives."

Berdie nodded and went on. "The evidence was hidden in a small metal box. But not at Lavender Cottage. The box was with the cousin in France."

Hugh spoke up. "The box was brought to Aidan Kirkwood only after Miriam's death, at the time of the funeral. It was kept in a safe place. I'm not at liberty to say exactly where."

Berdie and Lillie exchanged a quick glance and coyly smiled.

Hugh, still maintaining his code of honor, went on. "No one, not even those who were unknowingly safeguarding it were aware of what it held. They were simply doing a quiet favor."

"Until, that is," Berdie continued, "the box was opened using numbers that were carved into the candleholders of Miss

Livingston's Advent wreath. The phases-of-the-moon candles gave the order: waxing, full, waning, new."

Lucy Butz's lightly agitated teenage voice interrupted, "Why put all that important stuff on a silly wreath? Seems kinda' naff."

"Not for Miss Livingston," Berdie retorted. "Remember her real name was Miri Avent. Lillie?"

"*Avent* is the French word for *advent*," Lillie informed.

"Oh!" Dawn broke across Lucy's face.

"Quite clever perhaps?" Berdie told more than asked.

Preston Graystone knitted his brow and grumbled, "Clever? Why didn't the old woman hand the evidence over to legal long ago?"

Berdie had a cautionary tone. "It wasn't quite that simple, Preston. The information she possessed also indicted someone who was considered a great Resistance war hero. Someone very dear to her—Marquis Avent, her husband."

A flutter of whispers rose and fell.

"Without putting too fine a point to the matter," Hugh expounded, "it seems there were some unsavory alliances made by him that she believed were best kept silenced."

"How extraordinary," David Exton spoke. "Quite amazing. I have another inquiry. Can you tell us when you began to suspect Lewis—Luedke—wasn't who he pretended to be?"

"I think it started with Ivy's drawing room really," Berdie answered.

Ivy yelped, nearly dropping her tray of goodies. "My drawing room? Why it *just* qualifies as a room a'talel." She chuckled. "How did it help?"

"That's the thing, you see. It had most the trappings of a drawing room: lovely paint, furnishings, and window. It appeared as much for the most part. But it just didn't *feel* like a drawing room. I should say it almost wished you away. That's what first tickled my thinking that perhaps Gerald Lewis wasn't all he appeared."

Lucy Butz, who sat admiringly next to Jamie Donovan's seventeen-year-old brother, piped up again. "In your solving things, did I help a'talel?"

"Ah, well, Lucy, you were the reason I was in the drawing room, if you remember." Berdie was discreet.

"Oh." The young woman bit her lip. "Quite." She flushed and turned her attention back to the lad who was staying over from the wedding. Everyone agreed he was the image of Jamie.

Berdie proceeded. "Of course, there were other clues if we heeded them. His mobile ring, for one. When it sounded, we heard the tune for the hymn 'Glorious Things of Thee Are Spoken.' He heard Germany's national anthem, the same tune."

Edsel reared his head. "What I want to know is how Lewis framed our Jamie." His words had a bullish tone.

Rumbles of agreement swirled around the room.

Berdie began, "From conversations with Jamie in a feigned friendship, Luedke knew the lad was working at Lavender Cottage, trying to correct the problem Luedke had put in place. He was also aware that Jamie had Livingston's key due to a slipup in the Upland Arms."

"Aye, I remember that," Dudley Horn injected. "The key tumbled to my shoe."

"Jamie's outburst at the caroling party fitted Luedke's purposes perfectly. A lad fresh from a brush with the law, new to the area, certainly not wealthy, and with a one-of-a-kind screwdriver, all of it was a sure thing in the diabolical mind of the villain."

"I hope he's put away for a hundred years." Jamie's brother blew the words out.

Villette Horn voiced agreement and continued, "There was talk of some masterful plan you conspired, Mrs. Elliott, to catch the fake vicar. Well?"

"Indeed. It's true, Mrs. Horn, but it's a moot point now. Just like Gideon and his small band of men, God won the victory His own way."

"I must say." Mrs. Plinkerton wore a bewildered look. "This all sounds like a Miss Marple novel. Quite frankly, it's a bit too much to take in." She ran her hand over the bodice of her winter-white silk suit.

"All we really need to know, dear Mrs. Plinkerton," Berdie explained, "is that the scoundrel responsible for the whole affair is safely locked up."

"Here, here," Dr. Meredith prompted.

"Here, here!" The vicarage sitting room resounded with the cheer. David Exton was even so bold as to clap.

Hugh came next to Berdie. "Now that my wife has brought this case to a close, she can give herself wholly to the tasks of the church," he announced.

"I have to say," Dudley Horn acknowledged, "I didn't expect the wife of our parish priest to be so skilled in crime solving. Mrs. Elliott, you are full of surprises."

"Speaking of surprises," Edsel Butz trumpeted. He winked at his wife who immediately relieved herself of the serving tray and nestled comfortably against her husband's side. He went on. "That is to say. . ." He paused. "Well, Ivy has something."

"Yes." She matched her husband in volume. "Our Duncan's going to get a *D*!" Her face was alight with joy.

"What is this *D*?" Mrs. Raheem queried.

Edsel explained, "Lucy and Lila start with *L*, Milton and Martha with *M*."

"Duncan's going to get a *D*," Ivy repeated.

"A baby?" Mrs. Raheem sparkled.

Congratulations swirled around the room like a bright Christmas ribbon. Even Mr. Graystone had to smile and shake Edsel's hand.

"I s'pose we'll both be busy, won't we, Preston?" Edsel bubbled.

Lillie approached Berdie and spoke quietly. "Ivy expecting. Now that certainly explains her emotional state."

When hubbub began to subside, Hugh tapped a holiday glass with a fork. The eyes of all fell upon their parish priest.

"Congratulations to the Butz family," Hugh acknowledged, "and I'd like you all to adjourn to the kitchen."

The horde filed into the awaiting room uttering murmurs of glee.

"Hugh," Berdie whispered to her husband, "our guest hosts have been manning the kitchen. It could be well out of order."

"Perhaps, perhaps not."

"Why on earth?"

Hugh took his wife by the elbow. "Let's just go have a look-see."

When Berdie stepped into the kitchen, the ocean of people stepped aside like the opening of the Red Sea. And there, where the untamed machine of old had been, a shiny new dishwasher stood in all its splendor with a giant red ribbon attached.

"Oh my." Berdie put her hands to her chest. "I say! It's lovely."

Atop the machine a jolly Christmas card, adorned with a Christmas robin, held a handwritten message.

Dear Mrs. Elliott,
    Thank you for your relentless quest for the truth. We salute your bravery and courage. Happy Christmas.

It was signed, *The Members of Saint Aidan of the Wood Parish Church.*

"Oh thank you, thank you!" Berdie felt the heat rise on her cheeks. "It's lovely, thank you."

Hugh gave her a kiss and the whole lot fell into a round of "For She's a Jolly Good Fellow."

After moments of admiration for the new appliance and several murmurings of "I must get one myself," the party moved back to the sitting room.

Berdie, however, already set to loading the new dishwasher with soiled party plates and cups.

Lillie, who had left with the others, burst back into the kitchen all aflutter. "Berdie, you'll never guess. Loren just told me about something he heard at work today."

"It certainly wasn't from the voice of one of his clients." Berdie put a plate in the rack.

"There's talk of fraudulent practices in the Timsley City Council."

"I don't want to hear this, Lillie." Berdie picked up another utensil. "I'm not hearing you."

"It goes all the way to the Lord Mayor."

Berdie stopped. "Truly?"

"They say one of his council members, a Colonel something, has embezzled thousands."

"Not Colonel Orson Pierpoint."

"That's it. You know him?" Lillie's eyes sizzled.

"He served with Hugh in the Falklands. Sterling character. British cross. No, Colonel Pierpoint is not an embezzler."

Lillie danced. "Just your cup of Christmas tea, Berdie Elliott!"

"Ladies." Hugh entered the room with mugs begging for more wassail. He must've sensed the electricity of the atmosphere. His left brow lifted. "Ladies? What are we up to?"

"Just loading the washer, dear," Berdie offered.

"Just loading the washer," Lillie chimed in.

"Berdie, you aren't getting your nose into something again. Tell me you're not." Hugh was stern.

"Did I say anything of the sort?" Berdie asked.

Hugh set the mugs down. "Come you two, back to the celebration. It's Christmas Eve." Hugh opened the kitchen door. "After you."

"Lillie," Berdie said, "what are you doing Monday? I believe I have some errands to tend to."

Lillie tipped her head. "Monday?"

"In Timsley," Berdie offered.

Lillie shook her head. "Oh yes, in Timsley."

The friends hooked arms and walked into the sitting room.

And a Merry Christmas was had by all.

Marilyn Leach has enjoyed writing for the stage as well as for publication. She became a "dyed in the wool" British enthusiast after visiting England, where she discovered her roots. She currently teaches art at an inner-city school near Denver, Colorado, and lives lakeside near the foothills.